T0193650

But Not Without Hope

Prison Time at Devil's Island

James Haydock

authorHOUSE®

AuthorHouse™
1663 Liberty Drive
Bloomington, IN 47403
www.authorhouse.com
Phone: 1 (800) 839-8640

Published by AuthorHouse 09/19/2018

ISBN: 978-1-5462-5983-1 (sc)
ISBN: 978-1-5462-5982-4 (e)

Print information available on the last page.

Also by James Haydock

Stormbirds
Beacon's River
Victorian Sages
Mose in Bondage
Against the Grain
A Tinker in Blue Anchor
Portraits in Charcoal: George Gissing's Women
On a Darkling Plain: Victorian Poetry and Thought
Searching in Shadow: Victorian Prose and Thought
The Woman Question and George Gissing
Of Time and Tide: The Windhover Saga

Not without hope we suffer and we mourn.

-- William Wordsworth

Man's inhumanity to man
Makes countless thousands mourn!

-- Robert Burns

Contents

Chapter One

Growing Up Parisian

My name is Arthur Maurice Bonheur. I was born in Paris in the early years of the twentieth century. I had an uncle who went by the name Arthur, and so my parents chose to call me Maurice. My father was the chief conductor on the Paris-Orleans Express, a position he won after many years on a train he dearly loved. As I recall, he was handsome and proud in his elegant chief's uniform. My grandma, who was never generous in her remarks, said it made him strut like a rooster. Maybe so, but why not? He was a good man, a good father and husband, and a reliable railroad man. His work required him to be away from home most of the time. Late in his life he married a pretty young woman, a clerk in a bank, who had a running joke among her friends that her husband was really her father. I, of course, was not able to judge the validity of that observation because a year or two after their marriage I became their first-born and only child.

I am not able to say whether my mama was a good woman or not. I like to think she was, but I do know from what my papa has told me that she left us. When I was not more than three years old, my dear mother abandoned us and left the country for Russia. She took a job as a nanny in the family of a rich and powerful politician, caring for his children rather than her own. She sent my papa a couple of letters to say all was well with her and life was good, but we never heard from her again. I can't say whether she liked her job, or whether her life in Russia was a happy one. I know only that Papa in spite of his demanding job struggled to keep me with him after she left. I was a toddler at the time and needing care around the clock. Eventually he had to turn me over to my grandparents who agreed to raise me. It was necessary to do that or lose his beloved job on the train.

My grandparents, Leon and Elsa, owned a small restaurant located near the station, and so Papa was able to see his little boy on a regular basis though without the bonding that usually comes with living in the same house. Until I was twelve I was a good boy living a good life even though at times I was in trouble with Grandma and often felt like an orphan. I went to a good school and learned some English, history, math, and other things. I liked learning new things every day and was beginning to think I might even be a teacher when I grew up. Then at twelve a disastrous event occurred in my life that left me feeling afraid, empty, and lonely. Both of my grandparents died. My grandma died at seventy-one while taking a nap one rainy afternoon. Five days later Grandpa died also in his sleep. All the people who knew the couple said the old man loved his wife so much that when she died he couldn't live without her. They said the threads of life that had bound them together for half a century grew old with them and snapped. They said when that happened and the old man realized his wife couldn't be with him, the will to live quickly departed. Well, I won't go out on a limb and disagree with what all their friends were saying, and yet I know from living with the old couple they were not all that close. Days would go by with no conversation between them whatever. Anyway, for a time I had no adult in my life, no guardian to guide me or tell me what to do, and I roamed the streets of the city as a waif. A few months later my Uncle Christophe of Lyon moved to Paris and became manager of a nightclub known to Parisians as *Le Chat Orange*, or *the Orange Cat*.

The club was located at 89 Rue Pigalle in Monmartre, a famous district of Paris where artists and literary figures lived for a season.

Some who found fame in later years were Henri Matisse, Salvador Dali, Pablo Picasso, Gertrude Stein, Cole Porter, Scott Fitzgerald, Ernest Hemingway, and T. S. Eliot. Monmartre was also notable in an earlier time — *La Belle Époque* they called it — of Toulouse-Lautrec, the impressionist painters, and *Maxim's,* a restaurant in business even now. The *Moulin Rouge* or *Red Mill,* the cabaret where so many of them gathered, was only a block away from the *Orange Cat.* Uncle Christophe generously allowed me to live with him in his tiny apartment above the restaurant and club, but only if I did my part to help him earn a living. During the late afternoon after a few hours at school and well into each evening, I worked as an errand boy. I was only thirteen at the time but alert and observant. Well-heeled ladies and gentlemen of leisure and wealth patronized the *Orange Cat.* Women of the demimonde, attired in elaborate evening gowns and made up to look younger, also frequented the place. The men ranged in age from young lads on a bender to sophisticated old gentlemen, agile and debonair in white ties and cummerbunds.

Montmartre was the center of Parisian merry making, the place to visit noisy, bawdy, unrestrained "Paris by night." In clubs called *La Lune Rousse* and *Le Désert Sec* by the French and *The Red Moon* and *Dry Desert* by English celebrants, Django Reinhardt wowed audiences with his guitar. In most of the clubs couples drank their fill and danced riotously until dawn. On the Boulevard de Clichy were numerous sex shops for deviant tastes. Pigalle was a vulgar neighborhood, so earthy in fact that visiting Americans began to call it "Pig Alley." On one section of Rue Pigalle were orange circles painted on the sidewalk. When a gentleman stood in a particular circle, it told the lady at the window above that she had a customer willing to pay well for her presence. The *Orange Cat* put on naughty shows that drew wealthy playboys and loose women with plenty of money from all over Europe and America. A florid woman calling herself "the Queen of Paris" visited the nightclub with her coterie of young girls every night. A middle-eastern Prince once gave me a tip of 100 francs to deliver a message to one of her girls. He didn't know the girl belonged to the Queen, and the indiscretion got him banned from the club. I couldn't be blamed, of course, and was soon earning more money in one week than my papa was earning on his train in a month.

I had never seen so much money, so many people splurging as if convinced their last day on earth was just around the corner. I can describe it only as wild, careless, lavish spending in the passionate pursuit of pleasure. All the people I had ever known, all my close and distant relatives, worked hard for a few francs and spent them frugally. They struggled to obtain their money and often went without necessities to save it. But at thirteen I was sometimes in a different world altogether though truly not a part of it. I merely hovered on the outskirts, a servant of sorts, and yet I'm not ashamed to say I seized my share of the wealth any time the opportunity offered.

It was an amazing reality in which people didn't work an hour a day and yet had plenty of money to spend. They slept all day and partied all night and spent lavishly on anything that caught their fancy. They believed legal tender in Paris could buy anything, and they denied themselves nothing. They were consummate pleasure seekers, conspicuous consumers clothed expensively in silks and satins and finest broadcloth. They dined on rich cuisine: caviar, *pâté de foie gras*, and truffles. To gratify sensitive palates and release inhibition, they ate rich food and drank rivers of champagne. At thirteen, viewing that extravagant scene with admiration, I concocted dreams of living that way. However, destiny or necessity or whatever it's called had other plans for me.

I liked what I was doing, but alive and active during most of every night didn't make for an alert student during the day. I wanted to learn but was often sleepy. In most of my classes the teachers droned on and on and put me to sleep. Then when they saw me slumped over my desk and paying no attention to what they were saying, they felt insulted and angry. More than once I was put on detention with a warning that if it happened again I would be expelled. It did happen again, over and over, and very little was done about it. They tried to shame me, telling me I was bright and capable but wasting my life and hurting my health. With each reprimand I solelmnly promised to do better but soon began to consider dropping out of school altogether. The place had become a hostile environment for me, toxic except for a couple of girls I knew, and I wasn't learning anything I didn't know already. Also I was making more money in my early teens than any of my teachers, and that didn't set well with them. I talked it over with my uncle, and when I turned fifteen he agreed I could leave school and work full time. Though in later years I regretted not going further in school to become a teacher or tutor, the decision to be on my own doing a job I really liked made me happy.

However, it wasn't the kind of work I can write about with pride. I was a messenger boy delivering messages of lustful longing from rich old men to nubile young women. Sometimes I helped to arrange a love tryst between a gentleman of wealth and a lady of the demimonde. They called me their *entre-deux* or *go-between* and rewarded me well. My uncle only sniffed at the immorality that oozed from every pore of the *Orange Cat,* justifying the activity by saying it was happening in every nightclub of the neighborhood. A special class of people lived in Montmartre, struggling artists mainly, and they allowed raunchy behavior because of their own liberal way of thinking and living. My papa by contrast was a staunch conservative, believing in old-fashioned values. He became very angry when he learned I had dropped out of school and was doing a borderline kind of work. He wanted his son to get a good education and perhaps train to become a railway employee. His dream was to turn his job over to me when the day came for him to retire. He quarreled bitterly with Uncle Christophe, and they never spoke again.

The club was often referred to as a nightclub, but it was open during the daytime too. Some people came in the afternoon and remained until midnight or later while others trooped into the establishment after dining and remained most of the night. A few came in for coffee and pastry every morning. Those patrons consuming Colombian coffee and rich pastries often discussed the races. A fair number at the *Orange Cat* were in the habit of placing bets on the horses. I carried their money in a leather pouch to the bookmakers, and when a horse won I got a piece of the take. One fateful day I was told that because the group had inside information, they would be placing a large stake on a horse the experts were calling a sure loser. The horse would pay twenty to one if it won. So a modest bet of 500 francs could net an astounding 10,000 if the dark horse came in a winner. Even though some were saying it would be a miracle, those in the know were convinced it would happen.

I was only the errand boy and had no opinion whatever. Wealthy men could afford to take a big risk. Unlike me, they wouldn't miss 500 francs at all when the horse came in a loser.

"Oh, they're throwing their money away!" a friend of mine at the track told me. "Don't be a fool, Maurice. Put the money in your pocket. Take it all. It's better they lose it to you than to the bookmaker!"

He seemed to know what he was talking about, and I got to thinking that maybe he was right. I counted the money and it came to 8,000 francs. I figured I could live quite well on that for a long time. So after thinking about it long and hard, greed got the better of me and I pocketed the stash. On the day the horse would be racing I didn't go near the track or the bookmaker. I went to the house of the friend who told me to keep the money and spread it on a table in his room. I told him that when I was certain it all belonged to me I would buy him a gourmet dinner. We laughed and talked and counted the money. For a brief time I felt as rich as any person who frequented the *Orange Cat*.

But as a cruel fate would have it, the dark horse won. I didn't return to the club that night. I couldn't face my uncle and admit that I had not placed the bets of his patrons but had kept the money for myself. I knew he would become furious and call me a thief. I walked the wet streets of Paris all night in a cold drizzle, trying to think of what to do. No workable solution of any kind came to mind. Near dawn I sneaked into the *Orange Cat* through the rear entrance but couldn't avoid my uncle. He had always been an early riser and wanted to know why I was up so early. When I tried to explain what had happened, he glared at me with intense anger and slapped my face hard. Then he rolled up a fat newspaper and hit me over the head with it several times as though punishing a naughty dog. In a stupor I handed him his patrons' money in its original pouch. He grabbed it cursing and hissing vengeance. I ran from his blows to encounter my dear papa on the sidewalk. I explained what I had done and begged his forgiveness. Instantly I saw he was not in a forgiving mood, was becoming very angry.

"Get away from me!" Papa screamed. "Get out of my sight, you cur, you dirty little thief! You dropped out of school to become a thief? Your grandmother always said you had a load of thievery in you."

He was causing a scene. Pedestrians on the pavement, though in a hurry, paused to be amused by what was going on. He had called me a mongrel cur, and his language was on the mark. I felt exactly like a beaten puppy. I scurried away from the snickering crowd as fast as I could. Before turning the corner I looked over my shoulder to see my father walking stiffly toward the station. I was certain he would be seething with anger for hours. I lost him that day. I never spoke with him again and saw him only from a distance. And what is more, on that same day I lost all the trust and confidence my uncle had placed in me. In a fury he demanded I collect my stuff and leave his residence. I couldn't be trusted he told me. He would find another boy to do my job.

So with no home and no job, I was forced to endure several brutal months on the streets of Paris living from hand to mouth.

Then one day out of sheer desperation driven by hunger and no place to sleep, I joined the army at seventeen and went off to war. It was another terrible experience for one so young. It became the job of a mere boy to kill Germans or be killed. I was too green and too soft to kill, and yet my country demanded I do it or die. More than once I thought death would be better than living to kill. I thought I might let a German sniper shoot me down, but the will to live even in bad times was strong. In an ambush that became a skirmish I was wounded by a bullet in the left shoulder and sent to a hospital. While convalescing I met a slender young nurse overflowing with warmth and fell in love with her. We decided to marry as soon as I was well again and out of the army. But of course I had to be settled in a good job first. So at twenty-one I was again walking the streets of Paris, looking for a job. I looked and looked day after day for at least a month and found nothing. At the end of each day I went to the hospital to walk Gabrielle home. She assured me that in time I would find a job. I needed only to keep trying and be patient.

Weeks glided by and I had no job and no money. The little I had saved as a soldier was spent, and my pride wouldn't allow me to be supported by Gabrielle. I took a job as a dishwasher, but the owner of the restaurant wouldn't pay more than eight francs a day plus room and board. I slaved in a steamy kitchen many hours each day for ten days. Then entering the owner's office on an errand I found a wallet stuffed with cash. I grabbed it without thinking and put it in my pocket. I should have hesitated to consider the consequences of so serious an act but didn't. Deeply troubled, I had become a common thief. I had broken the law and would be punished. I could go to prison for a long time. Old Benedetti would bring in the police. They would find me and arrest me. Though the court would call it a petty theft, an unbending judge would deliver a stiff sentence. I would go to prison for a long time.

Young and foolish, I quickly put those thoughts out of mind and went shopping. I bought a new suit, two expensive shirts, new shoes and a spiffy cravat. Dressed to the hilt, I went to see Gabrielle. She looked me over and laughed gleefully, admiring my looks in new clothes. She said I was every bit as handsome in my new duds as when I was a soldier in uniform. She wanted me to have dinner with her parents and set a date for our marriage. I hesitated because I knew they wouldn't accept a thief as a son-in-law. My uncle had called me a thief and my father had called me a thief, and so had my grandma. As a child when I raided her cookie jar, she scolded me and said she would not allow a thief to live in her house. Now with this last indiscretion I knew that my genes, or whatever sets the pattern of a person's behavior, had conspired to make me a thief for life. With that thought in mind I couldn't face my girl's parents. Until I knew myself better I couldn't face the future with my love, and so I ran. Saying not a word to the one person who mattered most in the world to me, I left Paris for an undisclosed location.

Chapter Two
Sentenced to Hard Labor

W hen I was growing up and in the habit of purloining cookies from a jar in the kitchen, my grandma often quoted a Spanish proverb when scolding me. In English it went something like this, "Once a thief, always a thief." Then she would solemnly add, "You didn't become a thief, my boy, because you steal. You steal because you are already a thief. I want to get it through your head, I won't have a thief living in my house!"

"I know, Grandma," I would always reply. "I won't steal again." But of course I did, and it threw me into terrible trouble. Much later I found it absolutely necessary to steal. I had to steal to survive.

As I grew older I believed thievery was in my blood. I stole when I was a child, I stole when I was a teenage messenger, and I stole from my employer Benedetti as a young man. So perhaps there was truth in the old proverb. Acting on impulse, I had seized the restaurant's payroll and quickly I went into hiding. The police were surely looking for me, and I felt I could be arrested at any time. But as soon as I got to a town some distance from Paris, I applied for a job as a valet to a wealthy woman who lived in the countryside on a large estate. She was a good and gracious employer. No one on her staff was overworked, and we had time to enjoy life. The authorities couldn't have reached me there, and I could have saved enough money to marry Gabrielle. But I viewed myself as a menial and that brought discontent.

I had been in the service of Madame Bordeaux only a month when I saw on her dressing table a delicate ivory case containing her pearls. Near the pearls was a packet of money brought to the estate to pay the servants the following day. Again the thievery in my genes or just plain greed — even now I don't know which — nullified rational behavior. Without hesitation I stuffed the money and pearls in my pocket. Quickly I changed from livery into street clothes and hopped on a train for Paris. I spent the night in a cheap hotel and the next morning, as I was going for breakfast, two policemen began walking close beside me. When I turned to speak to them, they clapped handcuffs on me and announced I was under arrest. Madame Bordeaux had concluded I was the only person who could have taken her valuables, and she lost no time reporting the theft. In jail awaiting trial, I wrote a letter to her begging forgiveness and assuring her that her stolen property would swiftly be returned. I didn't get a reply. Later I learned she hated thieves and justifiably felt angry and betrayed. I wasn't feeling too good myself.

After two weeks of jail time not altogether marked by discomfort, I was hustled into a paddy wagon and carted off to a town thirty miles from Paris to answer a charge of thievery. My crime, the cause of subsequent suffering in the worst prison on earth, was stealing money and jewelry from my employer. It didn't matter that every single sou and every pearl was returned to her. I had committed a crime and had to pay for it. I had to be punished, and that was that. In less than a week I found myself in a courtroom with a hard-faced judge perched on a pedestal looking down on me over the top of his spectacles. He had a full docket of cases and was all business. Within minutes he reviewed my case and pronouncd sentence. I got no trial.

"It's a matter of crime and punishment," he intoned. "You stole from Madame Bordeaux, known in these parts as a kind and

11

generous employer. That was a big mistake, sir, a serious crime and a silly one at that. Now you must do time for your crime. I sentence you, Arthur Maurice Bonheur, to five years' hard labor in French Guiana."

I couldn't deny that I had committed a crime, but in body and soul I knew the sentence was too severe. Benedetti, for reasons I never understood, had not even charged me. But for a crime that hurt nobody, a theft with all the stolen goods returned, I got a harsh prison sentence. Angry and despondent, I broke loose from my captors and ran like a rabbit. I was quickly apprehended and frog marched back to court. Two rawboned policemen stood close beside me, each gripping an elbow. They wouldn't allow me to sit. The judge scowled at me for a full two minutes without speaking a word. Then shaking his head, he pounded his gavel hard and loud. With obvious satisfaction, he gave me seven years' hard labor for theft. Pounding the gavel hard a second time — I thought it would surely break — he added another year for my trying to escape custody. I would serve the eight years not in France but at Devil's Island near the equator. I knew the climate to be unspeakably hot and the prison cruel. Reports of scandalous abuse were often in the news. That odious prison colony was built by slaves in 1852. It became in the course of a century one of the worst in the entire world.

Within a few days I was taken by rail to the Atlantic coast. There in what the police called "a holding tank" I would have to wait several weeks for the convict ship to arrive. The car in which they placed me had several compartments measuring just large enough for a man to sit on a crude bench and lie down when curled up. When another prisoner was placed in the cell opposite mine, the two guards demanded silence. As they began to play a game of chess at the end of the car, I began a whispered conversation with the newcomer, Anatole Durand. The man was in his middle fifties and was sentenced to ten years' hard labor for violating an old woman. Although he had spent several years in an African prison for another offense, he insisted he was innocent of the crime. He said he entered the woman's house when drunk looking for a place to sleep. She began to scream, and he tried to shut her up by cupping his hand over her mouth. They fell to the floor with him falling on her, and she was injured. He fled as she screamed rape and was arrested the next morning. He wasn't physical with her in any way, he claimed, but the authorities believed her side of the story and branded him guilty. I had my doubts as I listened to his story. Later I heard it was rare for a rapist to admit guilt. Maybe Durand convinced himself he was innocent.

The cell car stopped the next day in another town, and three more convicts became my companions. To my eye they looked very young, and I was amazed to learn that all three were going to Guiana. Julien, Claude, and Lucas were farm boys who drank too much at a village tavern one evening in summer and got into trouble. On the way home they passed another tavern that had closed for the night. Drunken and merry without caution, they instantly decided they wanted more to drink. So crying, "Open, open! The night is young!" they banged on the oaken door. Getting no answer, they broke open the door and helped themselves to the bottles behind the counter. The owner heard the ruckus, came running from the loft in his nightshirt, and confronted them. He was a feisty little man but no match for strong, rangy, drunken teenagers. In minutes he suffered a few well-placed blows to the head and belly and fell groaning to the floor. The three boys ran with bottles of booze and a few francs they found in the till. The next day they were arrested on charges of breaking and entering, criminal assault, and theft. Each was sentenced to five years of servitude in French Guiana. Within thirteen months, as I was to learn later, the harsh environment took the lives of all three. Julien was sixteen, Claude and Lucas seventeen.

The prison car ended its journey at a seaport on the Bay of Biscay. There we left the stuffy car that was beginning to stink and were placed in a spacious room within a government building.

Three guards stood by to keep order but paid little attention to us. As far as I could tell, they were sharing on the sly a bottle of rum. It was good to have enough space to walk a few steps before turning and good to be able to lie down at full length. We were together now, no longer separated and not required to remain silent. Destined to be in the same boat, the grisly convict ship bound for the tropics, we wanted to support each other as friends. I had been told that when facing danger the group is forever stronger than the individual, and I believed it. Yet I found myself practicing the caution of one who can't trust anyone entirely. It was the lesson life had already taught me.

Anatole, a seasoned convict, was more talkative than the rest of us and told ugly and sensational stories of the prison experience. Though he directed his remarks primarily to the three youngest among us just to see their reaction, his stories made me think about my own condition and what lay ahead. I had been convicted of a crime and was doomed to pay for it. In those years after World War I, France was a squeamish and skittish nation trying to put down confusion and chaos. Hating disorder, the legal system was rife with anxiety, and the courts were quick to send men across the seas when they didn't deserve it. I was just one of thousands unfairly sentenced because of the times. Whether deserving it or not, I would have to spend eight years of my youth in a brutal prison among rough and desperate men away from any woman. Rejected by society and filled with hate, those with brawn and muscle and no moral code whatever were known to prey upon the weak. I was a small man not very tall, tolerably well built, but weighing only 132 pounds. That made me a perfect target. I couldn't be weak. I had to be strong to fend off degenerates. I resolved to be alert and cautious at all times.

Lying full length on the concrete floor of our cell and breathing the stench of dirty feet, when sleep wouldn't come I thought of what lay ahead. I loved a young woman and wanted to marry her. I wanted to live with her for the rest of my life and raise a family. I wanted to work hard to support her and our family, and I wanted her to love me as much as I loved her. Because she was doing good work as a nurse, I wanted to go back to school and study for a profession too. That way, like her, I could make a contribution to the community in which we lived. I wanted to improve it and myself so she would be proud of me. I wanted to be a respectable citizen proud of myself. With more education I could perhaps obtain a job in the same hospital where she worked or maybe become a teacher. My dream was to find a well-paying job that would allow for advancement. We would never have to worry about money.

But to please Gabrielle and marry her as soon as possible, I stooped to thievery once more, committing a crime against an employer who had treated me well. It was a foolish crime of youth and passion driven by tainted genes. "Once a thief," my grandma had said, "always a thief." Even today I regret that it ever happened. But I have never regretted loving that serene and beautiful girl. Thoughts of her lived in my mind and heart for many years; her image sustained me. To return from exile and prove myself worthy of her gave me hope and strength. I would escape from that tropical prison as soon as I could. Somehow I would find a way to travel thousands of miles to stroll with my girl on the boulevards of Paris. I would dine al fresco with her at one of the sidewalk cafés and luxuriate in her musical laughter, her smiling face, and the funny way she held her fork. The state was poised to punish me for stealing. I wouldn't let it steal from me the best years of my life.

When morning came we were shackled and marched by gendarmes through the town to a small prison on the outskirts. Never in my life had I been an object of curiosity, and so I was surprised to see people looking at me as though I belonged in a zoo. We entered the prison to stand in a large courtyard. Guards ordered us to undress for a thorough body search. They looked for any substance we might conceal in a body cavity. Afterwards we were given showers, striped prison uniforms, and very short haircuts. Then to the bleak cells we went to wait many days for transfer to the convict ship. After a week or so we were vaccinated against tropical diseases. Each of us got three inoculations and a temporary prison number for the ship. As we waited for departure, we spent our time untwisting old tarry rope to make oakum for caulking deck seams and plumbing on ships. It was a job that brutalized thumbs and fingers in minutes, causing blisters and black hands. We worked in dead silence. They say the Chinese invented water torture, a single drop falling every five seconds on the forehead. The French invented silence. Any man who mumbled a few words got lashes across his back.

Even though the big ship sailed for French Guiana early in the year, not a person in my group was on it. We were stuck in that stinking little prison, that so-called holding tank, for several months enduring daily abuse. During the daytime when confined to our cells we were not allowed to lie down. The bed folded against the wall, and there it remained until one hour before lights out. To sit and slump against the wall was also forbidden, and so when not working at useless labor we walked in continuous movement. When the bed was finally lowered on command, we were so exhausted from work and walking we fell immediately upon it and slept like the dead. The tiny cells had chamber pots for use during the night. Rules called for emptying the pots every morning, but that seldom happened. When the stench became unbearable, one poor wretch was ordered to empty all the pots. The job was so nauseous that most of the men ordered to do it couldn't eat breakfast afterwards. By the time we were ready to ship out, because we were made to suffer long before our prison sentences began, most of us were bitter and fiercely determined to cause trouble later. Every man among us was prone to escape from French Guiana as soon as he got there.

When the authorities heard the ship would soon be in port, more than three hundred convicts were selected as cargo. We were the chosen ones, separated from the other prisoners and not required to work. Prison officials gave us more and better food and even old magazines to read. Later I learned treating us better was intended to prepare us for the rigors of the voyage. A few days before we left, army doctors gave us a cursory physical examination and pronounced us fit. Only a few of the three hundred were deemed unfit. One was the strapping son of a millionaire factory owner in Paris. Another died of a clogged artery to the brain, and still another of a lung condition. A dozen or more were dead before the voyage ended. Those last days of waiting were wretched, especially for those with loved ones who came to see them off. Many were seeing wives and children for the last time. Some older men were certain they would never return. A sentence of ten years for men in their mid fifties was a death sentence.

I desperately wanted Gabrielle to see me off, and I wanted to tell her to wait for me no longer than two years. If I had not returned by then, I wanted her to be free to choose another man. I was going away for eight long years but firmly believed I could escape and return within two. Even though she wouldn't be able to leave her hospital duties to say farewell, I wanted her to know I would be coming back into her life. I kept telling myself it was *not* wishful thinking. I would see her again. I was lonely for her. In a dense crowd I was lonely. It was painful to see my fellow convicts saying goodbye to friends and relatives, for I had none. Thoughts of a quick escape consoled me. I didn't know that even after serving his sentence, a man wouldn't be allowed to leave the penal colony. France had passed a law that required convicts to remain in French Guiana for a time equal to their original sentence. Almost to a man that amounted to prison servitude in a vile place for life.

In the first week of September the day came for departure. The old convict ship stood quite visibly off shore, her hull a tall black wall as formidable as any prison wall. Her stacks were belching black smoke that drifted skyward. She was there to take on cargo, a human cargo of miserable men who would be even more miserable before her voyage ended. In the courtyard we saw for the first time the guards from French Guiana, all muscular and swarthy and about twenty in number. They were dressed differently from the guards we had known on French soil. They wore blue uniforms of a military cut and looked like soldiers or policemen. Circling their waists were wide leather belts with holsters containing pistols. Those of higher rank carried batons weighted with lead to be used when necessary. All walked with a quick military step resembling a cocky strut.

The chief guard, fit and handsome in his crisp blue uniform and wearing stripes of rank on his left sleeve, demanded we stand at attention to be counted. When four convicts turned up missing, a prison official immediately led the guard to a small enclosure where four men lay huddled on burlap bags. Three of them had lost a leg. The fourth man was white as a sheet and sweating profusely. Though too weak to stand or walk, he was included in the count. All of us were now the property of the Penal Administration of French Guiana. But we would not be serving the sentences meted out to us until we arrived in that place of torment on the other side of the Atlantic Ocean. We would certainly be prisoners in a prison ship but not yet serving time. Grimly we shouldered the bags allotted us and marched through the town to the waterfront. Again people turned out to gawk at us as if we were on parade. Guards prodding us along with nightsticks cautioned us to maintain silence and keep our faces locked forward. At anchor the old ship patiently waited.

Chapter Three
Crossing the Atlantic

A crowd of sympathetic citizens came together to watch our departure. Among them were parents, wives, children, sweethearts, and friends saddened and alarmed by the sight of exiled men taking what could be their last steps on the soil of France. Several women called out to loved ones, urging them to remain strong and return soon. Not a man among us believed any one of us would return soon. I wanted to be home again in two years, but that I didn't consider soon. We had been cautioned to say nothing to those in the crowd, not even to acknowledge them. So we tramped along eyes riveted ahead until we reached the pier. Some of the people were laughing and hooting as though enjpying a festive event. Barking dogs nipped at our heels and mean little boys threw mud balls at our legs and feet. We were told to ignore it all and we did. Half a mile from shore, gently riding the waves, was the ship that would take us to a place known to be a possession of France and yet another world. The old vessel stood so high in the water even a man with poor eyesight couldn't miss her. Throbbing engines spewed black smoke from her stacks, and on her decks were young mariners preparing to sail. Her name was displayed in large white letters at her bow. Someone had named her, perhaps with tongue in cheek, *Saint Mary's Challenger*.

A barge of vast size waited to take us to the *Challenger*. Expertly it came to the side of the ship just under the gangplank that was quickly lowered. On board we dropped our bags through a hatch. Below in a dim and tight compartment sailors stored them by number. In single file we went down a narrow stairway to be shoved into a huge cage made of steel. It was large enough to hold sixty men, and the guards counted each of us as we entered. Other cages held an equal number, and within an hour the hold with five steel cages was stuffed with human cargo. A smaller cage near the ship's boilers was reserved for troublemakers. In another hour the stink of sweaty, unwashed bodies was overwhelming. By command all portholes had been closed until the ship was at sea. With little ventilation, the air we breathed was heavy and noisome. When I felt a vibration beneath my feet, I knew the ship was moving. The desolation I felt, believing I might never see Paris or Gabrielle ever again, canceled all thoughts of the future.

I had thought the hold of a ship was always cool, even cold depending on the season, but the hold of the *Challenger* was steamy and hot and stinking. Outside the harbor on the Bay of Biscay the portholes were opened to make conditions more tolerable. I was able to breathe again and caught a glimpse of the shoreline quickly receding. A guard told us that every morning we would spend half an hour on deck. I looked forward to that, thinking it would be a respite from the stinking hold. Then I learned we were there to be washed by a high-pressure hose while sailors below sloshed water in the grimy cells to clean them. Standing on deck in the early morning, just as the sun tipped the eastern horizon, we breathed the salty air and felt invigorated. Yet for fifteen minutes we were not allowed to talk and had to stand facing the sea. Then came the order to strip in chilly air, stash our clothes on the quarter deck, and be washed. Blasts of cold water knocked us down but washed away body odor. Guards with rifles ready watched us closely. In the past insane prisoners had tried to jump them, and some equally insane had thrown themselves overboard into the roiling sea.

I was soon to discover just how bad the food was and just how little we got for each meal. The captain claimed half the men were seasick and eating very little. I could vouch for the seasickness, for sour puke was everywhere. But that had nothing to do with the meager rations measured out to us from a large metal pot. The old scoundrel was buying less food to enrich his own pockets. A similar fraud occurred with the daily half liter of wine each convict was supposed to get during the crossing. Aggressive guards charged wretched men with misconduct and seized their ration of wine for themselves, calling it retribution. In time I learned that most of the guards had chosen to work under harsh conditions simply to line their pockets. Unlawful graft was rampant. Every guard seemed to be taking advantage of the young and weak. Julien, Claude, and Lucas, the farm boys, got very little wine. A Corsican guard named Giacamo managed almost every day to accuse all three with bogus infractions and take their wine as punishment. We knew it was happening but could do nothing to stop it.

Even though discipline was strict in other places, it was lax in the cages. We were able to talk, play cards, read in poor light, and smoke. Invariably the conversation turned to French Guiana, what we might find there, and how soon we might escape. Some in my cage had tiny maps of South America they had torn from an atlas after conviction. They spent hours poring over the small print and memorizing names of towns and villages in Dutch Guiana and other places. It all seemed futile to me but gave them hope. I too was beginning to shape plans to escape as soon as I got there. I would go with a seasoned convict who knew the forest and the lay of the land, and with him to help me I believed freedom would be possible and perhaps easy. I didn't know at that time how difficult even a carefully planned escape would be, how the unforgiving jungle and other factors would militate against it.

As the ship moved along, getting ever closer to the tropics, I endured each day as best I could. I managed to get enough to eat and kept the brutes away by flashing the knife I carried always on my person. I got enough sleep and began to make friends with one or two men I thought I could trust. Then of a sudden violence erupted in the cage. Two convicts began stabbing each other with daggers made of spoons sharpened on the floor. Though the fight lasted only ten minutes, blood oozed over their naked bodies and made a mess. The man who seemed to be winning suddenly slipped in the muck and fell; the other man pounced to finish him. But before it could happen guards entered with weapons and a bullwhip. One crack of the whip ended the fight. A man with numerous puncture wounds was taken to the infirmary. The one who appeared to be the victor was sent to the hot cell with a burning whip mark across his back, a welt that later festered. There he remained until the voyage ended. When finally released, he was too weak even to stand and yet had managed to stay alive. Two young men in our cage died en route. As many as six perished in another cage.

When the old ship crossed the equator, the heat and humidity was worse than any I've ever known. Most of us wore only a damp towel around the waist and a smaller towel supplied by the ship's crew to cool our sweating heads. Some men passed out and lay as if dead on the dirty floor. If they were not up and walking after a few hours, they were taken to a holding room adjacent to the infirmary. Medical personnel looked them over and pronounced their condition either fake or genuine. When the water became contaminated, the ship's stewards poured rum in it to make it potable. Later it got worse, and they replaced the rum with permanganate, a strong oxidizing agent that turned the water purple. The bad water, carefully rationed, left a metallic taste in the mouth. Just about every day as the ship moved into the tropics and the weather grew hotter, the steam engines stopped and the old vessel lay silent. That told us at once that one or more men had died to diminish the *Challenger's* human cargo. When a man died, his corpse was hastily dropped into the churning sea. A brief ceremony of a few printed words took place, or so we heard, to observe his passing. He was a convict unworthy of more, and the captain had a tight schedule.

One morning after almost three weeks at sea an officer on board called out, "Land ho!" I rushed to a narrow porthole to view land in the distance. Within two hours the ship was entering the mouth of a wide river and moving gingerly against the current. Gawking at the sights and jostling one another for a better look, we could see monkeys in the tall trees and gorgeous birds. Sliding slowly along was the green and vibrant jungle. An elbow pushed me away as I realized I would be surrounded by that jungle and would have to penetrate it somehow to escape. I slumped to the dirty floor and got away from the present by means of memory and imagination. Beneath my closed eyelids I saw with extraordinary clarity the days of my childhood and the years I spent as my uncle's errand boy in Paris. I felt the ambience of the cocktail lounge in the *Orange Cat*, heard the orchestra playing lively jazz above the murmur of happy voices, and breathed the exotic aroma of wealthy people having a good time. As I was strolling the streets of Paris, absorbed in the glare of neon lights, a heavy boot kicked my thigh.

"Get dressed and make ready to land!" a guard ordered as the ship came to a crude dock and stood still.

Slowly with striped prison garb covering our bodies we climbed out of the stifling hold to find ourselves in bright sunshine, blinking like water rats. A small city with gleaming white buildings and red rooftops lay before us. It called itself Bella Vista, *beautiful view* when translated, and it did have a beautiful view of the ocean, river, and jungle. Its streets were narrow and dusty but clean looking. People of several races sauntered along the walkways in the tropical heat to reach the waterfront. The entire population of Bella Vista, or so it seemed, had turned out to see our arrival and were making it a festive occasion. Officials in white and wearing pith helmets, some with their wives and children, were gathered on the pier. Although the town's colonial appearance seemed pleasant enough as we stood on deck and gawked, many of us turned our heads to look at a small Dutch settlement on the other side of the river. There close at hand lay the promise of freedom.

Corsican guards herded us into a military line to be counted. As many as thirty who couldn't stand or walk lay in the shade to be taken to a hospital. The administrative head of the prison, a tall and swarthy man in civilian clothes, stood on deck to observe the procedure. Down the gangplank we went in military fashion to the long pier. As we began to march toward the city streets, a group of black women in gaudy but pleasing dresses waved handkerchiefs of welcome. One called out to us in accented French, "Soyez forts, messieurs!" Another called in Spanish, "Se fuerte, caballeros!" *Be strong, young men!* We heard no English. Then as we marched along toward a huge gate in a high wall, we began to see fellows like ourselves, convicts serving their time. They were brown as chestnuts and wore stripes, straw hats, and sandals.

"Anyone from Marseilles?" one of them asked. "Marseilles?"

Because we were not allowed to speak, he got no answer. We filed through the gate into a spacious, sun-washed courtyard. At first the yard seemed pleasant enough, but the sun was intolerable and the odor of unwashed bodies sweating in the heat assailed us. A mongrel dog so thin I could count its ribs ran from a corner to the gate. A rat larger than any seen in Paris scurried along the base of the wall to dive into a hole.

"Oh my god!" I heard a very young convict moan. "Am I to live in this god-forsaken hole until I die? Oh please, God! I want to go home!"

Robbed of hope and stunned by the ghastly reality that now confronted him, his narrow shoulders trembled and he sank to his knees. A guard with a heavy nightstick whacked him hard across the back.

"No squatting, you maggot!" the guard shouted. "No sitting in this place! No laying down! You only stand or walk here!"

The young man's anguished cry of despair went unheard by anyone who might have helped him. In less than a year, though apparently in good health, he would be dead. From the courtyard they moved us to cramped barracks. It was a lesson I learned fast in Bella Vista. Human beings value space, and when they don't have it they grow vicious. The Administration deliberately crammed the barracks with too many convicts. Violence inevitably broke out and young men died. Savage behavior kept the prison population in check.

Chapter Four

Inside a Monstrous Prison

T he prison units at Bella Vista were known as camps, particularly the ones in the jungle. They would be ready to receive us after a couple of days of orientation. Guards marched us into structures they called barracks. Each building, designed to hold forty men, had fifty-five or more. So once again I was fated to live in close contact with too many convicts. My group went into a building someone had christened *Nid d'oiseau* or *Bird Nest*. With heavy bars on all the windows it was more like a birdcage, and we were the birds inside — jailbirds. Though no weary soul was laughing at that moment, humor in the place wasn't lacking. Some of the older convicts firmly believed it was humor that kept them alive. The barracks were a forum for bawdy jokes and off-color stories. Laughter, sometimes hysterical but often hilarious and infectious, was never lacking. The person who could tell a good story with humor became an entertainer earning popularity and respect. His story eased listeners away from reality when he told it well. Any time he told it poorly he was taunted. Some stories divulged information worth knowing.

A few hours after lockdown an older convict began a story based on what he had gone through in another prison. We listened quietly until a clanking on metal interrupted him. Several liberated convicts had come to the barred windows and were tapping on them. We went over to see what they wanted and heard them whispering. They had luxury items for sale — tobacco, bananas, and coffee.

"How can we pay for that stuff?" someone asked. "We don't have any money, and I'm sure you ain't here to give it to us."

"Your clothes, hotshot! They're like money! Them guards don't care whether you have clothing or not. And you won't neither when you start working like beasts of burden under that hot sun. If anyone should ask, you can always say the stuff was stolen."

With some misgiving we did business with them, and that night we had fewer clothes but cigarettes to smoke and bananas to eat. The next morning several men who had not traded their clothes discovered most of them missing. The thieves who came in the night to steal our stuff on the ship were busy with the same scheme in the barracks. Later I learned that clothes were very necessary when a man was trying to escape but often a burden when working like oxen in the heat. In some camps nudity was common. In most the men wore ragged shorts or loin cloths with no shirt. Quickly the tropical sun turned them brown.

The next day the warden assembled all newcomers in the courtyard and made an inspirational speech to allay any fear or anxiety we might have concerning prison life in French Guiana. He wanted also to emphasize how impossible it would be to carry out a planned escape.

"In this place," he said for all to hear, "you may go one way or the other. Those of you who give us no trouble will serve your time free of undue suffering. The second way, trying to escape, is plainly foolish and not recommended. I know most of you dream of escape. But you should know before you try it that either the jungle or the sea will stop you dead in your tracks. In the jungle you'll die of hunger, heat exhaustion, snakebite, or betrayal by a comrade. On a flimsy raft the sharks will get you if heat, thirst, sun, and drowning don't take you first. I know many of you won't listen, but I do not advise you to go the second way."

It was a good speech and convincing but not convincing enough. In spite of what he was saying and even as he said it, I knew I would try to escape the first chance I got. It was simply a matter of waiting for the right time, and time was passing. Our names were placed in the registry and we were given identifying numbers. Mine was 51080 and it burned into my brain an ugly fact. Since 1852 when the prison was first established by Napoleon the Third, more than fifty thousand doomed men who might have contributed substantially to French society had come there and suffered before me. The farm boy Julien was given the number right after mine, and that placed us in the same barracks. But as soon as I was able to talk to him I learned he was going to the barracks of a degenerate who wanted him as a lover. Julien went off quietly and I never saw him again. A month later I heard he went to the hospital complaining of stomach pain. A week or so after that he was dead. The doctor in attendance never knew exactly why he died. The thug sent his personal effects home to his mother and asked her to send money for a tombstone. She gave the devil that killed her son several hundred francs.

After three days of orientation involving a medical examination and endless paperwork, I was marched to a labor camp in the jungle. That meant separation from a man calling himself Gérard with whom I had planned to escape as soon as possible. He went under guard with five other convicts to install electrical lights in a village close to the Brazilian border. News of his death reached me later. With another man he had drowned when trying to escape by sea in a dugout canoe. A wave capsized the canoe, hardly more seaworthy than a heavy log, within sight of people on shore. His body washed up on the beach. Sharks feasted, according to the report, on his friend. Gérard's intense longing for escape made him careless, and the escapade ended before it began. The incident underscored a relevant fact. I would have to be patient when planning an escape and very careful when executing it.

Men of every walk in life worked side by side in the sweltering labor camps. The penal Administration made no distinction between old and young, murderer and petty thief, laborer and executive in civil life. Degenerates from vice dens worked side by side with defrocked priests and crooked scam artists. Unlike the guards who prided themselves on rank, no convict was above another. We were all on the same level and required to work to exhaustion at the same task. Men with clean fingernails and soft palms who had never held an axe in all their lives were put to work chopping down gigantic trees in tropical heat. For them and for me it was a deadly game, and yet the warden had said we would not experience undue suffering. More than half of the men sent to a jungle camp would find the labor beyond their strength and die. It was common knowledge that hundreds sent to the colony died in the first year of overwork, abuse, or dread diseases. Dysentery causing dehydration, severe abdominal pain, and bloody diarrhea killed two or three men every day in just one jungle camp.

In the timber camp where I worked, the guards sounded a klaxon to jar us awake at five in the morning. At five-thirty as daylight approached they marched us into the jungle to labor all day with only half an hour's rest for lunch. Each convict had to produce a sizable stack of wood to be fashioned into lumber. If he fell behind and didn't meet his quota, he received on coming from the forest only dry bread for supper. Each man had to cut down a tree, chop off its limbs, and leave the heavy trunk away from standing timber. Late in the afternoon the guards checked to see that all the men had done the job. If a convict came up lacking, he went hungry. Though small of stature, I was young and strong in those days and managed all right. But downing a tree with only an axe was a daunting task for the strongest of men. A bucksaw would have made the job efficient and easy, but no administrative officer cared to make a convicted man's work easy. We had been sentenced to years of hard labor, and that's exactly what we got.

Any person with a warm and good heart, rare in French Guiana, might have wept to see us ragged wretches trooping barefoot and half naked into the jungle every morning. In our bellies to sustain us until noon was only coffee and a hunk of black bread. Some mornings we had for breakfast a tasteless mush or gruel with a thin slice of meat, but on most days we got two pieces of bread and a pint of coffee. On that we worked until a guard came with soup in a black pot. Flies swarmed around the pot and often fell into it as he put the warm liquid into tin bowls. We ate it anyway, joking that the flies added protein. At times the soup had bits of rancid meat that were eaten anyway. Drenched in sweat and suffering from painful mosquito bites, we chopped trees so hard they blunted the axes. Then returning weak and wet we had no dry clothes to change into because we had bartered them away or had them stolen. For supper we got a glass of water, a piece of bread, and a few ounces of rice covered with a sugary brown liquid. Frenchmen love their bread, but good bread in a jungle camp was not to be had.

It was a miserable life — I hesitate to call it a life at all — that was now beginning for us. We had no money even to buy a pinch of tobacco. We bartered away the bar of soap issued to us monthly. We got a tepid shower once a week when it should have been every day, and we had to reckon with diseases that laid even the strongest of us low. We had come from a temperate climate and were not equipped to work under a burning sun in a humid jungle where the heat was intolerable even in deep shade. We were bitten incessantly by bloated mosquitoes and by insects I had never seen before. Any man swatting a mosquito had to reckon with human blood spurting from it.

When we were not slowly killing ourselves at hard labor under a blazing sun or downpour, we were badly treated by inhumane guards or dying of disease. I saw my companions falling sick and dying, one or two, almost daily. I saw their corpses rotting in the mud half a day before removal. I saw my own swollen feet oozing blood after vampire bats had gnawed on them in the night. Also

I ripped my skin to scratch away tiny insects that bored into my flesh. Every morning I woke up sick to my stomach and short of breath but wouldn't give up. To do so meant to die, and I wasn't ready for that. Somehow I found the strength to carry on. Soon, I told myself, I would leave that horrid place and find a life. A small nugget of hope I could have lost sustained me.

Adding to the physical suffering in a hostile climate was the mental suffering that assailed us. I quickly learned that French Guiana had no social order and no moral code. The towns had churches that citizens attended, but they were off limits to convicts. If a prisoner or liberated convict got religion and wanted to attend church, most likely he was turned away. The only moral guide among convicts and for the town as well was a crude philosophy insisting that every man had to shift for himself. Reduced to an ugly struggle merely to exist, every man was in revolt against the system and governed solely by self-interest. Each of us became an island, never part of the main, and the isolation made us all intensely lonely. We hungered for normal and friendly conversation, for harmless horseplay at times, and for camaraderie. But not able to trust each other in that jungle camp, we shut ourselves away in a world of our own and viewed everybody with high suspicion. With nothing pleasurable to look forward to after work and too tired to hear or tell a good story, we suffered from boredom. Some men inevitably sank to the level of animals and tried to lose themselves in lustful longing. In all the jungle camps immoral behavior was rampant. Coarse, older convicts desperately sought younger partners for sex. The guards turned a blind eye to it, especially when a bribe was available.

Most of the newly arrived convicts listened dutifully to the warden's speech but made up their minds to escape as soon as they could. More than a few left with a few lumps of bread stuffed in their pockets and a bottle of water slung around their necks, certain they would succeed while others had failed. Some tried to swim across the river to reach the jungles of Dutch Guiana. In a current stronger than expected they drowned. Others fled into the French jungle trying to reach Brazil. A few unfortunates got lost and wandered in the hostile jungle for days and weeks before perishing. Most returned beaten by natural forces and shaken by acute pain in their joints. They suffered also from dysentery and diarrhea, and from malaria transmitted by mosquitoes larger and fiercer than any they'd ever seen. Many were gravely ill on returning and died in the ill-equipped hospital. One could count on the fingers of one hand the number who gained freedom for a few months. Not one desperate soul managed to secure a permanent freedom. It was an object lesson quickly taken to heart.

As the weeks passed I gathered other important lessons. Living on a level that swiftly became primitive, after a few weeks we began to go barefoot and nearly naked. Wooden sabots were issued to us but caused huge blisters on our heels. Leather shoes were available only to those with money and quickly stolen. Clean underwear and fingernails, even a clean neck and face, belonged to another place and time. Any attire that made a man look presentable, that made him look as though he lived in the current world, ceased to exist. We didn't bathe in the morning or at night because water in the barracks was mainly for drinking. Very few of us had the luxury of owning a toothbrush, and toothpaste just didn't exist. So in the midst of dirty unwashed bodies one began to curse his sense of smell and hope it would soon diminish and disappear. The coarse food, reeking of bacteria and too often half spoiled, quickly damaged taste buds as well as stomachs. Drinking the water often brought diarrhea. Also we had no magazines, newspapers, or books to read. We couldn't receive packages to remind us of home, and so the gulf between present and past grew larger and larger.

Snickering guards told us that any man determined to adapt and remain alive after six months, would exist as an ape even though his dear mama happened to be an angel. To accept the brutish existence thrust upon us would make life easier, they said, but not for long. Then slapping their thighs with glee, they hooted derision.

"Even the fittest among you will die within a year or two. Life in this place as you must know already is nasty, brutish, and short. So if you have anything of value, such as a stash of money in your bowels, let us know so we can be there to take it when you go."

And they laughed at their little joke, laughed as if they had made a rare and funny and very clever jest. Three of the eight men I first got to know were already dead, and the other five would die in just a a little more than two years. I was one man in a cargo of 300. Within five to seven years nearly half of that number would be dead. I had never experienced such hardship in all my life, even as a waif on the streets of Paris. I lacked the physical strength of many who fled and died, and of some who didn't but died anyway. I soon began to wonder how long I could last but quickly shoved those thoughts behind me. To survive I would put my trust in brain instead of brawn. It wouldn't be easy.

Chapter Five

Transfer to Hollow Reed

Not long after my arrival in Bella Vista I was sent with nine other convicts to a camp called Hollow Reed deep in the jungle. Under guard we crossed the town and were soon tramping down a dusty street to the outskirts. We came upon a quaint little shop where a Chinaman sat relaxing in the shade. Hanging on a string in the tropical sun were six golden bodies of deep-fried chickens. Only the feathers and entrails had been removed. In the store was a strange assortment of everything one could imagine. The chief guard said we might buy something if we had the money. Although only two or three of us had money, we crowded inside to stare stupidly at tobacco, bread, canned meat, and bottles of rum. Two skinny clerks watched with eagle eyes to be certain we didn't steal anything. Yet despite their vigilance, several men walked out with goodies in their armpits and pockets. That's when I realized rapists, child molesters, and murderers live by a moral code that allows them to commit any sort of crime with impunity. I didn't buy anything, for I had no money. Though branded an habitual thief and convicted, I didn't steal a thing. I could see the little store was struggling to stay in business.

Half a mile from the shop a narrow path entered the forest. From there until we reached the camp, the guards told us, we would be on our own. We stood amazed. They were leaving us on the outskirts of town at the edge of the jungle to make our way unattended.

"Just follow the path," they told us. "The camp's only a dozen or so miles from here, and you can take your time getting there. But be there before the sun goes down. You don't want to be in the jungle after dark. It gets cold and damp, you won't be able to see a thing, and predators go on the prowl as soon as the dark comes."

Across the river within easy sight was Dutch Guiana. Should we bolt toward the river, swim across it, and hope to find freedom? We quickly agreed it had to be some sort of trick to test us. If we ran for the river we could be shot. So we took the path, trudging resolutely, expecting to find a guard around the next bend to escort us. For a couple of hours we walked deeper into the jungle, the canopy above us blotting out the sun. We found no guard waiting for us. After a while we came upon a camp the inmates called *Chien Galeux* or *Mangy Dog*. Nearby were gaunt men in loincloths hacking away at underbrush. They wanted to speak to us, but their guard ordered us to keep moving. Later we met a group of half-naked men coming toward us with axes slung over their shoulders. They seemed to be in good spirits after completing their day's work. One convict, however, suffering from insect bites and grotesquely skeletal, told us the work was killing him. Then in a raspy, hollow voice he added we would have it better at Camp Hollow Reed.

"You won't be cutting down trees with dull axes there," he muttered. "That's what kills a man, that and the fever. I was a lawyer back home and never owned an axe, never touched an axe. Here on the equator they make me chop trees hard as steel ten hours a day with a goddamn axe not sharp enough to cut a banana in half!"

"What crime did you commit to be sent here, counselor?" a young man we called Julot asked with a wry smile "Were you unjustly sentenced like all the rest of us?"

Emaciated and exhausted but retaining a sense of humor, the lawyer managed to chuckle softly before replying. "I got mixed up in a Ponzi scheme even more lucrative than the one old Charles Ponzi pulled off shortly after the big war. Made a lot of money, lived high on the hog, had my pick of sexy women and fast cars and fancy houses. Then a bitter old dowager complained I had stolen thousands of francs from her. I was hauled into court to face charges of fraud, theft, and elder abuse. Argued my own case and did a good job of it too but lost."

"And now you lose again, you dirty old crook!" Julot taunted as we strolled away. "Too bad, nasty old bastard! You just can't win, can you? I hope your victim, the little old lady, got her money back but doubt it. I'm sure she needed it more than you."

"Oh, another smartass! Don't be a smartass, youngster! You'll be in my condition soon enough!"

The skeletal man shook a bony fist behind Julot's back and muttered with hissing discomfort, "Always a smartass in every bunch."

As the day wore on we moved slowly and rested more often. We sat at the foot of gigantic trees, their roots serving as benches, and caught glimpses of monkeys scurrying from limb to limb above us. Brightly colored birds — parrots, toucans, macaws — were there too, singing notes of downright joy. In a place made deadly and terrible by men for men these so-called lower animals seemed to be living happy lives free of restraint. That thought was with me as we straggled into Hollow Reed in late afternoon. It was a sight I vividly remember. Forty acres of big and tall trees had been cut and burned. An army of hapless convicts had sacrificed themselves to remove stumps the size of a small truck. The backbreaking labor of many months in searing heat eventually killed them, but in time a jungle camp was erected. Five decaying buildings with tin roofs sizzled in the sun. Their yellow paint had faded to a baby-poop tan and was almost gone. A cursory glance assured me that wretched men in the hundreds had lived and died there.

After signing in with name and number we entered the mess hall and ate supper. It was a noisy place. Unlike the prison eatery in France where silence was the order of the day, at Hollow Reed we could talk and even complain. Guards leaned against the wall with rifles loaded but paid little attention, allowing free activity within reason. The food was abominable, but after walking all day through the jungle I was hungry enough to eat it. Half an hour later we were escorted to a barracks that smelled of urine and dead rats and was in dire need of a thorough cleaning. Grime on the walls indicated it had not been cleaned in decades. Arranged in a long row were bunks made of rough boards without a mattress. When darkness came I found a bunk near a window and lay down. While attempting to fall asleep I surveyed my surroundings. An oil lamp in the center of the long room threw shadows on the walls of dark figures moving eerily about like phantoms. The keeper of the barracks, a rat-like little man with narrow shoulders and a potbelly pranced in and turned off the lamp. Tired men slept.

Every one of the barracks in the compound had its keeper, a convict who looked after the building when its occupants were away at work. One of his duties was to keep the place clean, but he seldom did more than merely sweep the floor. He brought coffee to the inmates every morning, filled a barrel with river water that had to be strained and boiled, and remained in the building when all the others had left to see that nothing was stolen. Between supper and bedtime he sold or traded tobacco, soap, sewing thread and needles, food items, shoes now and then, and clothing. The trade was profitable and the job much sought after. Above all, he had to be trustworthy. When tempted to steal another man's property, he wrestled with right and wrong to convince himself it wasn't worth it. He would lose his job and be assigned hard labor in stifling heat. The fear of severe punishment kept him honest. On this night he called out, "All present! All thirty-six present!"

I wasn't able to sleep. I lay on the hard board staring into the gloom for hours. Then a shadowy form rose and moved toward the unlocked door and was soon outside. Moments later a slimmer shadow flitted outside. I thought the men had left to use the latrine but then remembered that facility was in a smaller room in the same building. When they didn't return I could sense something was up. The hours dragged on and when the day began with a blast of the klaxon, I got the full details of what had happened. Two men were missing from my barracks and three from another. Five men had escaped! I was young in those days and full of hope, and that gave me even more hope. I promised myself I wouldn't be suffering in that jungle camp for long. At the right time when factors were favorable, I too would escape.

I was curious about the job I'd be doing there in the middle of the jungle. The next day they told me I would be assigned to a workshop where straw hats were made. On arrival in Bella Vista I had seen convicts wearing the wide-brimmed straw hats to protect their heads, ears, and faces from the tropical sun. Now I would be doing my part to manufacture them. I sat at a table with a pile of fiber from palm trees in front of me and was taught how to braid the fiber into a sturdy material that would be passed on to another convict to fashion into hats. On a good day I began work early in the morning at first light and finished the job with blistered fingers near noon. The rest of the day was mine to use as I saw fit. My co-workers went back to the barracks to rest, but I got into the habit of going into the jungle to walk a narrow path. There alone, witness to sights and sounds new to me, I realized trying to escape with others was too risky. It was harder for authorities to track down one man than several. I would have to go it alone.

I did go it alone for more than three weeks but slowly made friends with other convicts. I learned that one had to belong to a group to survive assault by crazed convicts intent on rape or robbery and not beyond actual murder. I was living with vicious, angry men who settled a mild disagreement with a fist in the face and a kick in the groin.

"Stay away from the toilets at night," I was told, "even if you have to piss in a can. Violent brutes lurking there will pounce upon you and squash you like a bug when they see you ain't very big."

At least once a week I heard screams coming from the toilets at the end of the building. When morning came, a guard would find a body or badly wounded man in a pool of blood on the cement floor. Two or three unlucky convicts would be ordered to clean up the mess. The body couldn't be removed until examined by someone from the hospital. I followed the good advice offered me and managed to survive as a newcomer without becoming a victim. At all times I kept a low profile and remained close to my group. At night it was inevitable I would think of Gabrielle and the few happy days we spent together. Then one day to my surprise a letter was handed to me. It was brief, only one paragraph, and I read it carefully. Even today it sticks in memory.

"My dearest Maurice," it began. "When you were unjustly sentenced to spend many years in a prison that is being called hell on earth, I felt my life at twenty-two had ended. You were only twenty-three when you left for that tropical hell, and we both knew you might never return. You assured me, however, that while it's unlikely you will ever see the soil of France again, you intend to escape as soon as possible and be with your girl in some other country. Wherever you go I will follow. Regardless how long it takes, please don't lose the hope that nourishes you and gives you strength. If we can't embrace once again after two years, you want me to live my life as fully as I can perhaps with another man. Well, my love, as long as you live that will never happen. I shall wait for you, because without you I am half a person. Write to me, my love."

It was the only mail I ever got from Gabrielle. Even though I sent letters as often as I could, I believe she never received even one. Because she never heard from me, she probably went on with her life to marry and have a family. I have always hoped she did exactly that. Prison officials surely opened my letters, decided they revealed too much of their operation, and threw them away. Rampant double-dealing and the attempt to hide it made that a certainty. It ranged from top-ranking officials to the lowest guard and from the guards to savvy convicts. It was a fact of life and a way of life for just about everybody.

Chapter Six
My First Attempt

As time crawled tediously at a snail's pace, I became more acquainted with the muggy jungle and learned to respect its terrible power. I came to believe it would be folly to blunder deeper into that strange and dangerous world in an attempt to reach Brazil. Others before me had tried it only to get lost in the jungle and die. I would take the easier route and escape into Dutch Guiana. At the Hollow Reed camp I quickly came to know convicts who had made it to the Dutch colony but had been caught and brought back. One man had spent several months in the settlement posing as a Dutchman. He had acquired the manners and language of Dutch people when living in Holland. Yet somehow he was exposed as a Frenchman by the way he held and smoked his cigarette! I found the story a bit hard to believe, and yet it could have happened.

From those who had escaped I learned important strategies to put into use: where to go in the uncharted jungle, how to identify a jungle path, how to detect signs of danger at a water hole, how to find edible food and untainted water, and whether to move by night or by day. Also, when moving by day, how would I become invisible when approaching a primitive village or civilized town? That requirement was the most difficult of all. Any time I asked about it, I got half a dozen different answers. When my comrades heard the details of my plan, to a man they advised me not to try it. Repeatedly they told me any chance of succeeding was small indeed. I would soon be arrested, returned to French Guiana, and punished with years added to my sentence. I didn't listen to them.

In time I gained the trust of a young Sicilian who was even more passionate to escape than I. Russo was the butt of cruel jokes and homosexual proposals from older, vicious convicts. They were making his life miserable and he had to get away. He told me he would save himself from the brutes surrounding him or die trying. So with some misgiving I took him on as my partner in pursuit of freedom. Within days we began to build a raft of bamboo down by the creek after work and planned to flee within a week or ten days. In the meantime we gathered provisions: water in a barrel, bread, rice, sardines, onions, canned ham, condensed milk, and a bottle tightly corked filled with matches. All these things we pilfered surreptitiously from shops and the prison pantry. Bolstered by the arrogance of youth, we were happily certain we would soon be free. Going with a congenial companion was better than fleeing alone.

It was raining the day we had chosen to leave, torrential rain one finds only in the tropics. We thought we might postpone the trip for a better day, but decided to go anyway. After supper and when our work was done, we went to the creek and uncovered the raft. Quickly we pushed it into the water and let it drift with the current. A very dark night made navigating down the creek difficult. After giving it a try we paddled to the bank and found shelter under a tree. Mosquitoes attacked us with freight-train force, and within minutes our hands were bloody from swatting when bitten. The pesky insects made their way into our ears and even up our noses. We couldn't make a fire to fend them off, for anyone pursuing us might see it. In a dry area we had no mud to smear on our skin, and we had no tobacco juice to cover our faces. So we suffered painful bites through the night. It was our first night in the jungle and not a good one. We lay among the roots of the tree and hoped no roaming animal would make a meal of us. Near morning after sleeping very little, howling baboons in the canopy above us jolted us awake. Then at last the sun filtered downward, and all was suddenly very different. In daylight the bugaboo jungle was tolerable.

After a meager breakfast of coffee and bread hard enough to crack a tooth, we pushed off again and drifted into the river's current. It began to take us away from the bank into the view of anyone who might be standing on shore. That caused alarm, and so we paddled furiously back to the bank and decided to move only in darkness. When it began to rain again, sheets of water reduced visibility almost to zero. Under cover of the heavy rain, we tried crossing the wide river. That's when we found our paddles were too small to buck the currents and allow us to steer the raft. We swirled toward the French shore and could do nothing about it. Then after hours of struggle a favorable current caught us and carried us toward the Dutch settlement but not to it. By then the rain had passed on to another location and the sun was out. We paddled to shore and chose a little inlet for landing. Clutching our bundles, we crawled up the slippery bank and let the raft go. In no mood to celebrate our freedom (if indeed it was freedom), in clammy clothing we ate something tasteless and tried to sleep. We would have to tramp through a dense jungle and knew we couldn't do it in the dark. So with two hours' rest, three at most, we were up again and moving.

Convicts in camp had told us we might find a path that would take us through the jungle to a native village some twenty miles to the west. With no compass and not even the sun to guide us, we found no path and no direction whatever. To put it with painful directness, we got lost in a deadly maze and came out abruptly into a clearing where a group of Indians were at work. They spotted us as soon as we stepped from the trees and came trotting toward us. All of them carried machetes for cutting bamboo and some had rifles. Russo grabbed my arm and tugged at it; he wanted to run. I persuaded him to stand as still as a statue, saying to him that if we ran, they would surely overtake us and kill us. Up they came, close and menacing, gesticulating and jabbering. We understood not a word of their language. They were naked except for loincloths and wore white markings on their faces. Breaking into a chant, they danced around us as though celebrating.

We tried to buy them off with a few coins and even our shoes. They took the coins and shoes and anything else that caught their fancy. Jabbing us with their rifles and threatening with grotesque movements to slice us into little pieces with their heavy machetes, they marched us into a nearby town where the authorities threw us in prison. Later I found out the penal Administration in Cayenne paid them well for captive runaways. They were "chasers of men" (chass*eurs d'hommes*) in a long-standing program supported by the French. We languished in the damp and dark cell for several days, eating almost nothing and drinking polluted water that brought a severe case of diarrhea to Russo and a moderate one to me. When officials sent us back across the river and dumped us on the riverbank at Bella Vista, we were weak and sick and barely able to walk. The warden debated whether we should go to the prison infirmary for rest and recovery or to the hole on bread and water. Supported by guards as we tried to walk, we went to the hole.

Charged with attempting to escape, we got solitary confinement without delay. I remembered the nice little speech delivered to us when we first arrived. The warden apparently had forgotten his closing remarks about not administering punishment for any first attempt to escape. It was our first attempt, and he punished us severely. We remained in the disciplinary section of the camp for two months, locked in separate solitary cells on coarse food with not enough nutrition to sustain normal weight. The only exercise I got was pacing the tiny cell for hours each day. Within a week I found myself rapidly losing weight and talking to myself. A big black spider somehow crawled into my cell. Half crazy, I tried to make friends with it. Contact with any kind of living creature, I reasoned in my fevered mind, was better than nothing. When a talkative guard finally came to release me, I was so disoriented I couldn't understand what he was saying. Only later did I learn that he was complaining about a strong odor, the stench coming from my unwashed, emaciated body. I never saw Russo again. I asked about him but got a scoffing, nonsensical response and silence. Maybe the ordeal of confinement killed him, or maybe he killed himself. I never found out.

From the hole I went into one of the four blockhouses located in the section of the camp hell-bent on discipline. Each blockhouse held forty convicts waiting to be tried for offenses ranging from trying to steal a porcelain coffee cup from an administrator to outright murder. Some were charged with theft as petty as stealing a toothbrush, others with refusing to work or insulting a guard. Most were there because they had tried to escape and were caught. One man was sent back from as far away as Cuba. They asked what I had done to be there and lost interest when I replied, "failed to escape." In the flickering light of a small lantern I lay down on a bare board, as did the others, with one ankle in a shackle attached to an iron rod. The board was hard as concrete, the heat was stifling, the shackle rubbed my ankle raw, and a terrible odor assailed my nostrils. It came from a large bucket of human waste. The bucket was emptied once a day supposedly, but only when it was full. A host of insects seemed to like it. All night I slapped mosquitoes, sweated profusely, struggled to breathe, and slept very little.

I soon discovered that life in the blockhouses went on day after day miserably and without change. We lay around nearly naked in tainted air and terrible heat, mumbling to ourselves or to each other. We paced the floor for exercise but never got enough, and strong men soon became anemic. More than a few waited and suffered and died before their day of trial. An old convict with a dread disease that had distorted his face grotesquely pleaded in a hollow voice: "Kill me, kill me, please!" We heard it for hours night after night.

The old guy was longing to die but couldn't do what he hoped others might do. He got no sympathy from anybody. Every night an exasperated voice would cry out, "Take my knife, you evil old bastard, and do it yourself! Why do you think anyone here owes you a favor? Jab my knife deep in your gut and give us some peace!"

In time, suffering from dysentery and loose bowels, I lost all desire to eat. I needed medical attention but never got it. The Administration viewed me as rebellious and troublesome and placed me last on the list for any kind of medicine or a doctor. Fearing the slow starvation I saw all around me, I forced myself to eat whatever god-awful food I could get my hands on. I even choked down a handful of fat cockroaches known for their protein. Even though our daily rations were miserably small, I managed to eat anything others turned down. I wrestled with the moral question of taking the food other inmates needed to stay alive. But always I told myself that if left untouched, it would go back to the guards. I ate to survive, to stave off the debilitating weakness that was killing so many. One enduring passion possessed and sustained me: *I would live and remain strong to escape a second time.* It was my destiny.

Each day seemed to become longer and longer, dragging by in the stench and heat with no end in sight. Our one distraction was the mail boat that came once a month. Some of us got letters from home. Others sobbed behind clenched fists on receiving nothing. I felt like crying too but didn't know how. On occasion a mail boat brought escapees back from neighboring countries, and for several days they were the center of attention. We crowded around them to hear their stories, and I learned from them. I was able to obtain from another inmate a little book with blank pages in which I jotted notes. Eventually I received word that because it was my first attempt to escape, the tribunal would go easy on me. I was amused by that and wanted to laugh, but any laughter I was capable of at that time burned in my throat. I was given thirty-seven more days in the blockhouse and sent back to Camp

Hollow Reed. The place was dirty, damp, intensely hot, and very uncomfortable. Also my fellow convicts were not much better than those in the blockhouse. Yet compared to what I had endured in that awful place, my existence at Hollow Reed was easy living in moderate safety. Even so, I made up my mind to escape as soon as I could. Done with Dutch Guiana on the river, I would do it this second time by sea.

Chapter Seven
Money Comes My Way

At Hollow Reed I went back to my old job and worked for a couple of weeks in the hat shop. Then as things seemed to be going well again I found that a tropical insect had bored into the soles of my feet. I had to be taken to the infirmary on a stretcher because both feet were so painful and so badly swollen I couldn't stand or walk. The condition was new to me and scary. The pain was so intense I thought I might lose a foot or even both. In the camp were men hobbling about on one foot, yet still required to work. Dozens in rags with every human deformity imaginable shuffled about in that camp. Not a single one was excused from work of some kind. For a time it looked as though I might become one of them, but in the infirmary they killed the bugs in my feet to allow for a full recovery. Even though I went back to the hat shop to resume my usual work, the chief guard decided to put me in a jungle clearing where men were trying to grow vegetables. My first day there was a disaster. Huge black ants attacked my half-naked body and left my flesh swollen, raw, and bleeding. On top of that, the sun beat down on my neck and shoulders with the force of red-hot hammers.

The next morning, suffering terrible pain and feverish, I asked again for admission to the infirmary. The doctor in charge rejected my request, saying I could soothe the damage to my skin with tobacco juice. When I replied I had no tobacco and no money to buy any, he gave me a small plug, told me to chew it to make it wet, then rub it on the sunburn and lesions left by the biting ants. I followed his instructions and found some relief, but the guard sent me back to the clearing for more bites. So for two weeks I tried to escape work, claiming sickness every morning after coffee. Unknown to me a guard of unsavory character was keeping a record of my infringements for the warden's disciplinary committee. Ten days passed and I was summoned to stand before them to answer questions as they reviewed details of my conduct. They sat in comfortable chairs behind a table. I stood, awkwardly shifting my weight.

The chairman was speaking: "Number 51080, Arthur Maurice Bonheur. You feigned sickness after drinking your coffee thirteen mornings in a row. You made a pest of yourself at the infirmary. You refused to work, and you responded with insolence when required to do so. Well now, Arthur Maurice, what do you say in your defense?"

"He has nothing to say in his defense," said the guard who had recorded my infractions and made them known to these esteemed wielders of power. "All that you see in that little notebook is true and accurate, a daily record of misbehavior."

"That may be so," retorted the chairman, "but I want to hear from the defendant himself. Let's hear his side of the story."

I tried to explain I was sick and feverish because an army of black ants had devoured me at the vegetable garden. They laughed at my hyperbole, saying I could do better than that, and meted out punishment of ninety days in the cells. An hour later I lay in irons on cool but slimy concrete. It was better by far than nursing a gaggle of vegetables under a scorching sun and suffering the bites of ants and other insects. If I had to say one good thing about tropical French Guiana, I would tell the world it's a place favored by insects. They love it there and thrive. As for me, except for an occasional cockroach, I hated the insects and where they lived. Every morning a guard gave me a piece of bread and a glass of water instead of coffee. On the rim of the glass and on the bread were insects. It was hard having no coffee at first, but after a while I lost my craving for it in the morning, and I didn't mind having dry bread one day out of three. I was never a heavy eater. Also I learned to live with the irons. Even though they left bloody sores on my ankles, I was able to walk about for exercise.

I scratched off the days on the grimy wall with marks that looked like this: /. And I drew a line through every four marks to make a unit of five. So I knew exactly how long I had been confined when on the 55th day the chief guard announced my sentence was complete.

"Get all your stuff together and get back to camp," he said in that loud, commanding voice all guards used. "You're a lucky sonobitch! You got ninety days but you're out much sooner."

All my stuff, he said? What stuff? I owned nothing but the clothes on my back, and one could hardly call them clothes. My sweaty and very dirty shirt was in tatters and my trousers in rags. I had no socks and no shoes. I told the guard to go to hell and refused to leave. He demanded I pull myself together. He thought I was crazy, and so he paid no attention to what I was saying. Insults from crazy men were usually ignored.

"You're right about it being sooner, *Asticot*! In fact, I still got thirty-five more days to serve in this rat hole, and I'm staying!"

"You calling me a maggot, you bag o' scum? You'll be staying longer all right, but right now you're leaving!"

"If you drag me out of here expecting me to work, you got another thought coming!" I shouted. "I won't be going to work tomorrow, and it means you'll be hauling my ass back here. So save yourself the trouble, Ape Guy, and leave me alone."

"So it's ape guy now, huh? Looks like I evolved real fast from maggot to ape. Yep, it's likely you'll be coming back tomorrow, but you're coming out today. So it's up to you, Bozo. Go without a beating from good ol' Gus or not go and take the beating."

I knew what Gus was capable of giving, and so I went. Since I had been away from the barracks for more than two months, not even one man seemed to know me. I thought I had made friends with two or three, but they were no longer my friends. I was a troublemaker and a glutton for punishment. To be seen with me meant trouble for them, and quickly I became a pariah. With nothing else to do, I lay down on a board and waited to go back to my cell. Not an hour went by before two men hustled me to the chief guard's office.

"Bonheur!" he demanded. "What in hell is going on with you? I'm hearing you refuse to go back to work. I want to know why."

"I refuse to work in that clearing because I don't like vegetables and I don't like that blazing sun and black ants eating my flesh. In the cell I'm in the shade with cockroaches — no mosquitoes, no ants or malaria, and no tropical sun beating down on me."

"You don't mind speaking your mind, that I'll say for you! If you had another job, would you simmer down and stay out of trouble and out of my hair? You won't be in the sun, and no insects."

"I think I would simmer down, sir. I guess I would."

"All right. I'll hold you to it. Tomorrow you'll go into the infirmary to work as an orderly. Behave yourself or it's back to the clearing."

"Thank you, sir. That job has to be better than digging in the dirt and smelling rotten vegetables and fighting insects under the hot sun. I'm from a temperate climate, you know, and I can't tolerate a tropical sun and creatures like ants the size of puppies."

It wasn't a glamorous job being an orderly. I had to sweep the floor, empty bedpans, help the sick take their medicine, help them with eating and drinking, and bathe some who couldn't do it themselves. Whenever a patient got really sick and made a mess of his bed, I had to change it. Some were incontinent and woke up with soaked mattresses. Airing the stinking mattress in the sun was an ornery job. I've never liked being around sick people, but being there when they needed me was different. So I didn't mind the job all that much.

One day while going for water I saw an orange tree loaded with fruit in the backyard of the chief guard. The next day I filled my buckets with oranges instead of water and sold them to inmates. I made enough money with that one batch of oranges to buy myself a shirt. The next day I confiscated more ripe and juicy oranges and made enough to buy a pair of used trousers. On the third day as I was eagerly picking oranges high up in the tree, the chief guard himself surprised me.

"So, Bonheur!" he said. "Is this how you behave yourself?" I could tell he was very annoyed with me but suppressing his anger.

"You must know I had no clothes, sir, until I found this tree. When the doctor shows up, do you want him to find a half naked orderly tending patients and casting aspersions on his dignified profession?"

"I didn't know you had no clothes. You make a good point, Maurice, but you will not be stealing any more of my oranges. I have chestnut trees. You can have chestnuts."

So I began to do business in chestnuts. I roasted them on a piece of metal and sold them in the barracks. As my capital increased I dealt in bread, tobacco, and small bottles of rum made in Guiana and bought from a guard at prices lower than I demanded.

The chief guard, as I recall him now, was a good and generous fellow. Somehow he had managed to hang on to his humanity in a place where inhumanity was the rule of the day. But I must tell you now he was unlucky. He got mixed up in a scandal involving a bribe from a convict who wanted to escape. Prosecutors claimed he allowed the man to leave the camp, gave him an hour to get away, and then set the dogs on him. My chief guard was tried and convicted, and most of us thought he would get off with a light sentence. But one morning before the sentence was handed down a guard found him dead in his cell. The poor fellow had made a rope of his shirt and trousers, tied it around bars in the high window, and hanged himself. The incident caused a lot of chatter in the barracks. I didn't like to hear it, for the man had done well by me.

Within three months I had made and saved a handsome sum of money and was thinking of another escape. I had clothes to protect my body from the elements and even a pair of good leather boots. I would keep them in a canvas bag while at sea and use them as soon as I touched shore again. I began to sound out some convicts who had saved money from selling butterflies, and we began to work out a plan. My second attempt to escape would have to be more than a mere attempt; it would have to succeed. I had been in the penal colony for more than a year and knew a good deal more about the place and its surroundings than during my first attempt. I knew the climate and the primeval forest, and I thought I knew something of that vast blue ocean just waiting for us. I would go not with one ignorant man, but with a savvy group of men seeking freedom at the risk of dying, and I would not fail. It didn't pay to escape and get caught and serve time and escape again and serve more time. I knew hapless convicts who had fallen into that dreary pattern, but Arthur Maurice Bonheur wasn't about to become its victim. Well, at least that was my thinking.

Chapter Eight

My Second Attempt

It was Christmas in tropical French Guiana. The sun-baked town of Bella Vista was celebrating the season. Citizens of several races decorated palm trees on the main street in a rather futile attempt to make them look like Christmas trees. In the penal colony the guards were jovial and celebratory, but only a few convicts spoke of Christmas and what it was like back home. One group, and I was part of that group, was thinking of the holiday as the perfect time to escape. For days we had planned our departure, parsing every detail, and we had spent time gathering necessary equipment. Just as darkness came on Christmas Eve, six desperate and driven men slipped into the blackness of the jungle and hurried to a canoe in thick bushes near a creek. We answered to Bonheur, Bigelow, Georges, Lapin, Marcel, and Pierre. Our time on earth ranged from twenty to fifty-seven, Georges being the oldest and Bigelow the youngest. The chance to get away on this night was better than any other time. Prison officials, already drinking prodigiously, were lax in their duties and eager to celebrate. They would be drunk within the hour.

Our stolen canoe, made from the trunk of a rubber tree, carried a makeshift sail and supplies of coffee, rice, beans, condensed milk, dried beef, and bananas. In a large keg we had several gallons of clean water. We had managed to buy the supplies at minimum cost from an old convict who had gained his freedom but often visited the camp. From the creek we reached the river and traveled down it several miles to enter the open Atlantic. This time I was not in a flimsy raft at the mercy of wind and current but in a sturdy canoe with five strong men. Three men on either side made it seaworthy and powerful. The ocean was eerily calm with swells that gave us no problem. The tide was going out, withdrawing, and with it we went without effort. Away from the shore we hoisted our sail, but in calm air we had to paddle again. In dangerous water we knew nothing about and in the dark of night, we were as giddy as children on a well-equipped playground. And like children at play we chatted in friendly, excitable conversation.

"In a few days we'll be seeing a lighthouse that marks the entrance to the Orinoco!" Marcel exclaimed. "Didn't Columbus discover that river on one of his voyages to the new world?"

"Well, maybe," said old Georges who had been a schoolteacher. "I seem to recall he wrote about coming to the mouth of the river in 1498 on his third voyage. And about a hundred years later the Englishman Walter Raleigh sailed up the river looking for El Dorado."

"Damn right!" said the man we called Pierre. "And we'll be sailing up that river too but not looking for a city of gold. We'll be looking for something better, a big hunk of freedom that will last for the rest of our days! I'm of the opinion we'll be free men within a week!"

"You don't believe you're a free man already?" I asked.

"Only for the moment, Maurice. I'm looking for permanent freedom, the kind the bourgeois in France have always had. They were free before the Bastille went down and even more so after the Revolution."

"Are you giving us a history lesson, young man?" Georges asked with a sly wink in my direction. "Well, it does seem appropriate," he chuckled, "to reflect at this moment on liberty, fraternity, equality."

We were laughing when Pierre at the tiller spoke of a breeze from the southeast. The sail filled tight and we moved smoothly over building waves. Though taking on some water, the canoe was proving its worth. I was dead tired from all the preparation and planning and was thinking of sleep when I heard Marcel say, "Didn't I hear thunder? Listen! I think I hear thunder in the distance. Means a storm!"

"Couldn't be thunder," Lapin who had signed on as navigator replied. "No thunder and no need to worry about a storm. Thunder comes in cloudy weather. The night is balmy. We got stars up there."

"My god, Rabbit Man!" Marcel exclaimed. "Are you stir-crazy? You been locked away from nature too long. You came to show us the way, but you don't seem to know much about the sea. A storm could rush in and knock us in the water in minutes."

"I have to admit I wasn't entirely honest with you," Lapin muttered as Marcel glared at him. "You're right. I don't know much about boats or the sea. I was desperate to come but had no money. I'm real sorry, but I think I can pull my share of the weight. I'm sure gonna try."

Lapin's confession was startling as we heard it, but at the moment he was off the hook. We could see a storm approaching fast, and we had no time to consider his case. A good breeze was up and we were moving fast. Suddenly a rogue wave hit us broadside and almost capsized the canoe. Somehow it remained upright though swamped with water. Two men started bailing as fast as they could, using buckets brought along for that purpose. The dugout with Pierre steering rode the waves well, slicing through them or riding them down into the trough at breakneck speed. But soon we discovered our food was a sodden mess and our sail ripped to shreds. Daybreak came with a thunderclap, and we could see the jungle shoreline only a few miles away. We headed for it with paddling made easy by a good breeze behind us.

Not a person said a word. We were thinking people on shore might surely see us and raise an alarm. An hour or so later the canoe was racing through the surf, all on board holding on tight. Two of us jumped into the water, as the waves began to draw back, and pulled our craft onto the beach. Pierre gashed his thigh struggling with the canoe and was barely able to walk later. I ripped off a strip of cloth from the battered sail and wrapped it tight around his leg to lessen the pain and stop the bleeding. We had to wait for him to give the injured leg a rest. So we sprawled exhausted in sullen silence on the white sand. Minutes later we heard Marcel tell Lapin quietly and patiently, almost as a father speaking to a wayward child, that he had forfeited his right to be a member of our group. It came as no surprise.

"You misrepresented yourself," he said. "You lied to us, Lapin. Five good men were in danger of losing their lives because you lied. I ought to kill you for putting us in peril. I'm sure you know you deserve it. I'll do it in a heartbeat if you refuse to walk. Now go!"

Without a word Lapin picked himself up from the sand and toddled toward the trees. In minutes he disappeared, dissolving like a ghost in the thick jungle. We had not selected Marcel as our leader, and we might have gone against his decision to punish the offender with exile. Instead we merely stood by and watched a man go quietly and obediently into solitude and death. Then without comment we turned attention to our own predicament. Almost all the food we had taken so many risks to steal was gone, washed out of the canoe when the storm hit us with unspeakable force. Some bread remained but was sodden. We spread it out in little pieces to dry. Though salty we knew we could eat it, and we had some tins of condensed milk. Each of us got an equal share of the milk and bread before we sprawled on the sand and slept.

When morning came we decided we couldn't make it by sea. Not a man among us knew anything at all about sailing a boat, and moreover the battered dugout had no sail. We agreed to rest a while longer and then set out through the jungle, hoping to find eventually a village or town. There we might buy provisions, find a real and seaworkthy boat, and go on to civilization and freedom. We trudged along the beach, but at times we couldn't follow the edge of the water and had to retreat into the forest. On the beach swarms of biting flies had a feast on bare sin. In the humid jungle we fought mosquitoes that squirted blood when swatted. Other insects I had never seen pestered us. All day we plodded in water and mud, prying leeches from our feet and legs. As night came we tried to build a fire in drizzling rain that became a downpour. When swarms of huge mosquitoes attacked us after the rain, we smeared black mud over every inch of exposed skin. It helped a little but smelled like human feces. Breathing the odor made sleeping difficult.

Daylight came on fast as it always does in the tropics, and we set out again, struggling through jungle undergrowth and reaching the sea near noon. I climbed to the top of a mangrove tree to get a view of what lay ahead. What I saw was disheartening. We were trudging along a peninsula that jutted many miles eastward into the sea. We had to cross it to get back on track. That meant trudging through mud and water and tangled mangrove roots to firm ground. When we reached a clearing dry enough for sleeping, we built a fire (as we fought exhaustion) to keep the insects at bay. Though the night was warm, we slept as close to the fire as we dared. When morning came we had suffered fewer insect bites than usual but were sweating, disoriented, and hungry.

After a long discussion in which we found ourselves quarreling, all but I decided to give up the grand adventure and go back to French Guiana. I thought it was a foolish decision and insisted we continue another day or two to see what lay ahead. I argued they had signed on with me for better or for worse, and better times were bound to come soon. With stubborn resignation they emphasized the hard reality confronting us. Nature and the elements, fate or luck, and even our own bodies were going against us. We had very little food and a bleak prospect of finding more. Quite simply the time had come to call it quits. Contrary to popular belief, the jungle doesn't give up its edible riches easily.

Dazed and stumbling, we moved in the opposite direction, hoping to get back to the river in a day or two. Perhaps we could hide in plain sight on the Dutch side long enough to regain strength and plan something. Just as we were moving out, Lapin emerged from the jungle and stood at the edge of the clearing. All the time we were struggling to move forward, he was observing and following. We could tell he was sick, starving, and feverish but offered no help. He had to pay for endangering our lives, and though I suffered pangs of conscience later, we left him there to die. The way back was as much a struggle as moving forward. Our stamina was ebbing, and we could no longer dream of freedom and a good life. Any dream we might have had was shattered by the simple necessity to survive. After wading through waist-deep mangrove marshes, we found higher ground and began cutting our way through the jungle, slashing a trail with two machetes.

All day we pushed against lush, rubbery, and resistant vegetation, taking turns at swinging the machetes and resting every three hours or so. When darkness came we spent the night with empty bellies beside a creek. The next day with no food to sustain us we plodded again through jungle growth, passing trees that soared to immense height and gave us shade but nothing else. At noon we ate grub worms and beetles, the worms supplying moisture. Somehow old Georges caught a gorgeous bird and wrung its neck. In minutes he was plucking it while Pierre built a fire. Marcel fashioned a bowl of hard bamboo, filled it with water and got it to boil just as the bamboo caught on fire. With his shoe he swatted out the burning embers, and we boiled the bird after gutting it. Each of us ate a small portion of real meat and felt better. In late afternoon we reached a small stream and caught a turtle. We ate it with great satisfaction, each of us blessed with a portion of sweet and tasty meat. We had thought we might starve or die of thirst before reaching the river.

The next day we saw prints of human feet on a trail we had found and followed them. We stumbled onward and came upon an Indian village that let us know we were near the river. With due caution we crept into the village to find only women and children who ran away as we approached. A thin old woman sat cross-legged in front of a hut and looked at us without flinching. We must have been an awful sight to her eyes, for we had suffered terribly. I pointed to a couple of dry fish hanging nearby, and she gave them to me. Then she brought from inside her hut a large bunch of ripe bananas and a jug of water. We ate the food like ravenous animals and found more in empty huts. To our surprise and delight we found in one hut a large tub of turtle eggs. Instead of having a shell as with most eggs, the turtle eggs were covered with a layer of skin and larger than most eggs commercially available. I jabbed one with a pointed stick, and a thick yellow liquid oozed out.

"That's the yolk you're looking at," Georges, the ex-schoolteacher, explained. "Let the white of the egg run free and then suck out the yolk. It's high in food value, lots of protein! The white of the egg has even more protein but not very tasty."

We followed his advice and gorged on the eggs, punching a hole in each and draining the white. Then we sucked out the rich yolk in the same way I remembered sucking a Spanish orange in my youth. Each of us had our fill of turtle yolk and even left some of the eggs for the rightful owner. After days of near starvation, our bellies were more than full. No longer racked by hunger and feeling no pain, we lay in the shade to aid digestion and get some rest.

Some of us were dozing when the men of the village returned. They were not pleased to see us. Trying to gain their friendship, I gave them a few coins. With grunts of dissatisfaction they took the money, ambled away, and left us alone. But unknown to us several village men had decided to alert the authorities. They ran four or five miles to the white settlement and brought back five Dutch soldiers who took us by surprise. The soldiers were armed and we were not, and so we didn't resist. After all the suffering we had endured, it was no time to die. They tied our hands behind our backs, and took us to the station in a long and narrow pirogue. They wasted no time locking us up.

After breathing free air for a short time, once more we were prisoners. The Dutch authorities didn't abuse us but didn't coddle us either. They rousted us from sleep very early in the morning, gave us a breakfast of rice and beans, and made us wait hours to be processed. Later a police launch took us across the river. In Bella Vista we had to wait for the official transfer. With bayonet points pricking our swollen backs, we were hustled through the town and into a blockhouse. Again we waited to be assigned a wooden board with no mattress and a bucket. My second attempt to escape the hell of French Guiana had failed with even worse results than the first. I was too miserable, too sick in body and mind, even to think about a third.

Chapter Nine

"Too Weak to Stand, Hospital!"

In the blockhouse I had plenty of time to think. My comrades believed Lapin, our lying "sailor navigator," had wrecked our well-planned escape and blamed him for our failure. Whether he deserved it or not, he became our chosen scapegoat. Yet the group had never become during those few terrible days a cohesive, functioning unit. I had believed I would find strength in numbers, but I was wrong. I fled the prison with five other men, thinking I would need their help, but alone I might have done better. When things turned sour, we sacrificed a man for dishonesty, blaming him for all that went wrong. It was a moral question I wrestled with for a long time; we should have blamed ourselves. We failed miserably, and five wretched men defeated by the jungle returned as one to captivity. The prison authorities never found out what happened to Lapin. I believe that unforgiving jungle showed him no mercy. It beat him down after a few days. He may have lived a week.

Big and muscular Marcel had torn a foot on sharp vegetation, and the wound had become infected. Seeing that he was able only to hobble, an old acquaintance began to bully him. Bad blood existed between the two because Marcel at one time had beaten the man in a fight. So now Fabio was taking his revenge, badgering Marcel at every turn and making him even more miserable than the rest of us.

"I won't take this from you," Marcel warned. "You'll see!" Fabio let go a loud cackle and slammed his fist into his enemy's face.

When night came Marcel slipped his good ankle from the shackle and drove a knife into Fabio's chest. A brief investigation quickly targeted him as the instigator. However, before he could be charged with murder, gangrene ravaged the infected foot, turning it from red to black as the tissue decomposed. He went to the hospital where maggots were applied to save the foot. Three days later, just as a doctor was about to amputate, Marcel died of the condition suffering intense pain. He was a leader, that man, and I felt a sense of loss when he died. And yet, had he lived for a trial, he would have gone to the guillotine.

After a day or two I found the lack of fresh air in the blockhouse unendurable. Pacing the floor in the stench of urine, feces, and sweating bodies, I began to feel I should have gone off with Lapin to die in the jungle rather than return defeated to squalor and captivity. Yet neither the sea nor the jungle had been kind to us. Insensate elemental forms of nature were unaware of our presence, and it didn't matter whether we lived or died. Though perhaps conscious of their own existence, sea and jungle were unconscious of our presence. Even though both offered the promise of freedom, we had to view them as totally indifferent. Struggling against them, we had a measure of hope and could dream of living as respectable human beings. In the blockhouse we had no such dream and very little hope but plenty of danger. Marcel had warned us that a group of vicious and greedy convicts wanted to rob us of the money we didn't spend during our brief escape. They knew we had not reached a civilized post where we might have spent it, and they waited to strike. However, when they came to know we weren't sheep ready to be shorn but keenly on guard against them, they left us alone.

A motley crew of discontents I found in the blockhouse, men of all ages and from all walks of life. Professional men of high rank in civilian life existed side by side with street rats and tried to get along with them. Because most of the men worked under a blazing sun almost naked, their bodies were roasted to a dark brown. Some of the older convicts were burnt almost black and looked more African than European. Every person revealed watery, bloodshot eyes harmed by the intense light and heat of the tropics. Some were nearly blind but given no favors. Those belonging to a gang, or family as they called it, wore red and green tattoos on their faces and bodies. The tattoos, often gross or grotesque but intended to display meaning, affirmed allegiance to the gang. Though supposedly placed in irons every night, gang members often gathered in the shadows looking for a weakling (a man alone without comrades) to assault. If he opened his mouth to complain, they killed him. It could happen even in the daytime. I was told they received minimum punishment even when found guilty, but I never knew why.

As time passed the stench and heat in that god-awful place became more endurable, and even though I slept with one eye open I slowly began to relax and fall into boredom. Then one day we were told an execution was about to take place. In the courtyard outside our barred windows the executioner himself would feel the blade of the guillotine. His name was Culette and he had been the official killer of men for several years. I heard his story repeated several times before the day he was scheduled to die. He owned a small boat and for an exorbitant fee he took convicts trying to escape across the river to the Dutch side. That discovery would not have brought him the death penalty, but as the authorities began to find bodies on the riverbank, Culette was charged with murder. He had taken men across the river all right but had killed them and gutted them, looking for money in their bowels. He knew no convict would try to escape without money and would often swallow it to keep it well hidden while seeking freedom. He was not above gutting another human being for a few francs. Shaken by the grisly discovery, hardened officials who thought they had seen the full spectrum of human depravity, quickly sentenced Culette to die.

On the day of the execution it rained. It rained often. And when I speak of rain I mean a tropical downpour unlike any ever seen in temperate climates. The rain began as a steady drizzle, but within minutes the skies opened to pour down a cataract. The weather delayed the big show for an hour or more. We stood at a barred window to get a view of what was going on. When the rained passed on, the warden, a couple of guards, and the executioner sidled up to the hideous machine. A group of townspeople, some with their children, came into the yard to witness the event. The executioner dropped the blade with a loud bang to make sure it was working. Culette was brought from his cell and ordered to stand at attention until commanded to kneel.

Then in the arms of the guillotine I heard him say, "Do it neatly, *mon enfant*, and hurry! I'm not here to have fun!"

The executioner nodded and the blade fell. In seconds the man's head lay in the bloody basket. On its face was a half smile. The entire procedure lasted only a few minutes. Not a soul staring at that awful scene felt any remorse for Culette even while admiring his bravery. He had killed countless men officially and unofficially, and he deserved what he got. Three days later they executed a young Chinaman who took it all in stride. His offense, as I heard later, was "taking liberties with a white woman." According to prison gossip, the sex was consensual. Unlike Culette, the Chinaman probably did not deserve what he got.

Time. We were serving *time*, and the weeks went by one after another at a snail's pace. Many weeks in the blockhouse had left me ashen and anemic. I found myself not able to eat and got in the habit of drinking mugs of coffee instead of eating bread and meat. Slight of build and weighing little to begin with, I rapidly became thinner. Observing my condition, a doctor gave me medicine that soothed my troubled stomach, but left a bitter taste in my mouth and caused severe constipation. In time I couldn't drink coffee or even the water because of the repulsive taste. I began to think I was dying.

Again I went to the doctor who gave me quinine as a tonic, he said, but I think he believed I had malaria. I knew quinine couldn't cure my condition, and so I feared I'd be dead in a week. The next day, barely able to walk, I trundled off again to the doctor. He looked me over, clicked his tongue, and said I should be given milk and plenty of it. A guard lifted me from the examining table and put me on my feet. I tried to stand and walk, but in a dark whirl of flashing points of light I fainted. On his clipboard, the guard told me later, the doctor quickly scribbled, "Too weak to stand. Hospital."

I languished in the hospital, a unit apart from the prison infirmary and very different from the hospital on Isle Royale, more than a month. I vividly remember how inadequate it was, how unclean and smelling of death. Its staff of convicts was lazy, uncaring, and untrained. Only one doctor was on duty most of the time, assisted by another who came once a week. They seemed to be honest men trying to relieve pain and disease but were overwhelmed by the enormity of it all. The men who lay in those rickety beds on urine-soaked mattresses covered by grimy sheets suffered a litany of diseases: fever, dysentery, diarrhea, malaria, tuberculosis, hookworms, anemia, and more. Most were beyond medical help. When a person left dead or alive, the mattress wasn't disinfected as in most hospitals. To make it ready for the next man, it was simply aired for an hour in the sun. Each patient had a pot for bodily waste that when added to all the others smelled horribly every morning. Those who could eat sat in their beds to consume a few ounces of bread and meat, a vegetable, or porridge. Those who were about to die drank only condensed milk.

In the wards several men died each day. The cause of death could be traced to any number of diseases even though the death report in most cases was rendered in two words: *pernicious anemia*. It was double talk to explain how young convicts not more than twenty-five were dying of painful diseases, such as hookworms in the intestines, that resulted in the wasting away of a healthy body. One case I remember as though it happened yesterday. A blond young man with deep blue eyes lay sweating and shivering under a frayed and dirty sheet in the bed next to me. He tried to smoke a cigarette but was too weak to hold it and too shattered even to light it. He dropped the cigarette and slumped backward, his mouth gaping and his eyes in a fixed stare. A fellow convict pretended to check his pulse, pronounced him dead, and stole his shoes. Another took a small sack in which he kept his personal items, and a third stole everything else he owned. The attendant, also an inmate, on seeing the man dead and the victim of thieves, became noticeably angry. He begged a guard to punish those who had dared molest the dying man. Looting corpses was his time-honored privilege, a "special right" that came with the job and made it sought after.

"That poor guy was too young to die," said a spectral patient, struggling to sit upright in his bed. "It's a goddamn shame."

"Maybe it's better he died young," said another. "He won't have to suffer any longer. I curse my condition for not going with him."

"He told me only yesterday he'd have his freedom in a few days."

"Did you believe that? Not a soul in this god-forsaken hellhole will ever go free except through death! He got his freedom all right. It just came a bit sooner than expected!"

Macabre prison humor was alive and well in the most unexpected of places. It often focused on death and dying and was ubiquitous. The next day a new patient occupied the young man's bed. He would slip into a coma and die in of a fever in five days. The urine-soaked mattress would be aired in the sun for one hour on the day of his death to accommodate another patient. And so it went year after year. When one prison cemetery could no longer hold another corpse, another was built. Convicts died of exhaustion and disease felling huge trees and hauling away massive stumps. They were buried in the cemetery they had struggled to build, eventually escaping the death-dealing toil and finding peace.

Chapter Ten

The Charnel House

Near the end of my stay in the hospital, I was to be tried for my second attempt to escape. I would not be the only one on trial. Those who went with me would be there too. The number on trial in a single day would amount to twenty or more. The president of the tribunal would question me in his official manner, and then the prosecuting attorney would demand the maximum penalty. A guard with very little knowledge of legal procedure or anything else would attempt to conduct my defense. No legal argument would come from him and no exculpatory evidence would be presented. All he would do and could do was plea for tolerance, a virtue rare in French Guiana. Rapidly the procedure would be crowned by a harsh sentence.

"This time they won't go easy on you, Bonheur," my guard confided. "Two attempts to escape in so little time ain't good, you know."

So I was looking at many months of solitary confinement, or three to five years on one of the "salvation" islands offshore. They were called *Îles du Salut* or *Islands of Salvation* because in a former time residents on the mainland had taken refuge there to escape an epidemic of yellow fever. As it turned out, I was able to convince the tribunal, as shown by medical records, that my health was in decline. So I was given a lighter sentence but classified "Incorrigible." Had he not died before the trial, Marcel might have gotten off lightly too, though I doubt it. It was the first time for him to escape, but murderous revenge was a different matter. Old Georges, Pierre, and Bigelow got two years' solitary confinement, a death penalty for all of them. The old man was the first to go. Bigelow, though much younger was the second, and Pierre went later. Our man Lapin the liar, "Rabbit Man" as Marcel often called him because of his name, was tried and sentenced in absentia. The unyielding jungle had already given Lapin a harsh sentence, and so the judicial thing was merely a formality. Of the six who made the run for life and dignity, I was the only one to live long enough to plan another escape.

Later I learned to be branded "Incorrigible" was not a light sentence at all. It was, in fact, severe punishment. I was seen as rebellious and unbroken, a man with an unquenchable thirst for liberty. I wasn't willing to bend to authority. So I became a member of a notorious group hated and harassed by prison guards. Incorrigibles were prisoners who had tried repeatedly to escape and wouldn't give up trying. For a month we were confined on Isle Royale but were later sent to one of two brutal camps on the mainland, Camp Charnéle and Camp Godeberta. The former was often called the Charnel House and the latter with medieval history behind it was sometimes called the Lady. I was sent to Camp Charnéle, the worst camp in all of French Guiana. It was located deep in a swampy jungle where malaria and dysentery raged. Hapless men labored many hours each day at felling trees in mud and water. All were fair game for mosquitoes, leeches, snakes, and rot. Any man not working got a bullwhip across his back. We were also victims of too little food. The guards ate well enough and were protected from mosquitoes and dangerous water but not the convicts. Some had festering sores on their legs and feet and were missing toes that had fallen off. Some were dying even as they were compelled to work.

Charnéle had an inmate who was unhinged, driven mad I believe by what he had endured there, and determined to get out.

His name as I remember was Julius Sigaut, and his age was maybe fifty or fifty-five. One afternoon as we were locked in the barracks after a watery lunch, he came up to me holding a blunt needle in a calloused hand.

"Take this," he said, looking fiercely at me, "and punch me in the eye with it. Just a quick jab! Do it!"

"I don't even know you, man. How can you ask me to do something like that even if I did know you? One jab could leave you half blind."

"I mean it, goddamn it! Just do it. No talk, just do it!"

"I can't and I won't."

He scowled at me and went up to a more willing man who took the needle and stabbed at the bulging eyeball. It was either too slippery or the needle too blunt. After the third try Sigaut grabbed the needle, drove it deep into the man's wrist, and ran away laughing hysterically. The next day he poked his eye himself. Blood spurted from it to soak a dirty rag, and he was hauled off to the infirmary. With a patch on the eye, he was placed in a blockhouse to await trial for "self affliction." He was given a ruthless sentence and died in solitary confinement. Another fellow spread sperm mixed with toxic mud all over his eyes to get them infected. He overdid it, suffered blindness, and was given fifteen months in a solitary cell. Within two months a guard delivering bread and water found him sitting stiff and upright against the wall. Rigor mortis had set in to make a statue of him. His bulging blind eyes were wide open and staring intently at nothing.

Incorrigibles in Camp Charnéle were treated worse than any farmer ever treated an animal. I've heard of farmers forcing horses to pull up stumps until they dropped dead. I've heard of brutes driving animals so hard they fell to the ground, couldn't get up, and received lashes from a bullwhip. I've heard of innocent and faithful dogs tormented by their owners. Our treatment was harsher. At

Charnéle they forced us to cut down gigantic trees with dull axes, working all day without rest. After felling a tree every man had to chop off its limbs and stack the heavy wood high. For a strong man in good physical condition the work was hard enough, but most of us were suffering from malnutrition and/or disease. When a man fell and couldn't resume work, he lay there to bake in the sun, or drown in putrid water, or die of snakebite. In all the time I was in that Charnel House not once did anyone in authority show us kindness or mercy, and no medical person ever came to help us.

Every day began at five in the morning with the blast of a bugle. At night I tried to sleep on a hard board in a fetid room with leg irons around one ankle. The iron cut into my flesh to disturb sleep, and I couldn't wait for the morning guard to remove it. For breakfast I ate a lump of bread washed down with black coffee. A few minutes later with all the others I was marched off to work. We walked in single file, caring our tools on bare shoulders. Guards armed with rifles strolled along beside us prepared to shoot any convict who broke the line. Swift-footed Arabs ranked as trustees in the system were in every detachment. They were there to chase down with machetes any man who tried to flee.

Near six in the morning the weather was cool and we worked without a struggle. By ten or eleven the sun was burning hot and sweat was flowing from every pore of half-naked bodies. Yet it wasn't so bad to sweat profusely, even though it sapped our energy and required additional salt, because it tended to keep the mosquitoes at bay. At noon we had a few minutes to rest in the shade and eat something watery and tasteless. Then back to work. At the end of the day, exhausted, we straggled back to camp. Any person who hadn't filled his quota of work got no supper and was locked in a special room. Even though the food was almost inedible at times, the ration was just enough to keep us working. Unlike other cooks in the penal colony, the cooks at Charnéle never pilfered supplies intended for us. I never quite understood why. Maybe the stuff they fed us wasn't good enough for the guards.

Shortly after supper the irons went on raw ankles. As darkness came on fast — there is no twilight in the tropics — talking was prohibited. Even so, we talked but in low voices just above a whisper. And what did we talk about? In one word: *escape*. It was in the thoughts of every man among us. Each of us had tried to escape at least once, and each of us was absolutely determined to try it again. It was just a matter of finding the right time. Someone asked if any of us had heard the story of an old convict respectfully called Gordo the Sapient by all who knew him. He had been sentenced to five years hard labor in French Guiana shortly after the turn of the century and was still there when I arrived. He tried many times to escape, and each time he failed he was given more time in prison. Altogether thirty-eight years were added to the initial five. He vowed he would try again and expect to make his sentence fifty years if and when he was captured. After his second escape and capture after thirteen days he was labeled "Incorrigible."

From the camp named after medieval Saint Godeberta, old Gordo escaped into the jungle completely naked six times. The guards fired a fusillade of bullets at him, even turned a machine gun on him twice, but couldn't bring him down. One bullet ripped off an ear, but the old guy asserted later it didn't matter a whit to him. He stuffed a banana leaf against it to stop the bleeding and ran on, barefoot in the jungle. With every escape he melted into the forest like salt in water, and the prison community assumed he was dead. Then everybody heard the chasers ran him down and brought him back from as far away as Venezuela. The guards hated the man because any guard who happened to be on duty when he escaped was suspended a month with no pay. A Corsican guard asked Gordo — he was called "the Sapient" because he knew the jungle like the back of his hand — "Will you escape today or tomorrow?"

"Not any time soon, you old bastard," Gordo replied, cackling and dancing a little jig, "But don't you worry old fellow [the guard was twenty-three] I'll let you know when the time comes."

And he did let the guard know. He bashed him in the head with a shovel one day when he wasn't looking and was in the jungle before he or two other guards could fire a shot. All three were suspended without pay and swore they would kill the man who was causing them hardship and misery. Gordo was captured and returned but never tried to escape again. Three angry guards tried to kill him but failed. He was sixty-two when all this was happening, and by the time he reached sixty-seven he had found an easy life on one of the islands. I was told he had his own little house and cooked his own meals, and for most of every afternoon he lay in a hammock nestled in the shade.

On Devil's Island life was easier than in the Charnéle barracks. Yet at times, as on this night, a semblance of camaraderie emerged. In the darkness after the lamp was snuffed, someone lit a cigarette and passed it along from one to another. The idea was to take one long draw on it, savor the smoke in the mouth and lungs, and pass it on while exhaling slowly. Of course the cigarette didn't last very long even though several men got a taste. Half an hour later all was quiet, only a whisper here and there. Then exhausted from the long day's labor, we began to fall asleep. The only sound was the clank of shackles on the metal bar as tired men sought comfort. Then suddenly someone screaming pierced the quiet. Just about every night the barracks was jolted awake by the moaning, screaming, or sleep talk of some prisoner in nightmare. When I heard the racket for the first time, I thought come morning the offender would be severely punished. It didn't happen. Among the habitués in a barracks as brutal as Charnéle was an unspoken understanding of the mental agony some men suffered. It was there in addition to the physical misery and tolerated. Too soon the night went by to bring another day of hard labor and pain. It was not a good life.

Chapter Eleven

The Hospital on Royale

Not a single convict in French Guiana envied my life as an "Incorrigible." Everybody knew we suffered severely but somehow endured all that was thrown at us and had the courage, or foolishness, to try escaping again. Even though the guards hated us and tried to find excuses for shooting and killing us for the slightest infraction, the prisoners in all the jungle camps and on the three islands offshore were in league with us. They heard our stories and sympathized with us, and sometimes in desperation they emulated "the brave Incorrigibles" with disastrous results. Quickly I learned there was very little regarding our situation that could be called heroic or admirable. It was in many respects a deferred death sentence, for when a man was labeled "Incorrigible," he seldom outlived the label. As for me, I guess I have to say I was lucky.

I existed in that identity only three months, from the beginning of June until the end of August, and I must admit the months seemed like years. Then when a new Director of Administration heard my case, I had the good fortune of becoming an ordinary convict. I sent a letter to him describing in detail how poor my health was, how I was liable to drop dead at any moment, and to this day I believe the man saved my life. I was unwell, anemic, and worn out when I wrote to him. I would have died before finishing my sentence. He replied in a brief but pointed note in blue ink that he was releasing me from the incorrigible class. I would be leaving Camp Charnéle for Saint Joseph for a term of six months. Afterwards I would be sent to Isle Royale where life was much easier than on Saint Joseph. Because I was not a political prisoner, I wouldn't be going to Île du Diable or Devil's Island.

Even though I was liberated from Charnéle, that Camp of Death, I would continue to face harsh conditions on the island reserved for escapees and those who had committed serious offenses. Most of the time when a convict murdered a guard, his fate was the guillotine. A few, however, managed to escape the blade and were sent into solitary confinement on Saint Joseph. It was the island where convicts were kept in small solitary cells in silence and darkness. I wasn't happy to hear I was going there but took some comfort in knowing I wouldn't be worked like a beast of burden. On adequate rations I could rest and restore my strength. I was transported to the island on a boat containing more than thirty other convicts. Half a dozen were too sick even to walk unaided and so were not in irons. They suffered from severe dysentery, wore soiled trousers, and exuded an odor that put a barrier between them and all others. They were going to the solitary confinement cells in spite of their condition. Another man, I was told, was suffering from a fatal disease and was being sent by a doctor to the hospital on Isle Royale. That was where I wanted to go. I sorely needed rest in a good hospital but had no money to bribe a guard to send me there.

In late afternoon we were loaded onto an old night steamer two at a time chained together. My partner was a bald little man square in appearance but not bigger than me. I couldn't help but notice he had blisters on his face and neck. His eyes were bloodshot and bleary, and when he spoke in a voice that sounded like a woman's I noticed most of his teeth were missing. Guards shoved us into the hold and within a few minutes the vessel was in the river moving downstream. At the mouth of the river and entering the ocean our chains were removed. The ship's hold was damp and dark except for a dim oil lamp casting grotesque shadows as the men moved about. Tossed into the hold with bags of cement and other freight, we were going to Royale, Saint Joseph's, and Devil's Island for a long time. While some of us had achieved a good life before being sentenced to hellish French Guiana, only one had gained a bit of fame. A prominent judge widely known in Rouen, where Joan of Arc was tried and burned at the stake, was on his way to Devil's Island as a political prisoner. My thoughts centered on Captain Alfred Dreyfus, an innocent man once confined there for treason.

We got to the islands early in the morning at daybreak. They lie only ten miles off the mainland but as many as thirty miles west of Bella Vista, and so we endured several hours of tossing and shaking as the old boat chugged along at five knots through the night. On arrival I elbowed my way to a porthole and got a view of the "salvation islands," as they were once called. All three were beautiful, postcard lovely, typical tropical islands with palm trees swaying in gentle breezes. That image dissolved never to return as soon as I touched foot on shore. We were ferried ashore in a large rowboat to land on Royale, the largest island and the one most developed. Devil's Island, the smallest, was little more than a rock with coconut trees. It was customarily reserved for political prisoners, only a few at a time, who lived in huts on the island. They were required to do no work except collect coconuts for the Administration from time to time. They had to cook their own food brought in by boat once a week. Their confinement was easier than on the other two islands and the food was better. But judging from all I heard, it was a lonely existence that took its toll on a man. Most of the prisoners sat and fished all day and went off to sleep in their crude little huts at night.

I would soon discover that life on the islands was different than on the mainland. On the mainland every convict sentenced to hard labor got exactly that, forced to perform excruciating labor many hours each day in a prison camp. On the islands no convict worked at a job as hard as cutting down gigantic trees. A few trustees were paid by the Administration to keep an eye on things, and a literate man could earn enough for tobacco by writing letters. Most of the island convicts spent their time in restlessness and boredom, hoping eventually to get back to the mainland where they might escape. At night they gambled with anything of value they might own even though many had nothing other than soiled rags on their backs. Poverty-bitten convicts could only watch the card games. One "card shark" as we called him seemed to win every night. Some believed he was cheating, but not a person dared confront him. He was huge. He towered over everybody. His biceps were as big as the legs of some who gambled against him.

Approaching Saint Joseph, I suddenly became very sick. I thought it might be nothing more than seasickness, but just as the boat was docking I fell into a deep swoon and lay unconscious. When I couldn't be easily revived, the chief guard decided I should go instead to Royale. At the island's dock I was placed on my feet, and an orderly rousted me immediately to the nearby hospital. I was burning with fever and vomited on the way. The orderly, himself a convict, slapped me hard when I spewed thick amber vomit all over the pavement. Cursing under his breath, he threatened to make me lap it up with my tongue but relented when the skies opened for a downpour. In the hospital, soaked to the skin, cold and shivering and stinking, my temperature rose to an alarming 105 degrees. My head swirled and my vision blurred.

A doctor showing genuine concern gave me a bed reserved for the very sick. I couldn't swallow, could only sip a little water. Anything I tried to eat came up explosively from a sour stomach. He prescribed milk and eggs to ease my condition, but even that I couldn't keep down. I suffered from severe diarrhea and began to stink horribly. I lost weight rapidly, grew weaker and weaker, and became a bundle of bones. Early each morning I got a raw egg in a small glass of milk but couldn't keep it down. Later the egg came slightly cooked with a slice of toast. I could eat and digest a meal like that and slowly got better.

Mentally as well as physically I was sick. After all I'd been through I was certain my body and brain had just given up. Three and a half years had passed since my coming to Guiana. My former life, all that I held dear, was slowly fading from memory. France, the streets and clubs of Monmartre, the pleasant boulevards of Paris, even the pretty girl I had loved so dearly were becoming insubstantial shadows. Desperately I tried to hold on to her name, Gabrielle or was it Giselle? At times I struggled to recall and savor the good things of past years, hoping that would be a way of keeping at bay the bad things of the present. On rare occasions remembrance of things past seemed to comfort me. Most of the time it didn't because I felt the pain of all I had lost: my mother at an early age, my grandparents when still a child, my uncle, father, and possibly the gentle girl I loved more than life itself. I thought of those who had come with me on the convict ship and had to admit that many were dead. I was in a hospital bed and very sick. Would I be dying too?

Lying there in the best hospital of the penal colony and slowly getting better with each passing day, I understood for the first time that I had become a seasoned convict. I was familiar with the underbelly of the prison system, the graft and corruption among the guards running upward to the bigwigs of the Administration. I knew about the rackets dear to the heart of every guard and the abuses of the Administration. Also I had gained a good understanding of the prison population. I divided the convicts with whom I lived into three simple classes: those who thought only of escape; those who didn't think of escape because they were too old and tired; and those who were content and didn't give a damn about anything because they were animals. Only the ones bent on escape seemed worthy of respect. The animals were steeped in degradation and vile. In my early days I believed the prison had done that to them and viewed them with sympathy, but later I changed my mind. They were mean-spirited men when they came to Guiana. They got meaner of their own making. Self-respecting convicts, and I put myself in that category, despised them.

The doctor on duty to help me get well was a good man. The joke shared by hospital patients was that Dr. Linville was too good. The sight of strong and healthy men falling into ruin with diseases he couldn't fathom truly upset him. If a man came to him with only a slight wheeze, he was seen as tubercular and given a hospital bed. Patients received all the food they cared to eat and special drugs (when available) for their condition. Then the Administration got wind of what was happening and clamped down on the man with an iron fist. In fewer than three months he was sent back to France and replaced by another medical man with a different mindset. Dr. Fabroni found a hundred men in the facility and decided it could hold only fifty. So he emptied the hospital of all patients who were ambulatory. He also cut back on food and medicine for all patients. Some of the men protested but soon realized, as some us began to get well, that his practice was based on sound training. He wasn't a likable man, Dr. Fabroni, but competent.

When I left the hospital after three months, thankful it was far superior to the one in Bella Vista, I was sent to the Cochineal Barracks. It was located six miles from the hospital on Royale. I had never heard of the place and had to ask a fellow inmate about it. He said it was named after an insect that yields a crimson dye when crushed. And then he said it was nothing more than a fancy name concocted by the Administration to replace "Bloodstained Barracks," the name given the place by convicts. He told me about a savage fight between two convicts with the vital blood of the men soaking into the wooden floor. Those who witnessed the event said they fought each other half an hour with sharply pointed knives, stabbing and slashing until they died in a bloody heap at the same time. Guards tried to remove the bizarre stain with chemicals, but it proved stubborn and remained imbedded in the floorboards for a long time. Prisoners coming later saw it as a symbol of prison violence.

The story was anecdotal and not entirely believable, and yet some of us wanted to believe it. We had seen enough of raw and brutal violence to last a lifetime. We had witnessed man's inhumanity to man in all its disgusting and degrading forms and wanted peace. Even though not a person in our group was afraid to die, we wanted as little violence as possible. It was a small thing to ask, and yet we never got it. I remember staring at that bloodstain any number of times just before the call came for lights out. Each time I felt incredibly tired.

Chapter Twelve

The Cochineal Barracks

The men who occupied the Bloodstained or Cochineal Barracks were to a person the most dangerous and merciless convicts in the entire prison colony. They were known to slit a man's throat simply because they didn't like his looks. The inhabitants of that most depraved of barracks were there mainly because of crimes against an official. Some offenses were as petty as slapping a guard's face or calling him an idiot. Others included grisly torture of an innocent victim and murder. I learned that some of the worst criminals ever spawned by the French Republic were quartered in Cochineal. While I didn't view myself as a criminal of that magnitude, my record showed I was something of a troublemaker. I had tried to escape twice and would try again. So in the mind of the official who signed the order of transfer, I was justifiably sent there. It was a place of pernicious repute. Dangerous is a mild word by which to describe it. If wanted to avoid trouble, I would have to sleep with one eye open through every hour of every night. In the daytime I would have to lose myself in a protective group. Any man seen alone, regardless how big and strong he happened to be, was a target.

Cochineal was a large building about a hundred feet long and thirty wide housing about fifty convicts. The windows had enormous iron bars and the one massive door was made of iron. Every evening after the roll was called, guards bolted the door and didn't open it again until early morning. If a fight broke out in the middle of the night and a man had to be taken to the hospital, they grudgingly made an exception. Then the door was opened and quickly banged shut. Always when the great door was closed activity sprang up within that even the guards knew little about. In the darkness after all lamps were extinguished, tiny personal lamps were brought from hiding places and lit for reading or playing cards or writing letters. The men bought kerosene for the crude, handmade lamps from the official lamplighter who stole it from his ration for the three regulation lamps that hung from the ceiling. It was a lucrative little business he had on the side. His boss knew all about it but turned a blind eye because once a month he found a sizable kickback in his desk drawer. Prevalent throughout the prison colony on all levels was the unspoken understanding: *"Si tu me grattes le dos, mon ami, je te gratterai le tien."* Or to put it in English, "If you scratch my back, friend, I will make a point of scratching yours."

On entering the building a guard directed me to a rusty cot where I deposited my meager belongings. When settled I looked around at my surroundings. Across the aisle from me was a man in ragged shorts with blue skin. The blue came from tattoos covering his entire body. His face was blue and his bald head was blue with intricate tattoos resembling hair. On each cheek was an ace of spades and on his forehead an ace of diamonds. His arms and legs displayed scores of tattoos in that one bluish color. Some were writhing snakes so delicately done one could see their scales. I thought of the pain the man must have endured when the needle was active. Then I was told many inmates were driven to get tattoos because they craved the pain. Near him another prisoner carved a face on a coconut while several men played cards on the floor. A very thin man in nothing but a loincloth was writing a letter to his lawyer in Paris and asking how to spell certain words. In the passage between the cots a man with an audience was talking about his last escape and his plans for the next one. He would need money for his next freedom run. The one thing on his mind and on those of everyone listening was finding a way to obtain money for their next escape.

From time to time above the chatter came the cry, "Pascarelli, two coffees!" Bennie Pascarelli was the keeper of the barracks. He was sent to Guiana to serve six years for burglary. Seven attempts to escape cost him twenty-one additional years. The coffee he sold came from kitchen leftovers, its nutty taste only slightly that of coffee. Later I learned he sold tobacco, cigarette paper, matches, oil, toilet paper, and vinegar stolen from island supplies. He earned a premium on vinegar. It was always in demand, for many convicts drank it as a substitute for alcohol. On occasion he was able to buy a case of rum from a man on the mail boat, and that he sold by the ounce at a sky-high price. Also Pascarelli owned the only "library" on Royale, volumes on all subjects collected over many years. He rented them for a handsome sum, payment in advance. It was a library where Charles Dickens rubbed elbows with Victor Hugo, Maupassant, Nietzsche, Tolstoy, and Jack London. Also it boasted magazines in English, Spanish, and French. The old scoundrel had become so busy with his enterprises he gave up trying to escape.

As night came with darkness demanding personal lamps, several groups of men began to gamble. A group in a corner shot craps. Others spread a blanket on the floor and played poker for small stakes. On the islands gambling was the favored past time. Instead of sleeping, the men gambled through the night. Hard labor wasn't required on the islands, and so they could get their rest in the daytime. While stud poker was the most popular game, several different ones were played simultaneously, and quarrels often broke out. The conflict was usually settled by a strong-armed Corsican who called himself master of the games. The job was dangerous and required a commanding person with a strong arm and hard fist. Pascarelli, keeper of the house, sold candy, chewing gum, and cigarettes to the players at a profit of

100 percent. Near daybreak when bright streaks were appearing in the sky beyond the bars on the windows, the little lamps were snuffed, and the men slept.

When reveille sounded at 0500, three guards unbolted the heavy iron door and tramped inside. Their boots beat a tattoo on the wooden floor loud enough to wake everybody. Though few in the barracks had slept more than an hour or two, we clambered half naked from our cots to stand at attention for inspection. The guards looked for weapons, drugs, contraband of all sorts, and found nothing. Cards, dice, and lanterns had disappeared, and anything approximating a weapon was hidden in the rafters. They made no effort to look closely, and all three ignored Pascarelli when he shuffled off to his little room to make coffee. However, before leaving they were careful to check the privy at the north end of the building. Every morning they inspected, for they had found more than once a body sprawled on the floor. The Cochineal privy had gained infamy as one of the deadliest places on earth. In that one room with its floor subsequently covered with tile, countless murders had occurred. While in later years the floor itself revealed no bloodstains, the grout between the tiles was reddish-brown instead of white. Anyone remaining in the Cochineal Barracks longer than a month found himself hearing sharp groans that quickly became a death rattle. The grisly sound taught me never to relieve myself at night.

There were times when the privy was the scene of three killings a month or even five. And did the neck of the murderer touch the blade of the guillotine for his crime? The answer, I gathered, was almost never. When the assailant was discovered and tried, he had nine chances out of ten of being acquitted. An unwritten law among those in the barracks was to blame the dead man. Let the victim become the villain. After all, he was dead to all suffering and not able to speak. Let the victor live even when guilty. His enemy would take care of him in the privy when least expected. Never to my knowledge did any man speak out for the victim or name the murderer. To do so was to seal his fate as a snitch. That meant a quick slashing of the throat in the privy. Every man, myself included, hated a snitch. Invariably the snitch was a cowardly little man trying to gain acceptance by the guards and the Administration at the expense of his comrades.

As soon as the guards left, Pascarelli came back with weak coffee, mincing down the aisle with a steaming copper kettle and humming a little tune. He had diluted the issued coffee to accumulate a stash of beans that he could sell later and was very pleased with himself. A measuring cup was attached to the kettle, and every convict wanting coffee to begin the day dipped the cup in the kettle and drew out enough hot liquid to fill his own pewter cup. No person without paying could have a second cup of coffee and was urged to make it quick when taking the first. All of us knew the little thief was cheating us with coffee weaker than it should have been but did nothing about it. He was running a business, and we depended on him for hard-to-get items that made life tolerable. So while most of us despised effeminate Pascarelli, we tolerated him as a businessman. In a dangerous world he knew exactly how far to go, how close to the edge he could stand before plunging downward.

Instead of "Bloodstained Barracks," the denizens of that formidable building sometimes called it other names. Some labeled it "Bloody Barracks," for example, while others called it *la case rouge,* the red box. It was a stifling, stinking, very uncomfortable red box. It was a box filled with despair because no convict residing there could even think of escaping. We were on an island surrounded by water brimming with deadly sharks. All one could do was dream of a distant freedom and make nebulous plans for it. In time I would be able to leave Cochineal and be quartered in a safer part of the island. In the meantime I had to watch my back and my life. I endured sleepless nights there. I suffered almost as much there as in the jungle where I stood in leech-ridden water under a blazing sun chopping trees.

And yet in a way I was lucky. I managed to keep on living while some around me spurted blood in the privy, or in their beds, and died. I managed to keep on living without appreciable damage when the man in the bunk next to mine was beaten so fiercely he lost his front teeth, his right eye, and the use of his left leg. I managed to keep on living when another man close by was pinned face down on the dirty floor and burned all over with a metal spoon heated in the flame of a personal lamp. After seven months I left the infamous Cochineal Barracks for the other side of the island.

My life in the new place was never on the line, as I now recall, and therefore appreciably better. I fell in with a group for personal protection and in time became friends with some in the group. In the Cochineal Barracks where every man kept his distance, friendship was a foreign concept. Also in the new place I had the leisure to write letters. To Gabrielle in France I wrote, affirming my love and promising to return. Day after day I waited for her reply but received nothing. She might have answered every letter I sent. If so, her letters could have been lost, misdirected, stolen, or deliberately disposed of (after opening) by the Administration. All I know is I heard nothing whatever from her. So in time with feelings of loss and futility I ceased to write. Years later I wrote to one of her friends, hoping to get a full explanation of what had happened to Gabrielle, but got no reply. I got no mail from anyone. Even now, though I have never been able to prove it, I believe prison officials chose to destroy all mail addressed to Arthur Bonheur. the malcontent and troublemaker. It was punishment of a more suble kind. My name with scores of others, I believe, was on a NO MAIL list.

Chapter Thirteen

A Tryst and Trouble

All the time I was on Royale no official saw fit to supply me with a new shirt or a new pair of trousers. I wore the same ragged clothing day and night. When it began to smell, I tried washing the skimpy clothing under an outdoor shower, soaping it down as I would my naked skin and rinsing. At first it seemed a good idea, but then I discovered I had to choose between keeping my clothes tolerably clean or my body clean. I chose the latter, and so after several days of soaking up sweat in the tropical heat my clothing once again assumed the odor that pervaded the entire barracks. That's when I wrote to the Commandant, Colonel Rousseau, the big man in charge of everything on the islands. I told him I was half naked and in dire need of new prison garb. To my surprise he didn't ignore my letter or the entreaty it contained. He allotted for my use a change of clothes including underwear, a blanket, and a pair of wooden shoes. Later I traded the shoes, worthless as footwear, to a wood carver for enough tobacco to make a dozen cigarettes.

In another letter to the Commandant I urged him to find work for me, something to fill the long and dreary days and eliminate the boredom I felt. Two paragraphs presented a convict formally pleading for work! He thought I was joking and shared the joke with other administrators who found it ironical and refreshing. They persuaded him to give me a job as a bookkeeper keeping track of food supplies. It wasn't exactly the kind of work I wanted.

Entering tiny figures into a ledger several hours each day paled in comparison to writing letters or reports or a book detailing the strange history of a French penal colony in South America. Yet I enjoyed with the job an amazing amount of liberty, and I spent my afternoons on the shore looking at the sea. Even though I lacked a formal education, having left school at fifteen, I became known as a literate and well-educated man among men of little schooling. Then hearing of my qualifications, a guard of the first rank asked me one day if I would be willing to tutor his daughter. He offered generous payment for daily lessons. That same evening I went to his house for the first lesson. His daughter was sitting primly at a piano. She played a lively little tune for me before we began to talk.

Ella Louise had recently turned eighteen. She had lived all her life on the island and had grown up in the presence of convicts. From early childhood she had seen convicts in her home working as servants, and she viewed them as ordinary men. So when her father introduced me to her I was just another man come into the house and into her life. I was twenty-eight, small of stature but well built, and attractive in her eyes. She was young and fresh with a pleasant oval face, large and pretty eyes, and abundant dark hair. Even though her body was a bit on the plump side, she was nubile, sexy, and curious. She had a soothing way of talking and loved to talk even as I tried to tutor her. I got the impression she knew more about the birds and bees than a sheltered girl should know. After three weeks of lessons she began to turn the discussion away from geometry and geography to risqué topics. I had not been in the company of a female for many months, particularly one so young and desirable. Instead of teaching her as I was paid to do, impulsively her tutor became her first admirer. Really and truly I should have known better.

I did know I was taking a feckless and stupid risk. Her father was hot of temper, and if he had gotten so much as an inkling of what was going on, he would have put a bullet through my skull. Losing all control, I put myself in grave danger for a few minutes of pleasure every day. I knew the cost was high indeed, knew it shouldn't be happening, knew I could die should I be found out, but couldn't help myself. Ella Louise seemed not worried at all. She even came to the office where I worked to whisper little phrases in my ear and run away. Then one evening I suggested we walk along the path near the sea, dark when no moon was shining, to a grove of palm trees. She didn't resist, and as we lay on the grass close to each other, the chief man on the island came upon us.

The following morning I had orders to see him in his office. He was sitting behind a large desk, impeccably dressed in white and twirling a yellow pencil. He stared at me for a moment, a look that made me feel very uncomfortable. He didn't invite me to sit, and so I stood and grew more nervous with each passing moment. I could see he was angry and I knew he was powerful. My destiny was in his hands. He had the means to throw me into solitary confinement for a year. I waited for the verdict. Sweat began to dribble down the sides of my neck, and my palms were clammy. Making no attempt to hide his displeasure, he deliberately made me wait to know what he had in store for me. Then directly and firmly but without anger he spoke to me.

"I'm sending you to Saint Joseph this morning. You will go on the nine o'clock boat. You are lucky it was I who found you. Had it been the girl's father, you wouldn't be alive now. The sharks would be feasting on your bloated body at this moment."

He put the pencil down, laced the fingers of well-manicured hands, and eyed me sternly. "What do you have to say for yourself?"

"I'm very sorry, sir," I mumbled. "I'm real sorry to disappoint you. I can't defend my behavior. I was stupid."

"How did you come to know this guard's daughter?" he demanded.

"I've been her tutor now for a couple of months. Her father asked me to prepare her for schooling on the mainland. I did all I could to earn my fee as a tutor, but things happened, sir. Things got out of control."

"And so they did! You were tutoring the girl in the dark, in a grove of palm trees in the dark! You were sprawled on the grass very close to her. Is that the way you tutor math or maybe astronomy? Did you violate that girl? Don't lie to me, Bonheur!"

"I did not, sir. I swear I did not. She told me she was a virgin when I met her. As far as I know she's still a virgin. We fooled around, sir, but I did not have sex with her. I was crazy enough to cross the line, but all she wanted was smooching and kissing and being close."

"I believe you for now," he said in icy resignation, "but if you lie you die. I can't have a convict romancing the daughter of a high-ranking guard. That's conduct not to be tolerated. I cannot and will not allow it! I've a mind to tell the girl's father what you were doing with her but won't. This island has known enough scandal without adding more to it. Get your stuff together and be ready to leave."

So without delay that very morning, in the company of two brawny guards, I left for Saint Joseph. I knew the island was notorious as being far worse in its treatment of convicts than either Devil's Island or Isle Royale, but didn't know what it held for me. In the days that followed I learned enough to stay with me for the rest of my life. On lethal Saint Joseph the man in solitary confinement suffers most. Up against a slow and painful collapse of body and mind, he can do nothing to improve his condition. He finds himself entombed in a dark and tiny cell with a narrow bench to sleep on and a foul-smelling bucket for waste. If he is lucky, he'll get dirty drinking water with coarse food twice a day but not every day. For one hour every morning, after discharging the contents of the bucket or slop jar, he enters a silent courtyard where he walks in solitude. He is able to see the sky at that time, but for the rest of the day he exists in semidarkness and damp silence afflicted by tropical heat.

The man in solitary confinement has nothing to occupy his time, nothing to read, nothing for writing a letter, not a thing for any kind of positive activity. He paces back and forth or circles his cell for hours on end, and his mind wanders into a strange dimension unlike anything a sane person knows. He sees nothing but damp and dirty walls, hears only the sound of the sea and the howling of mad convicts in another building. Alone with his inner self he tries to remember the past, but for many the past is too painful to remember. Most of the men in this condition turn to the future and visualize. They begin to dream of better days, even happiness. Life becomes a mirage of lovely scenes, a fertile garden of green lawns and gorgeous flowers, and they find themselves slowly going mad. Desperate for human interaction, they wound themselves in various ways to merit a hospital stay. They risk killing themselves to rest in a bed, talk with another man, smoke, and read. They know they will in time return to their cells, but with pleasant memories and a small stash of tobacco to comfort them.

I feared I would be confined in one of three crude structures of solitary cells, but I had misjudged the Commandant's anger. Close to the pounding sea and surrounded by a high wall was the camp for men sent to the island for offenses not meriting solitary confinement, and there I was placed. About forty of us, maybe fifty, were imprisoned there. As in my case, most of my comrades had done something on Royale to upset authority and so were given punishment on Saint Joseph. Our seaside camp was more brutish than anything on Royale, and not far from us was the "Howling House" where the demented were kept. The place was called that because in the middle of the night, sometimes all night long, a screeching or howling kept the convicts in our camp awake and cursing and threatening to kill. It was a new experience for me and to some degree I felt sorry for the poor creatures.

"Don't pity them," a man with hideous sores on his neck and face said to me. "They have escaped this god-awful prison. They live insanely now in another and finer reality. They do no work.

91

They eat and sleep and howl. I really believe they are better off than you and me."

They were not. Hollow replicas of what they once were, I couldn't believe they were better off. They were helpless and exploited, and they were miserable. The guards stole a good portion of their food supply. The little left for them barely kept them alive. Few of them had clothes, even dirty or ragged, and stumbled about chittering and chattering as in a horror movie. Doomed human derelicts, they suffered as we all suffered in that detestable place. I was never in the presence of the crazy convicts but heard many stories about them, many anecdotes often told with bright eyes and a chuckle. Man's inhumanity to man, the poet Robert Burns has said, makes countless generations moan. On Saint Joseph it made for laughter and cruel jokes. One man in the Howling House counted during all his waking hours, counted even when trying to eat 31, 32, 33 . . . 31, 32, 33. Another in the one hour he had in the courtyard threw pebbles at the sun. He shrieked when required to stop.

Still another was a man with a distinguished degree, a man said to have taught the classics at the Sorbonne in Paris. He spent every hour of each day verbally composing a letter to be sent to authorities. Even the guards were moved by the sound of his rhetoric, nodding their heads in agreement with some of his claims. Because at an earlier time he had written letters of complaint to figures outside the prison system, a sane man was systematically driven insane and sent off to die. He probably died soon after I left Saint Joseph, and nobody inquired about his death. If for some reason someone did inquire, the immediate response on official stationery, used hundreds of times for many years, would have gone like this: *"Subject was made crazy by the tropical heat. Now deceased."* That simplistic explanation might not have satisfied the man's loved ones, but it ended nonetheless all further investigation.

Chapter Fourteen

Solitary Confinement

I endured the ravages of Saint Joseph for three months, carefully planning each day how I might escape. Then from the mainland came the local tribunal, self-important judges who would review my conduct during my stay on Saint Joseph and decide my punishment. I was told I had two serious reports against me. I would have to stand before the Court of Justice, state my case, defend it, and hear my sentence.

"Bonheur! Arthur Maurice Bonheur!" an officer of the court called.

"Here, sir!" I answered, stepping forward and standing at attention. Behind a temporary counter sat three fat judges in comfortable chairs. Their leader, a round little man sweating under a thin shirt, was thumbing through sheets of paper, looking for the accusations against me.

"Ah, here they are," he said in a monotone and then began to read. "Bonheur, Arthur Maurice, 51080. Spoke with insolence and impudence to a well-meaning guard who tried to advise him to accept his condition without rebellion. To the guard he reportedly said, 'I don't want to hear your stupid remarks. Now get the hell away from me, get lost!'"

The judge shuffled the papers, looked over the top of his eyeglasses at me, frowned and asked, "What have you to say about this? We want to hear an explanation for your conduct. Why did you speak that way?"

"I have nothing of substance to say, sir, nothing at all to explain. The day was hot. I was hungry and hurting. I spoke out of line."

He looked at me in silence for what seemed a long time, and then he read the second accusatory report. "Bonheur, Arthur Maurice, 51080. Asserted in vulgar language he was being cheated on his ration of food. Insisted it be weighed. His complaint was heard with patience but deemed grossly out of order and ultimately refused."

Again he shuffled the papers in front of him, looked over the rim of his spectacles, and frowned. I stood waiting as he sat back in his chair, sipped a glass of cold water, lit a cigarette, and began to converse with his colleagues on either side of him.

"What do you say to that?" he finally asked, clearing his throat and staring at me again. "Would you call it unseemly behavior?"

"They refused, sir, to weigh my portion of meat. They knew as I did just by looking at it that it was too meager a serving and wouldn't meet regulations. They could have quickly added an ounce or two more."

"You must surely know the stewards do not weigh every portion of meat or anything else that is served to you daily. On some days, depending on the way things go, you will get more. On other days less."

"That may be true, sir. But closer attention to what the regulations say appears to be necessary and might solve the problem."

"It might indeed, but who are you to say? As a condemned man you have no say whatever in this matter or any other regarding the way this institution is run. You should be thankful you receive any food and shelter at all. Moreover, if you know what's good for you and I think you do, you will not make a habit of insulting guards. Their lot is hard enough without hearing insults. You will spend thirty days in confinement for your first offense and thirty days more for the second. Should another offense be recorded against you, it will bring you more time."

I left the room crestfallen, knowing I had lost my temper before the round little judge, knowing I might have received a lighter sentence had I remained calm and deferential. They viewed me as confrontational and cocky, a man with gall trying to instruct them, and so it was necessary to use their power to put me in my place.

"How many, Maurice?" asked a fellow convict when I returned to my bunk in the barracks. "Five years in solitary for cussing a guard?"

"Not quite, my friend," I answered while making ready to leave. "Just two months in hell but believe me, two very long months."

A friend filled my suppository with tightly packed tobacco, cigarette papers, and matches. That way on the sly I could smoke in solitary. A guard came to take me to my cell just as I went to the privy to conceal the suppository. It was a device universally owned and used by convicts in Guiana, a small aluminum cylinder. Thievery was rampant, and no person had a trunk or chest that could be locked or bolted in place. So hiding one's money inside a personal cavity was a necessity. Hastily I jerked on my pants and left with the guard. For several minutes I was in sunlight, and then the iron door closed on me. I would have to endure sixty days away from the sun, away from light and life. I would have nothing whatever to do to while away the hours, nothing but a crude bench to look at, a foul bucket assailing my nostrils, a slimy floor attacking sore feet, and damp walls. I could hear nothing but silence. Memories of the past might console me, but even those were slipping away.

Coming in from the bright sunlight, my sight had to adjust to the somber darkness that cloaked the cell. Then as the darkness dissipated I heard a key rattling in the lock. The guard wanted to know if he could bring me something worth money to him. I gave him some coins to get me coffee and bananas. Half an hour later he returned. Even though the coffee was weak and the bananas over-ripe, I felt better after eating and drinking and began to pace my cell. In late afternoon the same guard ordered me to go into the courtyard for exercise. It was cooler there than in the stifling cell, and the air was fresher. But I was there only for half an hour before required to return. Some watery rice on a tin plate was shoved into the cell, and the door was locked until morning. Soon afterwards the blackness of night fell heavily upon me. The next day my meal was two slices of bread smeared with bacon grease. The stale bread and rancid grease attracted flies, but I quickly washed the stuff down with bitter and metallic water.

I lay down on the crude bench, the hard board, and tried to sleep. Thoughts of the present, the past, and what could have been the future flooded my mind and kept me awake. I thought of how it came to pass to find myself in so dire a situation. I thought of people I knew in the past and wondered whether they were still alive. My old flame, the girl I knew long before I met Gabrielle, returned to my thoughts now that I was so completely alone. Monique! So young and vital, so sexy, and so much in love! Then quickly my thoughts centered on Gabrielle, my true love, the woman I dearly wanted to marry. Joyfully I thought of what our life could have been together. Sadly I remembered the cause of all my trouble, how so prematurely I wanted to please her. Would she wait for me? Probably not. Perhaps she had fallen for another young man even before the convict ship dumped me like a sack of garbage in the tropics. And for that I couldn't blame her. The girl had but one life to live. She couldn't throw it away or damage it severely as I had done. One mistake had seized my life to destroy it. Even so, I would survive solitary confinement and find a way to live again.

Without names the tedious days passed one after another. Was it Tuesday or Saturday? It didn't matter. Slowly I became accustomed to the routine and monotony of isolation. Today would be a few ounces of rice on a tin plate. Tomorrow would be dry bread and metallic water. If I happened to be lucky, I would find no insects on the bread or water. I paid the guard to bring me coffee. Night again and the cell was pitch black. It was a time not for sleeping but for pacing back and forth, back and forth like a caged animal. With all the pacing on the damp floor, the soles of my bare feet became soft and sticky. Ignoring the pain, I thought of how I would cope with the future, and I spent an hour buying a suit in Chicago, or was it New York? Impeccably dressed, I waited in the lobby of a fine hotel for a graceful girl, impatient for her to arrive and joyous when she did. We dined in a first-class restaurant with a view, ordering the most expensive food on the menu. Sipping champagne after the dinner, we agreed on the size of the generous tip. I could see marks of surprise and satisfaction on the waiter's pale face and happiness in my love's gorgeous eyes. I could hear her musical laugher as she sipped her wine. My fertile imagination was allowing me to live a dream of life not entirely beyond a realistic view of life, and it kept me sane.

It wasn't long before I made up my mind to get out of that place. I was getting weaker by the day and had to go soon. I could no longer tolerate the stench, the bad air, and the dampness that damaged my feet. Then as I desperately sought a solution, I remembered an old trick used by convicts and hoped it would work. I mixed saliva with the dirt and dust of my cell floor and made a paste. I rubbed the gray-brown mess into my eyes to get them infected. When the doctor came the next day for his weekly visit, he found both eyes puffy, red, and watery. The paste had done its job and I could barely see. Without delay he sent me to the hospital. Under guard but confused and anxious because I was seeing double, I left Saint Joseph for Isle Royale and a clean bed. Nourishing food, clean water, something to read, and people to talk to made all the difference. I hoped to remain in the hospital a long time, but that didn't happen. My fake condition rapidly diminished and disappeared.

The doctor believed his medicine coupled with his expertise as a well-trained physician had saved my sight. I was in no position to argue with him, and to this day (if the old fellow is still alive) he tells the story of saving a young convict's eyesight only hours before he would have gone blind. It was the one big triumph of his career. Until then he believed there was little he could do to help the sick and dying men he saw every day in that hellish place. Believing he had saved my sight changed his attitude and made him more confident. He took under his wing any number of living cadavers and slowly restored them to health. He left the penal colony a contented man respected by inmates. In France, as I learned later, he gained prominence as an eye doctor.

In the hospital on Isle Royale I soon discovered that during my absence on Saint Joseph a scandal of large proportion had occurred. It was a scandal far more juicy that anything the guard's daughter and I might have brought about. It involved two notorious convicts and the wife of an old guard known as Corbin. Convict Jean-Paul had once been a chef in one of the finest restaurants in Paris and was something of a celebrity in the penal colony. On one of the islands, or so the story went, he had worked in the kitchen of the Commandant with two other cooks doing his bidding. Then one afternoon in altercation he split open a subordinate's skull with a heavy frying pan. Subsequently, he gave up cooking altogether and became a dissolute denizen of the Cochineal Barracks. His whole life centered on a young prisoner named Ethan who had become his lover. But one day Ethan was ordered to work as a servant in the house of André Corbin. His wife Lena found herself attracted to the young man, and within days they were having an affair.

She knew Jean-Paul was Ethan's homosexual lover but wanted the young man for herself. She called Jean-Paul to her house one afternoon and gave him an ultimatum: "See no more of Ethan if you don't want to go to a cell on Saint Joseph." The crusty old convict laughed in her face and turned to walk away. She shot him in the back at close range. The bullet lodged in his spine and paralyzed him from the waist down. It all came out in sordid detail at trial. Corbin's wife was charged with adultery, immoral activity, and the attempted murder of a well-known convict. A lawyer proved her guilt beyond reasonable doubt, but she was acquitted. It wasn't good for the wife of an official to have her life and reputation damaged by a lowly convict. Lena Corbin left her husband, a man much older than she, and went back to France. For weeks the scandal gave us something to talk about, and we wondered what happened to paralyzed Jean-Paul and Ethan. The rumor went that in spite of three additional years to be served by the younger man, the two eventually gravitated toward one another and resumed their friendship.

Chapter Fifteen

My Third Attempt

I completed my draconian sixty-day sentence of solitary confinement in the hospital on Isle Royale. In peak condition after the long rest, I was ordered to leave the island and return to the mainland. That was fine with me, for there I could put into motion my plan to escape. They gave me work as a bookkeeper but without a cent of pay. I needed to accumulate money for a sea escape with two or three other freedom seekers. But how could I get it working all day at a job with no wages? There seemed to be only one solution. I would give up sleeping and gamble all night. That way I might increase my kitty. Loss of sleep and rest, however, began to affect my health, and I gained nothing. At one point I thought I might stow away on an old freighter bound for Venezuela. I could possibly hide in the firewood stowed in her hold to feed the steam engine. Then a well-meaning comrade told me the stacked wood could fall and crush me if the old bucket of a ship hit bad weather. That got me to thinking, and reluctantly I gave up a plan that might have worked.

A couple of weeks later an inmate asked me what I thought of the American couple taking pictures of activity in Bella Vista. His question came as a big surprise. In all my years there I had seen nobody photographing anything, and certainly no Americans. Foreign visitors in the town were rare and carefully supervised when present. It was not a tourist attraction by any means. Prison officials adamantly discouraged the taking of pictures by anyone. Years earlier a handful of photographs showing half-naked prisoners dragging a huge log were leaked to the press. It caused a hue and cry as far away as France. The scandal drove administrators to keep a wary eye on anyone who might want to take pictures. So how could Americans show up years later and appear to have carte blanche asking questions and taking pictures?

"They must be reporters from an influential newspaper," he said, "people of some importance with special permits. I hear they've been asking ordinary citizens a lot of questions and taking photos of them. They are walking about everywhere in the town though apparently not in the prison. They're at the Commandant's house in the square."

"Staying at the Commandant's surely means they have permission from higher authority, maybe the Governor or even the Board of Justice in France. I'm thinking it also means they're here to write propaganda, a glowing report with pictures for European and American newspapers. Propaganda, you know, to improve the image of the place. But maybe, just maybe, they'd like to hear the truth."

On the spot I decided to see the Americans, if at all possible, and offer them some stories I had written about prison life in French Guiana. Because I had found no way to promote or publish my stuff, I saw the Americans as offering perhaps an opportunity. Early the next morning I left my job with a small bundle and went to the house where the newspaper people were staying. When I knocked on the door, another convict employed there as a servant left me standing on the stoop while he went to inform the couple of a visitor. He said he'd been told they represented a major magazine in America. In a few minutes a man of thirty or thirty-five appeared and asked me what I wanted. In broken English I told him I wished to sell him a few authentic stories about the place he had come many miles to visit. As he examined my bundle of papers, a tall and slender woman in her early thirties appeared behind him to look over his shoulder.

"How much do you have in mind for this material?" the man asked. "I'm not able to read most of it. My French is terrible. But it seems to me it reveals stuff about the prison we might be able use."

"Whatever you think is fair," I replied. "I've never sold any of my writings, never had a chance. So I can't put a figure on them."

"Just a cursory glance tells me your work deserves a closer look," said the woman. "Geoffrey and I will read through the material this evening. Come back again tomorrow, will you please?" She slipped into my hand a folded American bill with a value of 100 francs!

Expecting far less, I couldn't believe my eyes. I went immediately to a Chinese trader where I bought a few items so as to change the note into local currency. After paying off a debt that had nagged me for weeks I had eighty-one francs left, a small fortune for a lowly convict. The next morning I went again to visit the young woman and her husband. They were having breakfast and invited me to join them. For the first time in a very long time I felt like a free human being, and with a sense of gladness I hadn't felt in a long time I told them my story. Happily the woman was skilled in French and jotted down all I said. She gave me a list of questions about prison life in the colony and asked me to supply the answers. Then she gave me another American note worth 100 francs! Several times, until the Administration began to take notice, I met with Ellen and Geoffrey Thornhurst. For each story I gave them she paid me generously. Then one afternoon soon after I came to visit Geoffrey told me they would be leaving in two days for New York. They would be taking passage on a ship berthed nearby in Dutch Guiana.

I thought if they were willing to help me, I might be able to get to New York on that ship. On the eve of their departure I went to see them about it but lost my nerve and couldn't ask for help. I wanted all the help I could get, but stubborn pride intervened and left me on my own. After wishing them *bon voyage* I went to the shack of a liberated convict and bought from him a white suit, a good pair of shoes, and a pith helmet. Then I asked him to find me a man to take me to the Dutch side of the river. He said a person named Malcolm would do it for a reasonable fee. At high noon the next day when all the officials were taking their siesta, we went to Malcolm's little skiff and pushed off. Within an hour I was in Dutch country near a small town. I went to an open-air bar and ordered a beer. It was native beer and known to be rather bitter. Yet I remember even now how delicious it was to a tongue that had not tasted beer for many months. I sat around and had a few more, waiting for night to come. When all was dark I left for the seaport fifteen miles to the north where the ship lay in harbor.

I had plenty of money and my intention was to book passage as an ordinary, well-dressed traveler. Perhaps in that identity I would meet up with the Thornhursts and travel with them. Somehow I would have to get to the port and get on the ship without causing attention. It didn't happen. I was on the road not more than a few minutes when I came face to face with the Dutch police escorting a work crew back to their prison cells. A white man on the road at that hour seemed out of place to them. They asked me where I was headed, and I answered politely. They asked for my identification papers, which I couldn't produce. So they insisted I come back with them to the town, and within minutes I was branded a French escapee and thrust in jail.

What a sad night that was! As I recall it years later and reflect, I feel the same old sadness as then. My high hopes of freedom, my dreams of fleeing the nightmare of French Guiana to live with dignity again were instantly dashed. Three times I had tried to escape and had failed. They sent me back to Bella Vista on the same motor launch the Thornhursts had used to cross the river. For a moment as a strange sense of loss swept over me I could have sworn I got a whiff of the lady's perfume.

The authorities placed me in the blockhouse again and were planning to add to my sentence another three years. But getting wind of a new regulation that said a man had to be away for twelve hours to be considered an escapee, I decided to fight the charges. Some quick thinking told me I was absent from my work only nine hours. In a letter to Colonel Rousseau, Commandant of the penal colony, I explained my situation. For several days I waited for a response. When it seemed I would hear not a word from him, I got a formal reply on fancy stationery. He had brought my situation before the Disciplinary Commission and had made it plain to them that under the new regulation I couldn't be punished with more time. Even so, the Commission classed me as "Incorrigible" again and gave me sixty more days on Isle Royale. They could have sent me to solitary confinement on hideous Saint Joseph, but in deference to the Commandant they settled on Royale. I protested the treatment, trying hard to be heard, but everyone in authority ignored my letters and refused to see me in person.

So I found myself once again in the Bloodstained Barracks of the hardened Incorrigibles and watching my back at every turn. Sweating and stinking but snickering and scornful, the habitués wanted to know why I was back. I didn't want to get on their wrong side by saying it was none of their business, and so I told them. They laughed and laughed when I divulged all that had happened. I can hear the merriment even now. The scornful cackling of brutes burned my ears then and even now. The wise among us tell us memory is selective. We tend to forget the bad things that happen to us, they say, and remember only the good. Like all the rest of us, sages at times are prone to babble nonsense. Yet to be honest, as I thought about it later, I had to agree. I wanted to forget what had happened. That tantalizing taste of freedom for only nine hours, was ludicrous, impulsive, absurd, and embarrassing. My next escape would have to be carefully planned, meticulous, and longer.

Chapter Sixteen

My Fourth Attempt

In that tropical prison where men came to suffer and die a condemned man would do anything to get away, anything at all to get a taste of freedom, and I was no exception. I told myself this fourth escape would have to be longer than just a few hours. It would be longer than a few days or months, even a few years, for I was not coming back. I was on record for having strength of will, determination, and a penchant for giving officials of the penal colony tons of trouble. So when I found myself in a stifling, stinking, notorious, and dangerous barracks, I had but one idea: to escape one more time and make it final. It quickly became an obsession. I had to find a way to get out of Cochineal and into the hospital. So for several days I smoked hand-rolled cigarettes stoked with quinine supplied by a guard charging too much. The result, when the doctor examined me, was a nasty rash on my neck and face and a towering temperature. I thought that would get me sent to the hospital, but the shrewd doctor sensed the sham and sent me back to my cell. He was a very perceptive man and I despised him.

A day later I stuck a needle through my left cheek, rubbed fecal dirt into the wound, and slowly got my face so inflamed and swollen I looked to be on the brink of death. When the doctor came on his weekly visit and gave one look at my condition, he decided it was not a sham and sent me immediately to the hospital. The first step in my scheme to escape had succeeded on the second try. I had managed to get away from the dangerous red box, the barracks of brutes, to a place of ease and safety. Sprawled on the white hospital bed in clean underwear, I now pondered my next step: how to get away from the island and do it before the doctor pronounced me well again. It was miles from the mainland surrounded by waters filled with sharks. From it very few had escaped. Scores had tried only to die or be caught and given additional time. I would have to construct a sturdy, shark-proof raft to get to the mainland, but out of what? The island offered one material used invariably by other would-be escapees, bamboo. One desperate man had tried to escape on a large bag filled with coconuts. A hundred yards offshore a feeding frenzy turned the water red. If I were to do what they had not done, I needed something better.

Then one afternoon my eye fell on a pile of boards in the corner of the ward, twenty of them stacked on the floor. I knew at a glance they were used on the bed frames to support the mattresses. Made of hardwood and strong, they were four feet long, an inch thick, and seven inches wide. My raft was there before my eyes, the essential component waiting to be used. I would have to find a way to connect the boards tightly, forming a unit that wouldn't fall apart. The next morning, under the pretext of changing the grimy boards on my otherwise clean bed, I was able to put aside just the ones I needed for the raft. The problem now was how to get the planks out of the hospital and hidden in a safe place. The ward was on the second floor, and that made the job even more difficult. However, when I found out that beneath my bed was a room on the ground floor in which old mattresses were stored, I knew exactly what to do. I would drop the boards through a hole in the floor to the next level, but how would I make a hole in the thick floor?

On examining it, I found a spot close to my bed of soft wood decaying. Every night for a week I patiently dug away at the decay with the knife I always carried for protection. I made a hole just large enough for each board to slip through. Then working silently

I dropped selected boards through the hole. Landing on the old mattresses, they made not a sound. I rolled up a blanket and a sheet and dropped them down the hole also. When everyone in the ward was asleep and the orderly in the toilet, I raced downstairs and gathered up my boards. Within minutes I found myself in the yard running for the wall. I folded the blanket and threw it to the top as a cushion against the pointed pieces of glass, barbed wire, and nails. Then I made six bundles of two boards tied with strips of cloth from the sheet and threw them over. I climbed the wall where the blanket lay across the barbed wire and slithered down the other side with blanket in tow.

Working rapidly in half-light, I lashed the raft boards together with strips of strong blanket cloth. An hour later I was struggling against a surge of waves, trying to get the raft through the surf. Away from the building the night without a moon was very dark, and so I didn't have to worry about being seen. As I struggled in the surf a big wave lifted the raft, and suddenly I was free of the shore and in the sea beyond the breakers. It was exactly where sharks had grown fat on human bodies. I tied myself to the narrow raft so as not to be separated from it by the rough sea. I was daring night waters on a clumsy contraption in a sea filled with circling sharks, and I couldn't swim very well. One false move and I could drown or be torn apart and eaten. I looked back at the shore, thinking maybe I had made a terrible mistake. All was dark except for one flickering light, and all was quiet except for the pounding surf.

Morning came suddenly, stark and hot, and I knew as soon as a check was made the guards would find me missing from the hospital. They would question every convict in the ward but would get nothing from anyone. Not a soul had seen or heard me leave. Only one man had seen me fumbling with the boards but wouldn't talk. They would comb the island looking for me but would find nothing. Through binoculars they would scan the ocean and see nothing. The news of my escape would run like wildfire through the prison population. Every person who heard the story would have his own theory on how I made off. Then wild rumors would start. Word would come that a battered raft had washed up on the rocky shore of Devil's Island. A rumor, grossly untrue, would claim that my corpse, partly eaten by sharks, had washed ashore. I had suddenly become to the entire prison community nothing more than carrion on the beach. Even as I felt my throat becoming sore from the salt air and exposure, I laughed at that.

When day broke, the islands were out of sight and it appeared I was only a few miles from the mainland. My mouth was dry and the sun was already scorching my skin, but that was small change to pay for the cloak of freedom. All day long under a hot sun the raft drifted slowly toward shore. In late afternoon I was fewer than a hundred yards away. Then I noticed the contraption that was keeping me alive had come to a standstill. It was no longer moving toward shore but was beginning to spin a little and drift seaward. Low tide was setting in and taking me out! With oars I might have nullified the tide but had none. It took me so far out to sea that I lost sight of the mainland. I lay on my stomach sick and desperate. I wanted to curse the gods who controlled the sea. I wanted to sob like a little child but couldn't even do that.

The next day, hungry and thirsty, I drifted back to within a few hundred feet of the shore. Had I been able to swim well I might have made it to the beach in a few minutes but dared not try. Despair set in to compete with desperation. I pried loose a board at the risk of having the raft fall apart and began to paddle. But the tide was pulling the flimsy structure back to sea again, and I was too weak to fight against it. Once more I found myself far out on the open ocean and staring exhausted at the stars. Day came and I was sick with hunger and thirst and burned a torrid red by the sun. Four days passed and then seven. I grew sick and slipped into delirium. Sharks bumped against the raft, trying to flip it over. They caused me no harm, but I was slowly dying of thirst, hunger, and exposure. When the raft came within a few yards of the coast one night, I thought I might wade ashore. I struggled to get off but was too weak. The tide, relentless and indifferent, swept me back to sea.

On the seventh day a group of Indians fishing off the coast of Dutch Guiana saw a naked white man burned severely by the tropical sun. He was lying unconscious on water-soaked boards on the brink of falling apart. The fishermen silently approached and with their paddles drove away two circling sharks. They found the man just barely alive. They took him into their canoe and brought him to their village as a curiosity for the tribe to see. Except for soldiers who sometimes came to their huts looking for escaped convicts, they tolerated no white men in their world. They expected this sorely burned wretch to die before sundown. But an old Indian woman named Peche took it upon herself to care for the stricken man. She applied cooling wet cloths to his blistered skin, dribbled water down his parched throat, and fed him a mush of sea-turtle eggs to quell his hunger. In a few days he found himself awake in the midst of strange surroundings and regaining strength.

A week later an Indian girl named Leywa helped me climb into a hut where six women and four men were living. She hung from the rafters a hammock wide enough for two people. I lay in the hammock for only a few minutes before she came and snuggled beside me. Though I couldn't understand her language, she let me know her village had adopted me, and she was my keeper. She touched my face, ears, eyes, and mouth gently with both hands. Her fingers were long and tapered but rough with small cuts from the coral where daily she dived for oysters. I kissed her full lips and she returned the kiss with a painful bite, her way of kissing. After my sunburn healed we found an empty hut, set up housekeeping, and lived as man and wife. Leywa cooked nutritious meals for me in earthen pots, and quickly I gained the weight I had lost during my ordeal on the raft. As the days passed, we got into the habit of bathing each other in the sea. Afterwards we lay in the shade of palm trees to dry ourselves. Leywa speaking softly in musical cadence began to teach me her language, pointing to an object and naming it.

I had escaped the brutal penal colony in French Guiana to struggle against natural forces and almost die. Then miraculously I found myself living an idyllic existence with a beautiful young girl who called herself my wife. It was beyond belief, a wild dream of sorts, and yet an existence that continued without pain for several months. We made love and she found herself pregnant. Her younger sister grew jealous on seeing her swollen belly and wanted the same. One day Leywa placed her naked sister beside me and waited for natural impulses to take over. I made it known to her in the native words she had taught me that I was unwilling to have her sister. That made her joyous, for she was thinking because she was no longer slender I was losing interest. For a time she was happy, and then one day as the rain poured down in torrents, invincible and total grief struck her down. Soldiers on the prowl barged into the settlement with rifles ready and took her husband away.

Two days later I was back in prison. Two weeks later I was again on the island of Saint Joseph in soul-shattering solitary confinement. Three additional years had been added to my sentence. Eighteen months were to be served in the damp and darkness and total isolation of a solitary cell. My fourth attempt to escape had failed miserably. My loving wife Leywa I never saw again. Even worse, I didn't learn anything about the life within her that we had created. When the soldiers wrested me away from her, she wept with her head between her knees, and I wanted to comfort her. They wouldn't let me go near her. They prodded me with their rifle butts, made cruel jokes in gibberish I couldn't understand, and laughed like hyenas. The laughter I did understand.

Later on I came to terms with what happened and began to realize it was probably for the best. I rather liked living in that pleasant Indian village with Leywa and all her relatives but doubt

I could have remained there longer. During all the time I was a condemned man I had a hankering for civilization and the city. From the time the French judge pounded his gavel to pronounce sentence, I knew I would return some day to a big city. I would not remain in exile forever. On Isle Royale I often sat on the rocky shore for hours looking out across the water and dreaming of New York, Hong Kong, London — any big city other than Paris — where I might go and live peacefully. It was the dream that sustained me.

Chapter Seventeen

Corrupt Cayenne

During my long isolation on Saint Joseph I bribed a guard to let me write a letter to the Governor in Cayenne, the capital of French Guiana. Politely I explained to his Excellency that I was sick and suffering in solitary confinement and would soon die if I couldn't secure help from some humane person in authority. My letter must have moved him because soon afterwards he instructed officials on Saint Joseph to transfer me to the penitentiary at Cayenne. Within a week, wheezing and coughing, I was on the mainland again and seeing the capital city for the first time. It wasn't much to look at because to see Cayenne beyond its multi-colored buildings, red rooftops, and lush vegetation was to see human misery. When I was there it was the capital of a colony without colonists. Few wanted to establish themselves in a place peopled mainly by hard-pressed convicts seen everywhere. Hungry and bedraggled, they roamed the streets like demented phantoms. Most of them, the so-called "liberated convicts," had served their sentences and were free of prison jurisdiction, but a heinous law demanded they remain in exile equal to their sentence. They were a miserable lot, pariahs with no support from anybody or anything and no visible way to make a living.

Not a single street in the entire city was paved. The main street with a few struggling shops was sprayed twice a month with used motor oil. When pedestrians tracked oily dirt into their shops, the merchants complained but nothing was done about it. All other streets were raw and muddy when it rained and dusty soon afterwards. Although rain poured frequently from the skies, the tropical sun could make a street dusty within hours. The town stretched along the seashore for a few miles and was surrounded by sea and rain forest. Pelted by consistent heavy rainfall just about every day of the year, it was damp and hot. Flowering plants were abundant, but weeds and grass choked any street not tended by convicts. Putrid water lay in ditches to breed mosquitoes. Buildings were made of wood, mainly one story in height, and painted whatever color that happened to be available. In a town where fresh water ran abundantly through the streets with every downpour, households had potable water only twice a day. The water works was primitive at best, electricity scarce and unreliable. Convicts, I was told, ran the machinery of the plant and were known to cut the power to throw the town in darkness during escape attempts.

Cayenne had no sewers in the modern sense. Collecting sewage for disposal was a job done by convicts at night. They went through the town on wagons drawn by oxen. They crawled under the houses, took away the filled buckets of waste, and replaced them with empty buckets. To fleece their pockets with extra coin, they worked a simple scam. Regulations called for the buckets not to be entirely full, the aim being not to soil the hands of the carrier with waste. But dropping a heavy stone into the bucket filled it to the top. People in the house were awakened and told the bucket was too full to be moved. The man of the house would have to pay to have it taken away. I was thinking when a fellow convict told me this how awful the job must be. Then I learned that sewage collecting was sought after. Numerous inmates wanted the job because one could earn ten francs or more in a single night. Any job that allowed a man to make a little money was a good one.

Convicts were also in charge of garbage disposal. Every other morning two trucks with three men on each truck went through the town to pick up anything left in front of a house. Their eyes were carefully trained on every item they tossed into the truck. While they didn't expect to find treasure in the trash, often they saw value in what others threw away. Sometimes they found a lamp, table, or chair that could be repaired, and the stuff went to a penitentiary workshop where it could be refurbished and sold. Once they picked up an old piano on the curbside. It was severely out of tune and missing some keys, but they managed to sell it to a Chinese trader at a good price. They got similar prices from another merchant for an old washing machine and a used accordian. Clever wheeling and dealing was the order of the day. It was the way enterprising convicts made enough money for small luxuries they could buy most of the time from guards.

The population of Cayenne when I was there was far less than it is today. The town had only a few thousand people, and of those more than a third were convicts. Half of them were so-called liberated convicts living in exile. The other half were condemned men who had committed crimes ranging from petty theft to murder. They mingled with citizens of the town but had no say in the way it was run. The civilian population was made up of four classes. The officials of the penal colony, mostly white, were at the top of the social ladder. They lived fairly well on good incomes in comfortable houses often with servants. A few white merchants were placed under the officials even though many were poor and struggling. Below the whites were the Chinese merchants, larger in number and often more industrious. They ran most of the shops on the main street, including the town laundry. A few Chinese merchants lived better than some officials. On the lowest rung of the ladder were the native blacks, largest in number and seen everywhere. The men scratched out a living on small farms or performed odd jobs as handymen. The women often worked as servants in the homes of officials. As I remember, they seemed to be satisfied with their condition.

In the bustling market down by the waterfront all classes merged into one. There in the early morning people of every stripe mingled in a chatty crowd. I was not able to see or be a part of this scene until I was finally given leave to walk the streets of Cayenne as a prisoner. Then I went there every morning to enjoy the spectacle. Shapely black women oozing sexuality stood in groups chatting, laughing, and swaying their hips. Bedraggled free convicts wandered among the booths looking for a cheap bargain and often snatching a vegetable or fruit when the vendor wasn't looking. Condemned convicts in their signature straw hats and prison garb, and I was one of these, were there to buy something tasty to eat with their ration. A few white women could be seen in the crowd, some with their maids and others with a male escort. Also I noticed several stocky, well-fed cooks in civilian clothes but wearing the convict's wide straw hat. Later I learned they were the cooks of important officials. At least one before he got into trouble had been a celebrated chef in the kitchen of a famous Parisian café.

I was surprised to see convicts at liberty to blend in with the town's population anywhere they chose. The penitentiary on the shore with its back to the rain forest and other parts against the sea had no walls, only a tall metal fence with gates left open, and so the inmates had free run of the town. Most of them answered to roll call and spent their nights in the prison and part of each day on a work gang. Some with special privileges didn't return to their cells at night. They slept in the houses of their employers and enjoyed unusual liberty. Those employed often had leisure and money to spend. The storekeepers were told not to sell alcohol to prisoners, and yet each day those who could afford it had glasses of rum or wine with Cantonese food in a Chinese restaurant. At one time Cayenne had numerous black slaves to do the dirty work their masters wouldn't do. Then in time the slaves were freed and the penal colony was established. So when I was there as inmate 51080 a reversal of fortune had taken place. Convicts did the work of slaves and some descendants of slaves held key administrative positions.

Everything in lawless and poverty-bitten Cayenne was to my mind almost unbelievable. An old-timer whose only pleasure was narrating a good story told me of an incident truly hard to believe but worth recording here. Six and a half miles out to sea on a barren rock stood a beacon tended by convicts. Its purpose was to guide ships into the harbor at night. By day its bell emitted a clang that could be heard for miles, and the sound often disturbed the three men who lived in a hut near it. Then one day one of them began to scream that he was losing his hearing and also his sight. Fearing that the man was either very sick or going mad, his comrades quickly got him returned to shore for inspection by a doctor. Regulations called for replacing the man immediately, but that was never done. A week later the two remaining convicts began to worry when the launch didn't bring them food supplies.

So they covered the white light with red cellophane to raise the distress signal. They expected those on shore to respond without delay, but the light burned red the next night and again the next. Anxiously they watched and waited for the launch to put out from shore, but it didn't move. After several days they had nothing to eat and had to consume shellfish scraped from rocks. Several more days and nights went by, and the beacon ran out of fuel. That meant one of the main navigation lights along the coast was dead and shrouded in darkness. Three more days passed and still the port launch was nowhere in sight. For three nights an important light no longer appeared on the sea. Two weeks went by and the motorboat at last came to the rock. It approached to within hailing distance of the famished men but turned back in a stormy sea.

Knowing they had been left to die, the two stranded men stood on the rocky shore and watched the launch grow smaller and smaller. Now their concern was to save themselves any way they could. Rather than die on the rock, although one of them couldn't swim, they decided to dismantle the hut and make a raft of its wood. They waited all day for the dangerous sea to grow calmer, and when night came they pushed off into wild surf that almost flipped their raft. After struggling for hours in three-foot waves and shark-infested water, they reached the mainland. Half naked and bitten bloody by mosquitoes, they sprawled in a heap on the beach and slept through the night without moving once.

As day began they set off through the jungle and finally reached a settlement of soldiers. The soldiers gave them food and drink and transported them to Cayenne. They were arrested and sentenced in the Hall of Justice for deserting their post.

But the story doesn't end there. In a frequently visited room in the hospital at Cayenne I saw one day five large bottles on a shelf. In them, carefully preserved in clear alcohol, were the heads of five executed criminals. My curiosity getting the better of me, I examined the heads closely. Hair on them had continued to grow after the blade cleanly sliced the neck. The faces of three grotesque heads had grown stubby beards. The bulging eyes of two or maybe three were wide-open and staring back at me. I saw a glint in the eye of a well-preserved face but no sign of pain or anguish. Passing a mirror as I left the horrible place in a hurry, I couldn't help but see plenty of anguish on my own.

The third head belonged to none other than one of the brave light keepers. In a rage after surviving the ordeal of rock, sea, and jungle, as the story went, he killed a guard who had taunted him. After a month in solitary confinement, he was brought before the Tribunal of Justice to be tried and sentenced. Less than a week later the blade of the guillotine severed his head in a ceremony attended by the public. Why the preserved heads were placed on display I could never find out. I remember them as powerful symbols of the inhumanity that pervaded every nook and cranny of the prison in French Guiana. I couldn't believe and cannot believe even to this day how a civilized nation such as France could have condoned and supported so evil a system.

Once more the words of the Scottish poet came back to haunt me: *"Man's inhumanity to man makes countless thousands mourn!"* By then bitter and cynical, I began to question the truth of that statement. I wondered whether any one person at all had mourned the injustice, cruelty, and general barbarity of those who for centuries called themselves our leaders. And I wondered whether the masses at any time had really given a damn about what happened to a single victim so long as it didn't happen to them. The creature we call human is surely a work in progress, closer perhaps to somber darkness than eternal light.

Chapter Eighteen
My Fifth Attempt

Most of the condemned men in French Guiana had but one consuming desire — to escape as soon as they could. Within days I learned of four ways to escape: through the unforgiving jungle; across the river to hostile Dutch Guiana; as a passenger on a Brazilian pirate's boat; and by sea in a canoe or sailboat. Escape through the jungle into Brazil was very difficult. An attempt by way of Dutch Guiana was easier, but Dutch authorities soon began to send escapees back to French Guiana. To brave it as a stowaway on a pirate vessel was a big gamble. The pirates were known to abuse stowaways and even throw them overboard to drown or be eaten by sharks. Going as a passenger was safer but only if a runaway could afford the exorbitant fee. Even then he had only a fifty-fifty chance of making it to his destination alive. Escape by sea was also risky. Yet it offered the best chance to men strong enough to endure the ordeal and foolish enough to try it. Every would-be escapee knew any attempt to flee was very definitely a gamble and dangerous.

At the time I began to think of my next escape, I had served more than six years in French Guiana and knew how the penal colony worked. In a few more years with good behavior I could have become a free man. Yet even granted so-called freedom, I would have to live the remainder of my days in exile. Finding that unacceptable, I began to think about escaping by sea. I asked around confidentially if anyone bent on escape knew how to navigate a boat, but had no luck. Even so, because I had the necessary money, I decided it was time to go. I would embark as a passenger on a coastal ship moving southward. In Brazil I would get on a mail boat for further passage but would need a passport. I got one from Raoul, an old convict working in an office who charged me 100 francs for it. Also he made up false papers that looked genuine to show I had once served as a convict but was now a free man.

The ship was scheduled to leave on a Wednesday afternoon, and I had everything ready by Monday. At the appointed time I would leave my work gang, dress in civilian clothes bought earlier, and walk casually on board. Then I heard departure of the ship would be delayed, and that troubled me. It meant I might have to follow a different timeline that could make prison officials suspicious. Under supervision one had to be in the right place at the right time all the time. I was facing a predicament but thought it might be resolved in the end. If they didn't arrest me at the moment the ship sailed, I would have my freedom. At the fishing village on the Brazilian border where I expected to land, only one policeman would glance at my papers and find them in order. My plan would work, I told myself, and to falter would be lose everything. The only wrinkle in my scheme was the change in the departure of the ship. It was a bother, but I had to go forward anyway. After all the preparation I had done, I couldn't change the plan.

Wednesday afternoon near three o'clock I left my street gang as we worked at pulling up weeds beside the road. I told the guard I was dying of thirst and had to find something cool to drink. He pointed to a nearby gas station and said I could go there for water. I wouldn't have to return because our work was done for the day. I ambled off in that direction but circled back and went to the hut of my friend Charles, a liberated convict, where I had stowed my civilian clothes. There I spent the night too restless to sleep. As soon as first light I sent Charles to the pier to find out the exact time the ship would sail. I paced the floor and waited. He seemed to be gone for hours. Then suddenly appearing, he advised me to get to the ship right away because it would be leaving within the hour.

"Go now," he said, "before the streets become full of guards. You know as soon as breakfast is over they pour into the streets."

I got dressed in a clean shirt, a white suit, a good pair of shoes with dark blue socks, and a pith helmet. Wearing sunglasses, I crossed the town with Charles and arrived at the pier. Waterfront activity was already buzzing and the morning seemed quite normal. We stood at the gate. Beyond it was the long and narrow pier. At the end of it sat an impressive ship, her bow pointed southward. I shook my comrade's hand warmly, turned on my heel, and strolled nonchalantly past the gendarme at the gate. He glanced at me and nodded. Beyond him my knees seemed to buckle under the excitement I felt. I was on the pier, my runway to freedom, approaching the ship resting languidly in the morning sun. I managed to put down all feeling and draw from within a pervasive calm. Though walking briskly, the ship seemed far away and the pier endless. Then of a sudden I was mounting the gangplank. On deck I presented my ticket. A steward in uniform directed me to my cabin.

I breathed a sigh of relief when the steward closed the door and left me alone. Mentally I went through all the details of my escape to see if anything was missing. Everything seemed in place. This time I would be gaining the freedom I had dreamed of for so long. I stood behind my locked door and chortled with joy.

"It worked!" I said to myself. "I did it, by god, I did it!" And speaking in my native tongue, I muttered out loud, *"Vive la liberté! Vive la vie!"*

Moments later I began to ask why the ship wasn't already moving. I looked through the porthole and saw only little eddies of water glinting in the sunlight. If the ship had been moving, I would have seen a bow wave rushing by and turbulence in the water. I grew nervous. Maybe somehow prison authorities knew exactly what I had accomplished, knew I was on board, and were delaying departure. Then from on deck came a blast from the ship's horn, the signal that her mooring lines would soon be cast off. Beside myself with excitement, I found a secluded spot on deck to watch the boarding of the last passengers. Again the horn sounded. In minutes the ship would be free of the pier, and I would be free of French Guiana.

As a surge of joy again welled up within me, almost a foreign feeling, my gaze fastened on a gendarme running at full speed toward the ship. He flew up the gangplank, saluted the ship's officer at the top, and rapidly began asking questions. He was breathing hard, gesticulating, and speaking loudly. I saw him point to a paper he held in his hand and heard him ask if a man named Raoul was on board. I couldn't believe my ears! Raoul was the name of the convict who had made my escape possible. Somehow his name had gotten on the passenger list instead of mine! When they ran below in search of my cabin, I decided it was time to make myself scarce. In seconds, or so it seemed, I was down the gangplank and on the pier and walking its length as fast as I could. Again the pier seemed endless, and the little gate stood miles away. I heard someone call out to me, a polite but urgent M'sieur! I pretended not to hear and kept walking.

I heard footsteps behind me and glanced over my shoulder. A slender man in uniform, the gendarme, was catching up with me. He was suddenly walking beside me and asking me to slow down.

"Where do you think you're going?" he asked, huffing and trying to catch his breath. "And why so fast?".

"To the town before the ship departs," I replied as calmly as I could.

"But you are leaving the ship," he said, gasping. "Why?"

"I forgot something important and have to go back and get it. I must hurry, or the ship will leave without me."

As a good officer doing his duty, he asked to see my papers. He glanced at them and saw the name Raoul.

"But you are not Raoul!" he exclaimed. "I arrested Raoul yesterday dead drunk and stumbling down the street. What is this?"

In a moment I realized what had happened. That old sot Raoul had bought alcohol with the money I had given him and got arrested. Now the same officer was about to arrest me! I sought for an opening.

"You might say I'm Raoul because that is my name also. I have the same name, but I'm obviously not the man you arrested."

The ruse might have worked. But when he looked at the full name on my papers, he smelled something fishy. Raoul Bouchard was the full name on the passenger list and on my papers. I couldn't possibly have the same last name. That would be too much a coincidence. At the police station I was quickly identified and hustled to the penitentiary. Once more the fates had turned against me. I had come so close, so very close, to escaping French Guiana forever only to have circumstance wallop me hard. Some mental quirk had driven Raoul to put his own name on my papers instead of mine. Then drunk from rum bought with the money I paid him, he had insulted this particular gendarme and got thrown in jail. On a desk in the jail, for reasons no one could explain, was the ship's passenger list. On it was Raoul's name easily seen, and the policeman quickly concluded his prisoner was trying to run away.

"Oh, what a tangled web we weave when first we practice to deceive," wrote a disgruntled poet. Despondent and suffering the sting of another failure, I was in no mood to disagree. I had tried to deceive and had become a victim of circumstance. I was never a child of fortune, never a friend of fate. During all the years of my youth that inimitable force dogged my footsteps wherever I went. People speak of free will as a precious commodity of mankind. If the ability to choose one's course so as to go through life unimpeded were ever in my possession, it was surely an illusion. If the ship had sailed as shown in the printed schedule, my fifth attempt to escape would have surely succeeded.

Chapter Nineteen
The New Governor

I wanted to avoid years added to my sentence but knew any chance of that was slim indeed. The police had found my false passport and had caught me in the act of using it. Also they had become suspicious of other papers in my possession and had branded my offense an attempt to escape with false identification. I would go on trial again and could receive three to five years in solitary confinement. But when I came to court on Royale a month later, the tribunal added only two years to my sentence and gave me no solitary confinement. For once I got a lucky break from a person in power. My reputation as a literate man had reached the new Governor who asked me to write an essay describing the abuses he had heard about. I had sent the manuscript in several pages to him before the trial, and those pages he read carefully. His influence not only brought about the lesser sentence, but put me in a position to leave the island shortly afterwards.

When I left Royale to return to the mainland, I had a canvas bag stuffed with clean clothes, toilet articles, and a stash of money. I was also in good health. An earlier attack of dysentery was gone. The boat reached the mainland just as night was falling. I entered the penitentiary and found most of the convicts I had known the previous year. We had a little party to celebrate my return, and they were astonished to see me off the islands so soon. We drank pints of rum and played cards all night. My friend Gaspard, the keeper of the barracks, thought he would never see me again. I was glad to be a prisoner in Cayenne where most of the condemned had it fairly easy. When morning came I tried to get some sleep, but the chief guard woke me and said the Commandant wanted to see me. I asked him why but got no answer. So thinking I might be in trouble, I walked without a guard across town to his office. He greeted me affably as if we were equals and friends, but I knew better.

As I stood to leave his office he said he would try to find a good job for me in Cayenne if I promised to stop trying to escape. In the meantime I was to go to Government House to be interviewed by the new Governor. I walked rapidly in the tropical heat and got to his residence wet with perspiration. It could have been the dank humidity causing me to sweat, but plain excitement was a factor too. The doorman, clad in red and white and not much older than twelve, required me to wait at the entrance. After a few minutes that seemed more like half an hour, he returned and said the Governor would see me. I climbed the long stairway, mopping my face with a soiled handkerchief to look my best. The boy led me down a narrow hallway to an office with the door ajar. Outside in the hall was a cushioned bench where I sat and waited another fifteen minutes. Then standing at attention in front of me and dramatizing his patter with a snappy salute, the boy announced in military fashion that I might go in. I wasn't sure of the protocol governing my behavior, and so I quickly rose from the bench and stood in the doorway.

"Come in, Bonheur!" a man almost hidden behind a huge desk called out. I could barely see the flecked gray hair on the top of his head.

I dropped my straw hat on the bench and sidled into the well-appointed office, trying to be as unobtrusive as possible. The Governor was shuffling some papers on his desk and didn't look at me immediately. The office smelled of lavender and was very quiet.

"Have a seat, Bonheur! Make yourself comfortable. Be with you in a minute," he said in a mellow voice, speaking educated French.

The man was in his middle or late fifties. His shoulders were square and his lined face rugged, but in weight and height he was even smaller than me. His greenish-gray eyes depicted high intelligence but appeared too small for features accenting a large mouth and strong jaw. His hair, perhaps reddish-brown in youth, was already gray. His hands were clean, strong, and capable. I looked him over as he did me and instantly liked the man. Maybe I liked him because he was a little guy who had made it big in the world. He pushed the papers aside, filled his meerschaum pipe with tobacco, and began to puff on it. Even before he spoke he impressed me as a man of intellect, will, and energy.

"I wish to thank you for that interesting document you sent me from the islands," he said cordially. "Your style is honest and clear and you write with frankness. You seem to have a good ability to see things in this place as they really are, and that's important. How long will it take for you to complete your sentence?"

"Only a few years now, your Excellency," I stammered. "Not more than another three or four if memory serves me right."

Many times before falling asleep I had counted the years, months, days and even the hours that would bring me to the end of my sentence. But not used to being in the company of a man highly placed, I was too nervous to remember exactly. He saw my discomfort and tried to put me at ease, asking another question.

"I see by your record that you've tried to escape five times. Are you planning another any time soon?" I could see a glint in those gray-green eyes as he puffed vigorously on his pipe.

"Oh no, sir. No sir! No, your Excellency, I won't be trying to escape again. I've learned my lesson finally. I'm done trying."

I knew I was lying and I believe he knew it too. But he was a kind and generous man willing to give me the benefit of the doubt.

He shuffled the papers on his desk once more and asked, "What kind of work can you do, Bonheur?"

"I can do just about anything you assign me to do, Excellency. I'm not highly educated as you must know from reading my stuff, but I try. I was a bookkeeper on Royale but got into trouble, and later here in Cayenne I worked as a bookkeeper without pay."

"Yes, I can see by your record the kind of trouble you fell into on Royale, and the punishment on Saint Joseph could have been worse. You have to guard against that sort of thing, Bonheur. The girl could have her little adventure with only a slap on the wrist when caught. Not so with you. It could have been a deadly game for you."

"I understand, sir. It won't happen again. It can't happen again. The girl is away now in France to finish her education."

"Good! That takes you away from temptation. Now the job. I think maybe you'd like working on the waterfront. You will keep track of the supply ships that come and go. No work as a stevedore, no heavy lifting, mind you, just a bookkeeping job, and with pay."

It wasn't the kind of job I could really like but tolerable. I worked with an old convict named Sidney Bechet, a man who had been in prison so long he couldn't remember being free at any time during his adult life. The one thing that kept him alive and breathing was a slim hope that in time he would find a way to escape oppressive Guiana and die a free man. Getting away was the only thing on his mind, the only subject he could talk about as we entered figures into ledgers.

I had been on the job only three weeks or so when he came to me in the middle of the night all excited.

"Maurice! Wake up! Wake up, goddamn it! Let's go! You coming?"

"Coming where?" I grumped.

I was sleeping soundly and suddenly the silly man was shaking me by the shoulder and asking me a question I didn't remotely understand.

"With me and Bruno to free living! Two men left a sailboat at the dock, and Bruno knows how to sail it! She's a sweet little vessel just sitting there waiting for us! Too good to pass up! Gonna go!" Bechet's tired old eyes blazed with excitement.

"I can't come with you," I said as clearly as I could. "The Governor was good to me, and I promised I wouldn't try to escape."

"Have it your way!" old Bechet replied. "It's your choice, friend! But me and Bruno are gonna make a run for it. We gonna go! When they question you, just say we was gone when you woke up."

I watched them gather water in some empty cans and push off in the darkness. A mild breeze was stirring and the little sailboat caught it and moved quickly away into the night. I wanted to be with them in that boat. It wasn't big but looked sturdy and seaworthy. But I had said I wouldn't try to escape to a man who had treated me kindly. For the first time in many years an official had asked me a question expecting me to reply truthfully. All the others were certain they would get from me a string of lies. The new Governor was anything but gullible. He knew I would seize any opportunity to escape Guiana. Nonetheless, he had spoken to me almost as an equal and I felt beholden to him.

Daybreak came suddenly — in the tropics there is no dawn — and the day began like any other day. The waterfront quickly became busy with commerce. Then near 0800 the owner found his boat missing and set going a hullabaloo. He complained to the harbormaster who knew already that two waterfront convicts were missing. Assuming they had stolen the boat, he sent a high-speed launch in pursuit. Three hours later the men in the speedboat, armed with high-powered rifles, came back claiming they had not seen any sign of the sailboat. How they could have missed it puzzled me. The day was bright, the weather clear, and the men couldn't have sailed far offshore. Moreover, the boat was white on a blue sea, and they missed it? An Inquiry was held to look into the matter, but nothing came of it. Some of us believed the pursuers murdered the men and sank the boat. If so, Bechet died a free man.

Because I was Sidney Bechet's partner on the waterfront, investigators assumed I knew something about the escapade. Within days I was summoned to be questioned by a panel of three administrative officials. They asked a bevy of questions that I tried to answer honestly. I gave them the truth as far as my knowledge of the event allowed. Bechet had come to me in the middle of the night asking if I wanted to make a run for it in a small sailboat left at the dock. His friend Bruno had agreed to navigate. Half asleep, I mumbled I wouldn't be going with them. I went back to sleep and when I woke up they were gone. The owner had discovered his boat was missing, had raised a hue and cry, and a powerboat was launched for searching. The officials accepted my comments and let me go. They ended the Inquiry without knowing whether Bechet and Bruno lived to gain freedom or were murdered.

For another month I did the job of two men instead of one. Ships came and went, and dutifully I kept track of them. Several hours each day I recorded their movements in my ledgers. I tried as best I could to be meticulous and accurate. The auditors liked my work and put in a good word for me with their superiors. Somehow their report got to the Governor, who read it with interest. Believing I was qualified for work more challenging, he used his influence to get me a job I came to like more than any I ever had. It was a job that gave me more than a birds-eye view of French Guiana's prison system. I saw it from the inside.

At a time when things were looking up for me, I wondered whether Bechet and Bruno after years of trying had finally escaped. What happened to those two men and their stolen sailboat made for rumor and remained a mystery. Later, looking at penitentiary records in my new job, I was not able to find even one mention of their names. They had made a desperate run for freedom on the deep blue sea and were never heard from again. All knowledge of their existence had simply evaporated. I believed then as now that the two lost their lives just as their adventure began. They were murdered.

Chapter Twenty
My Sixth Attempt

For decades the records of the French Guiana penal colony existed in miserable disorder. Important documents were stacked in desk drawers, cardboard boxes, corners and closets, nooks and crannies. It was impossible to find anything without searching all day for it. The messy records irked the new Governor, and he thought I might be the one to bring order out of chaos. So with characteristic energy he ordered the chief guard to release me from my waterfront job and send me to Government House. That same afternoon I began my duties. It was interesting work. I had access to all the prison archives and was at liberty to read any of them, even those labeled classified. On occasion the Governor would put aside his daily labor to ask about my work. It pleased him to see I was truly interested in what I was doing and didn't view it as work. I had become, believe it or not, an archivist.

Governor Egremont had come to his post eager to reform abuses so old they had become tradition. He labored many hours each day when he might have accepted wild chaotic conditions and done nothing as others before him had done nothing. However, he was an idealist believing application on his part could change the place for the better. With very little support from any person in the Administration and none from the citizens of the town, he struggled alone to improve conditions. In the beginning corrupt officials ignored his proposals, making excuses for not acting. Later when he persisted, they began to hate and fear him. He visited the camps in the early morning, one by one without notice, and found conditions even worse than expected. In one camp the chief guard had not bothered to show up for work. When asked why, he was told the man had been drunk for three days. In another he found four guards drunk and passed out while convicts cooked their own breakfast. In still another camp he came across convicts in loin cloths laboring in the searing sun and gasping for water not permitted them.

He catalogued the abuses he discovered and reported each one in detailed reports to the high court in Framce. Alarmed by what he was doing, civilian officials joined the Administration to charge Philip Egremont with misbehavior in office sent directly to Paris. Along with the complaint they demanded the Governor be recalled and replaced. On trumped up charges of malfeasance they wanted him put on trial, but nothing came of it. The Governor remained to the end of his term, and by the time he came to the end he had probed so deep and wide into a hill of muck and dung that authorities smelled it as far away as France. Officials there grew increasingly worried about what was going on. They believed that at any time Egremont would uncover a ghastly scandal that would give the prison a worse reputation than it already had. They quickly made it impossible for the Governor to serve a second term.

A paunchy little man intent on making no changes whatever replaced him. The man was totally out of his element, apprehensive of his position, and unsure of his duties. He closed his eyes to the ugliness of the place, was seldom seen by anyone, and quickly returned to France. Among the shakers and movers in Paris he was celebrated as a very efficient civil servant. Within a month he was given a lucrative position in the Treasury Department and soon promoted. Philip Egremont retired from politics and bought a vineyard in Burgundy.

For nearly three months I worked at sorting and filing hundreds of documents in the Archives Room of Government House. I worked at my task all day long, stopping only to eat. I went back to the barracks often as late as ten in the evening with the excuse the Governor had kept me working late. In that musty old room I sat at a long table reading files and reports as old as the colony itself. I found books that no one in French Guiana had ever read, books in different languages about the notorious prison sent there to be studied but ignored. I examined every item carefully before filing it away and came to know the horrors of the penal colony past and present as well as the shenanigans of many officials down through the years. Then one morning Governor Egremont called me into his office and sadly announced he was under pressure to dismiss me and send me back to the barracks.

The next day I was called to the office of the Commandant. That double-dealing man leaned back in his chair and with a wide grin on his sallow face, exclaimed: "So, Maurice, you no longer work for Egremont! Did you quit all of a sudden or did he fire you?"

I hesitated before answering, for I knew he had something up his sleeve and wanted to tease me. Then slowly and calmly I replied, "I finished the job I came to do."

Of course I was lying and from his reaction I could tell that he too knew I was lying. There was much more to do at Government House, enough to keep me busy for another six months, but someone of higher authority had persuaded the Governor to let me go.

"I have a job for you as bookkeeper for the penitentiary here in Cayenne," said the Commandant. "The man on the job now is incompetent, and I'm told he's drunk three days out of every week. It'll be a lot of work for you, but you can earn some money and sleep in the office if you wish and not have to worry about abuse."

Of course I took the job, for to turn it down would have brought punishment. Even so, I was bitter at having lost the labor I really liked, the all-absorbing work with the archives. Later I learned I was removed because of warnings from the Commandant sent to his superiors in France that I was ready to expose the many abuses I had found. Negative or scandalous information about the prison, if published in leading newspapers of the United States, could harm the prestige of France itself. So Governor Egremont was put under pressure to pry me away from the records. Neither he nor the Commandant appeared to know that as the bookkeeper of the mainland prison I had an open avenue to many corrupt schemes lurking in the figures of my ledger. A guard, for example, would order food for a work party on a jungle mission lasting five days. He would dole out to the convicts maybe half the food ordered and sell the remainder later to an unscrupulous merchant. Schemes like that I ferreted out and reported. As a whistleblower I made no friends, but guards of every rank left me alone. They feared I might expose an unsavory or illegal activity that would cause them harm.

One sultry afternoon I was called upon to register the untimely death of a convict with special privileges. I learned when I entered the hospital with its strange antiseptic odor that the dead man had been a citizen of some renown in France. His name was Merle Pantoppian, and he had authored enough books criticizing political schemes to become famous. When he was sentenced to French Guiana, his supporters in the hundreds protested in the streets. He had become wealthy, influential, and powerful but had gained enemies as well as supporters. In Guiana he quickly exerted his influence among highly placed persons.

Now he lay dead after drowning while swimming off the quay at the waterfront. He had been condemned to five years on Devil's Island after trying to poison a powerful politician who wanted him dead. The victim with his legal team was invited to a sumptuous dinner at the author's chateau where he hoped to settle the matter. He lived luxuriously as Inspector of Forests for all of eastern France. It was an honorary position that demanded little of his time, for most of his time was spent in literary labor. Rather than put the famous man on trial, several prominent lawyers suggested he pay the politician, partly recovered, a handsome sum to account for his suffering. When the author renounced the deal as outrageous and said he wouldn't pay the crook a single sou, his victim's cronies pulled strings to have him sentenced to French Guiana.

Even though his adversary had shown himself as stronger, Pantoppian wielded influence wherever he went. He spent only three weeks on Devil's Island before his transfer to Cayenne. With plenty of money at his disposal, he bought with generous payment any number of favors from the Administration. To show their appreciation, he was given free run of the prison and town and did no work. So on the day he died he was free to enjoy a beautiful day of moderate weather. A day later it was my duty to register his death by drowning and notify relatives and colleagues in France. Minutes before the official letter was ready for mailing, the Commandant informed me that a full pardon had arrived from France. It should have been delivered to Pantoppian the day received, but delivery of any sort in Cayenne was often delayed. The letter was lying on the Commandant's desk the day of the drowning. Had it been delivered on time, Pantoppian might have spent his afternoon preparing to leave the prison rather than going for a swim.

I could hardly believe it, but in time my own prison term began to get closer and closer to ending. For trying to escape several times, seven years had been added to my original sentence of eight. Although I have never viewed fortune as a friend, in a way I was lucky. I had managed to endure fifteen years in that place while so many others, including some of the men I had shipped with, had died after one or two years. Also some who tried to escape got many years added to their sentences while I got, using my wits as a weapon, only seven. I knew full well had I been given additional years in those horrendous solitary confinement cells on Saint Joseph, I would have died.

When the time finally came for me to celebrate my prison release, I played cards in the barracks with old comrades well past midnight. A guard on duty sold us some rum, and we got a little drunk and noisy. I wanted to play poker all night, just to celebrate and because I was winning, but they were tired and had to be up at six to meet the prison grind. So I crawled into my cot too but couldn't sleep. I liked to think I had seen too much of the world to become excited by anything, and yet the prospect of release brought a pleasant stream of thoughts concerning my future. I lay awake in the early hours of morning feeling happy.

Then as the day broke with reveille sounding my comrades gathered weary-eyed around me to say goodbye and wish me luck. For the last time I watched them go out to labor in the sun. Then I went to the commissary to turn in my convict clothes though dirty and ragged. In exchange they gave me civilian clothes that hung on me like scraps on a scarecrow. I complained but they laughed and made jokes. I was also given a small sum of money and my "free-convict" certificate. That I had to have on my person at all times should a gendarme stop me. The moment I received the certificate I was told that by law I had to remain in French Guiana for another fifteen years. If I tried to escape I would be sentenced to five years hard labor in the camps. Also I could not remain in Cayenne as a resident but would have to live outside the city limits.

"If you are not out of the city by tomorrow morning," the police captain solemnly announced, "you'll be arrested and imprisoned. Now get out of my sight and don't come back."

I had been a free man for only a couple of hours when a pompous official was treating me like something less than human and threatening to lock me up again! Angry and somewhat confused by what was happening, I went directly to the Governor's office and found him working with many documents as usual. He looked up from the mound of papers on his desk and cast a friendly smile in my direction.

"Well, Maurice, you are now a free man. Congratulations!"

"Yes, your Excellency," I replied tense with emotion. "But I must live like a stricken animal somewhere on the edge of the jungle. Even though I can roam the streets by day, I can't lodge anywhere in the city. I'm told I must get out of Cayenne as soon as tomorrow morning."

"Well, maybe not. Do you have money to leave Guiana by boat?"

"I do indeed, sir, but if I try to leave I'll be arrested and sentenced to five years hard labor in a jungle camp. Like all the other so-called liberated convicts, I'm expected to remain in Guiana for the rest of my life. You know and I know that isn't freedom, sir."

"Indeed it isn't, and I've been trying to get that law abolished from the books. I'm facing opposition at every turn, but I'm hoping some right-minded person will give me a hand. No civilized country has so brutal a law as that. It places a life sentence on a temporary sentence and kills. I find it hard to believe my countrymen devised that law."

All the time he was talking he was rummaging through his desk drawers looking for something. An old adage tells us the best things in life come in small packages. He was a good example, a little man with a big heart, kind and compassionate. He found a printed form, looked it over, and handed it to me.

"Take this," he instructed, "and fill it out. It's a formal petition asking permission to leave the colony for one year. Say in the Comments Section you have found no way to make a living as a liberated convict in Guiana. You therefore wish to go elsewhere to find a job, save some money, and live free of abject poverty on returning."

Two days later the Governor called together a council to approve my request. Since he supported the petition, there was little the council could do but approve it. I was given a passport and formal permission to leave the colony for one year. With that document in hand I went to the consul of Venezuela to request a visa attached to it. To my surprise the Venezuelan, a portly gentleman with an aloof and distant manner, flatly refused my request. Thinking fast to persuade, I told him it wasn't my intention to take up residence in his country. I merely wanted to stop over on my way to Panama. All I needed was a visa allowing that. He gave me no more argument and stamped PANAMA on my passport. Within a few days I was breathing salt air among well-dressed people who couldn't know the value of human freedom until one loses it.

I booked passage on a small ship called *Poor Butterfly*. It was a curious name for a coastal ship transporting cargo and passengers to the tip of Brazil, and I inquired about it.

"Oh, I think the name has something to do with that opera by Puccini called *Madame Butterfly*," said the booking agent. "I've heard it's about a Japanese girl who falls in love with an American naval officer."

Years later I had a rare opportunity to attend a performance of Puccini's opera. Because I knew Spanish, the Italian wasn't altogether foreign to me. The music was striking and memorable, the story sad.

My ship was scheduled to leave the next day at two in the afternoon, and I made myself ready to be on board. I laid out for wear on the first day of the voyage my natty white suit, a clean shirt of light blue, and a narrow black tie. I wanted white shoes and socks to complete the outfit but had to settle for black. My ticket I tucked away in the pocket of my coat. I knew in the tropical heat I would have to remove the coat, but I intended to wear it until I could relax in my cabin. On the morning of my departure I went to the office of my generous benefactor to thank him again for all he had done. He shook my hand, wished me well, and said I had to remember three things of high importance.

I should make myself known to the French Consul in Panama; I could not extend the time given me beyond one year; and above all, I wouldn't publish any article whatever that might damage the prestige of France on the world stage. While I had no problem keeping two of the requirements, I had doubts about returning after one year. Nonetheless, I quickly promised the Governor I would certainly comply with all three. I had no way of knowing what the future held.

Precisely at two o'clock the whistle of *Poor Butterfly* sounded, and within minutes the ship was leaving the shores of French Guiana. For the first time in a very long time I felt relaxed and happy. I was on my way to the free world and a future. I was free at last, free at least for a year. By late afternoon, as the ship moved farther out to sea, the coast was fading away. I stared across the shimmering water, acutely aware of the problems I would surely face but ready to meet them head-on. A diminutive but powerful friend had granted me leave for an entire year, something unheard of in French Guiana. For reasons I couldn't quite understand, I viewed that generous gift as my sixth escape. Yet I knew I would have to return when the fast-moving year came to an end. Just the thought of returning left me dazed and worried. I was facing a complicated conundrum and saw no solution. If I didn't return, it would be my sixth and final escape. If caught, I would die in prison.

Chapter Twenty-One

Heavy Hammer of Justice

My first night aboard ship was creepy. The gentle motion of the vessel allowed me to sleep comfortably in a clean bed, but I was soon wide awake, in a sweat, and bolting upright. Thugs from the Bloodstained Barracks were somehow on board and trying to rob, injure, or molest me. Between two worlds and having trouble adapting to the new one, I was experiencing nightmare. After a few hours of fitful sleep, I left my cabin and paced the deck to greet the day. When sailors on the early watch found me lurking in the shadows to smoke, they began to call me "that crazy gringo." They thought I was American and crazy to leave a warm and cozy bunk for the dark and damp deck. I stood at the rail slightly seasick to watch the sun push away the gloom of night with pink and gold. Under the blue skies I paced the deck, constantly reassuring myself that my passport was safe. I ate breakfast in the dining room with the other guests, exchanged jokes with them and shared laughter, but couldn't relax and feel comfortable around them.

We put into a Venezuelan port and spent one night there. I went ashore but didn't go into the town. In the Customs House an official glanced at my passport and nodded. A pleasant voyage of another day took me to Colón in Panama. Wearing a smile, I walked down the gangplank in breezy weather with hat in hand. My heart racing, I was ready for a new adventure that would require me to use every day the rudimentary Spanish I had learned. From the ship I went to a cheap hotel and rented a room. The next day, as Governor Egremont advised, I saw the French Consul. Then I went job hunting. After a few days of searching for work in Colón and being rejected, I decided to try my luck in Panama City. I was ready to take a bus to the capital when the night manager at the hotel suggested I go with his cousin, who was leaving the next day in his own vehicle.

"Just buy him some gasoline. He'll take you there in no time. More pleasant and less expensive than taking a crowded bus."

I had heard what it was like to travel by bus in Panama, and so I gladly accepted the offer. Tomás arranged to meet me at the hotel early in the morning, and the two of us crossed the isthmus in an old car that put my nerves on edge as it rounded sharwp curves with tires squealing. In the city I filled its tank with gas and gave Tomás a good tip when he pointed out a small hotel where I could stay at reasonable cost.

Panama City was bustling and prosperous. In a few days I managed to get a job in the Records Department of the local hospital. I had papers showing I had worked as a bookkeeper in France and later as an archivist, but the experience gained in Guiana really got me the job. After my interview I worked there without incident, living comfortably in a small apartment and making friends in the town. It was a productive year for me. In my spare time I began to write about my prison experience. The notebooks I filled became source material for the present narrative. Although my year of freedom was fruitful, one thing weighed heavily on my senses and distressed me. The days and weeks rapidly became too short and passed too fast. Before I knew it the year was gone.

As the last week approached, I decided on the moment to travel to France and petition for a permanent passport. I reasoned if I could succeed in doing that, I wouldn't have to return to French Guiana but could live free anywhere on the planet. Later I had to admit I had made an impulsive and destructive decision. As it turned out, even though I had promised the Governor I wouldn't, I should have remained in Panama long enough to find permanent residence elsewhere. The voyage to France meant I didn't break my promise, but as soon as the ship arrived in Brest I was placed under arrest. As a liberated convict I had returned prematurely to my homeland and broken the law. I languished in jail two months before being hustled southward to the infamous convict ship lying at anchor in the Bay of Biscay.

A Corsican guard from Guiana, one who knew me when I was imprisoned on the island of Saint Joseph, prodded my back with the butt of his rifle to shove me along. Having heard I was returning after tasting freedom for an entire year, he snickered and snorted in derision.

"Well, if it ain't little Bonheur! Did you buy a round-trip ticket when you left the colony, Badass? And of all the places in this wide world for you to go, you little runt, you went home to France. Oh so stupid!"

Aware I'd be punished if I made even a joking reply, I kept my silence and joined the other luckless convicts boarding the ship. It was the same old scene of almost two decades ago, the same old rust bucket of a ship with its filthy cages in the hold, and its frequent stops. I lost count of the times the ship cut her engines to drift so the crew could heave a corpse overboard. We heard that a brief ceremony took place before "the burial at sea," a chaplain presiding, but believed it was phony and hypocritical. After seventeen days of rolling and rocking, the old tub dropped anchor off Bella Vista near the mouth of the river. The men in my cage rousted each other to get a view of the jungle from a dirty porthole, but I didn't bother. I had seen it before, and I knew it to be a very unfriendly place. I tried to remain calm but was ablaze with anxiety and anger. In a few hours I would be once again under the thumb of the Administration in French Guiana.

Unable to sleep when night came, I lay fuming with rage and drowning in self-pity. I cursed myself for being so stupid at a time when I should have been logical and reasonable and cogently aware. I had freedom and life in the palm of my hand and stupidly threw it all away. So while I hated the institution about to engulf me again, my anger was directed mainly at myself. Fierce mosquitoes came through the open portholes and tormented the wretches around me. They had a feast on my flesh too, but bitter thoughts made their attack less painful. I had convinced myself, as they buzzed in my ears, that I deserved the pain.

As the day began we were herded into small boats to stand and wait on the wharf at Bella Vista. I had but one thought in my aching head, and I mulled it over and over. It became an obsession. I would escape again and make it my final escape. I had no promises to keep, no feelings of loyalty any more to anyone, no thoughts of "doing the right thing" as the Governor had put it. I would simply bide my time, wait for the right moment, and walk away from that god-awful place to become human again. They had made of me an animal at bay, but it wouldn't last. I would find a way to taste freedom again. I would make it my one and only mission. I would lie awake at night formulating every little detail of a complex plan. At the right time I would carry out the plan with religious zeal and mechanical precision. I would not be recaptured.

Because of our number we were forced to stand on the long wharf in blazing heat for more than two hours to be processed. Some of the men fainted while others begged for water. My knees were beginning to buckle when a sweating guard marched me away to a blockhouse and locked me in a solitary cell. On the grimy floor was a tin cup filled with water. I grabbed the cup and drank the brackish water in one gulp. In a stupor I slumped against the wall. That moment was absolutely the end of my year of freedom. Again I was a prisoner in an army of condemned men. I had been a model citizen in the real world, had found a job and worked industrially at it. I had behaved myself and lived soberly in a town that had pulled out all the stops. I had broken no laws. Yet I made a mind-numbing and soul-shattering mistake: *I went to France seeking justice.* Without a doubt I should have stayed in Panama. I would have except for the need to keep my word. One man had treated me kindly and I couldn't betray him. Now I owed nothing to anybody. Come hell or high water, come pestilence and plague, *I would escape.*

They added more years to my sentence and placed me in a cell on St. Joseph. Except for the guards who had become more brutish, the island hadn't changed at all. Even though suffering convicts were constantly in conflict with the guards, I managed to hold my peace. Three months went by little by little, and the only way I kept my sanity was to pace the tiny cell all day long and often at night. Sloppy food was shoved through an opening to rest on the floor. My toilet was a chamber pot I had to empty during my half-hour of exercise in the courtyard. Day by day I did all I could to keep my muscles firm. I found a way to chin myself, and I did pushups. Finally a year closed in behind me, and I realized with satisfaction that I had managed to keep my body sound and my mind sane. I did it in spite of being shut up like a rat in a dark and stinking cage. They gave me solitary punishment for an entire year for entering France, my homeland, as a convict who had served his time.

As I grew weaker day after day in harsh confinement, the prison officials thought surely I would die before the year was out. But to their surprise I remained alive. *I had stayed alive!* That was the refrain of the song I sang in my head over and over again. I had not died, had not gone crazy, and had lost no part of my body to disease or lassitude. I was a walking skeleton, having lived on nothing more than bread and water, and yet every part of me was functional. I was thankful I had possessed the presence of mind to exercise in that tiny space. They gave me a chance to exercise in the courtyard on some days, but the place had no shade. Activity beyond a slow walk couldn't be done under a tropical sun or relentless rain, and they knew it. They didn't know I would find a way to stay fit even if I had to do it in darkness. I was fanatically determined to survive in solitary confinement, and I would find a way to survive when finally released too. That meant only one thing: I had to escape again and make it stick. Failure was not an option.

It was a well-known fact in French Guiana that no man could escape the prison without money. All the money I had earned during my year of freedom was gone. I was broke and needed money merely to survive. For a time I tried catching huge butterflies to dry, preserve, and sell their iridescent wings. Other liberés were doing the same, and so the money that came of it was just enough to buy cigarettes. I had to forage in the jungle for food or steal it from the garbage bins in town. Once I dug an armadillo out of its hole and boiled it for dinner in a clay pot. I looked in vain for turtle eggs, remembering how they once filled my empty belly. Money, hard cash, was the thing I needed most. I needed money to buy a canoe, to buy a sail for it, and to supply it with food for a couple of weeks. I was reminded of an old liberated convict who had found a way to live well. Just about every day he paddled his canoe across the river to bring back duty-free goods for the guards. Sometimes he brought them opium from China, cocaine from Colombia, and whiskey from Scotland. Once he delivered to his delighted customers a mulatto girl. I shouldn't have to mention he demanded a high price for her. The old rogue had found a way to survive and prosper. So would I.

However, my survival depended on a final escape. I had six behind me and was thinking night and day of another. Three failed attempts had taught me that escape through the jungle was impossible. Escaping by sea was the way to do it but required the assistance of competent partners I could trust. Also there was the matter of finding a seaworthy boat, food and drink for at least two weeks, and supplies such as fishing gear, a lantern, and a stove. Also we would require some kind of canopy to shield us from the sun or suffer terrible sunburn. The boat would be at sea for at least a dozen days and would have to stand against bad weather at times. We could hope for good weather, a steady breeze, and moderate seas, but our vessel had to be ready for heavy weather. Realistically, those requirements seemed out of reach, figments of wistful dreaming. Yet somehow I would find a way. I couldn't spend the rest of my life in abject poverty eking out a brutal existence on the edge of an unforgiving jungle. I would find a way out or die trying.

Chapter Twenty-Two

My Seventh Attempt

As it happened I was able to plan and carry out my seventh escape much sooner than expected. One scorching day approaching the noon hour in Bella Vista I was walking down a road that led to the sea looking for a place to fish. I was thinking if I were lucky I might catch a sizable fish and make a good dinner of it. Then from behind me came a baritone voice calling out to me. A long and lanky young man in the clothing of a tourist complete with white trousers and a pith helmet caught up with me on the sun-baked road. His hair was blonde and his eyes intensely blue behind horn-rimmed glasses. After some hesitation he struck up a conversation, his sharp eyes blinking in the bright air.

"I think you might have the means to help me, thank you very much," he said in textbook French. "I'm looking for a man the powerful people say is still a prisoner here. Do you speak English?"

His French was atrocious and made me chuckle. I knew if I had to listen to more of it, I would burst into laughter and perhaps offend him. So quickly I replied, "I speak a little English. How may I help you?"

"I'm an American journalist," he said, his blue eyes sparkling in what appeared to be an open and honest face. "I'm here on assignment for a well-known magazine in the States and looking for a good story. But no one wants to talk to me. All the prison officials rebuff me."

"If you are looking for something sensational," I said, "you've come to the right place. We call this wicked town 'the village of the damned.' In its streets so-called free convicts mingle with actual convicts and become victims of ill treatment wherever they go. They are ghosts, pariahs reviled and persecuted by everyone. They are called free men but are not free. I know what I'm talking about, sir, I'm one of them."

"Then maybe you've heard of a man they call Maurice."

"In that loathsome prison in back of you are scores of men called Maurice. This hot little place, as you must know, is owned by France. Maurice is a very old and honored name among the French. It's a very common name in France, much like James or John in your country."

"The full name," he said, consulting a little notebook, "is Arthur Maurice Bonheur. Last name means happiness. Goes by Maurice. If you tell me where to find him, I'll give you five bucks for your trouble."

"I can tell you exactly where to find him, but you must pay me first. I'm not saying you don't look honest, mister, but trying to keep body and soul together makes me wary of promises a stranger makes."

He fumbled in his pocket and found a fat leather wallet stuffed with American dollars. I was thinking what a fool he was to be wandering alone in this place with all that money but said nothing. He gave me the five-dollar note, chortling gleefully.

"Is the man nearby?" he asked.

"He is indeed," I answered. "You are looking at him!"

"Ah, no!" he replied, speaking louder. "You couldn't be him. You're too little, too frail. The man I'm looking for has incredible strength

149

of will and muscle. He's notorious for constantly trying to escape. Half a dozen times they tell me. Now don't con me, little man."

"I don't advise you to call me little man," I said with a wink, "and yet I am a little man and so won't take offense. I'm the person you're looking for, the chump with 'incredible strength of will and muscle.' I'm guessing you want information about the prison."

"Yes, yes! That's right! I'm eager to pick your brain for details! Sorry for misjudging you. I'll pay you plenty for a good exposé of Devil's Island or even a story about your time here. Can we go somewhere and talk? I've heard you have attempted more escapes than any other convict."

"I've tried a few," I said, "but maybe not more than others. Years ago a man they called Popo escaped a dozen times but was brought back each time. We can talk wherever you're staying, but at night I have to go because the authorities won't let me sleep in the city limits."

We spent the night at his hotel sitting at a table talking while he jotted down in a little notebook many notes in a crabbed hand. I told him the story of my life, the cause of my coming to so-called Devil's Island, a brainless mistake. I narrated in detail my attempts to escape by sea and jungle. Time and again with a look of fascination he asked me to slow down. He didn't want to miss a single fact. When daybreak came he was too weary to write any more even though I had more to tell him. He opened his wallet and flicked some bills on the table. I didn't bother to count them until he left. Within an hour he was on an airplane heading out. I would have given my right arm to be in his position, free to soar through the heavens to exotic places.

He had seen me not so much as a suffering fellow man, but as a source of information. On that table, however, as he shook my hand and hurried away, he left a hundred dollars! I counted it more than once and was amazed. With so much money to finance an escape,

I knew absolutely my seventh attempt would be my last. I would not suffer recapture as with all the other escapes but would gain once and for all the freedom I had sought for so many years. I knew a Chinese merchant doing business on the waterfront who could sell me as a package a good boat provisioned with food and water for a month. I was certain I could find men who would gladly join me but would have to search carefully for the right kind. We would make our way first to a Caribbean island for a taste of freedom, and then to the United States. Thousands of miles lay between French Guiana and the southern-most border of the States, but with each mile gained we would come closer to civilization and liberty. The authorities, appalled by the very existence of Devil's Island, would accept us as *free men* who had paid our dues.

Methodically for several days I searched for three men who would go with me. Each man had to meet several requirements though one in particular was paramount: each of the chosen had to assure me that either freedom or death lay before him. There could be no turning back, no decision it was bad to run, no surrender to anyone or anything. In time I selected Jules, a young man who had just completed a five-year sentence for robbery, and Ludo who had served fifteen years for killing a friend. Though both were capable men, neither knew anything about navigation. So after days of searching I found a third man who had been a sailor to join us. Cluseau in his late thirties had served five years for a rape he claimed he didn't commit. All he needed, he told me with a show of confidence, was the sun and stars to guide us to an island. He knew how to sail a small boat in all conditions, and he could navigate.

After the sun had set on a sultry day, the four of us met at the merchant's shop to put the plan in motion. Then as night came we crept into the jungle and made our way to the creek where the Chinaman had assured us a boat with ample supplies would be waiting. It proved to be smaller than the craft bargained for, not very long and not more than three and a half feet wide. In the light of a half-concealed lantern I inspected the supplies and found they were lacking too. The "reputable businessman" as he called himself had cheated us severely. I had paid for something I didn't get and had a feeling my grand escape had been dashed even before it began. My comrades spoke of beating the man silly to teach him a lesson and trying again at a later date. In such a craft, little more than a poorly made canoe, we could all die at sea. But determined at all cost to carry through with the escape plan, I sat down in the wobbly canoe and urged them to come along. With no little misgiving they gingerly took their places and we shoved off.

Within minutes, or so it seemed, we were out of the creek and paddling down the river in darkness. We kept to the center of the river to be as far from shore as possible. The current was with us and we moved swiftly. Before reaching the ocean we passed another canoe moving upstream. In it were three Indians, broad and strong. They called out in their language followed by a whooping sound, but we didn't answer. At the mouth of the river we hoisted sail. The "reputable businessman" had promised the sail would be strong and sturdy, but even in the dark it seemed worn and flimsy. Again a feeling of anger mingled with despair rose in my throat, but I kept silent. There could be no grumbling to mar the adventure. Cluseau seized the tiller attached to a crude rudder, and the slender canoe began to skip across the water. Then he pointed to a star and said it would guide us northward.

Although the sea was fairly calm, we took on some water and began to bail it out. Another man sat beside the man at the helm to be certain he didn't fall asleep. As the hours passed all of us began to come to our senses, to know we were flirting with disaster. Four men were on the open ocean in a canoe only eighteen feet long and too slender to be seaworthy. Yet we were driven to put penal servitude behind us and seek freedom at any price. All through the night the darkness was thick with an overcast blotting out the star that guided us, but I produced a small compass. Reading it now and then in the light of a single match kept us moving northward. The silence was heavy. Some of us tried to sleep and none of us spoke a word. When the black night surrendered to day, we could see no shore in any direction. We complimented Cluseau, and Ludo relieved him at the helm. I volunteered to cook.

In a saucepan I boiled some coffee on the stove and passed it out to the crew. The coffee was strong and bitter. It tasted awful but stoked us with energy. The Chinaman had cheated us grievously on the food supplies, but at least we had a stove and spare fuel. We ate very little that first day at sea, and nobody grumbled. As the sun was setting we made certain our supplies were safely secured should we encounter rougher weather on the morrow. It came during the night. The wind howled from the southeast, and the little canoe whooshed across the water at good speed. Cluseau remained at the tiller all night, singing snatches of French and Italian folk songs to drown out the wind and boost his morale. Ludo had to relieve himself and began to stand up. Fearing the craft would capsize, we demanded he piss in a can. I had to do the same and it became the rule. All night not a man dared move even a little. Then as daylight was breaking the wind died.

We sang a nostalgic little tune of Paris in the rain to welcome the calm and set about repairing the sail. Several old pillowcases with their double thickness had been used to make it. The wind had ripped it at the clew, the corner of the sail attached to the line that controlled it. We repaired it with cloth from a tough old prison shirt, thankful we had tools for the job. The tropical sun rose high in the sky to burn exposed skin. We took care to cover our bodies but had to leave face, neck, and hands bare. With tired and anxious eyes we swept the horizon all day but saw no sign of a ship. We were alone on a wide and merciless ocean and yet relieved to be alone. Night came and the wind blew hard again. Jules manned the tiller when he learned Cluseau's right palm had a big blister. He did all right steering through the night, the canoe riding the waves and sliding down them just when it seemed it might capsize. We made no attempt to keep a course.

The black canopy above us had not a single star, and a rogue wave washed the compass from my hand. At first light after a night in which no one slept we found ourselves soaking wet, stiff and aching, exhausted and thirsty but not hungry. And we were not at all so optimistic as the day before. I dipped some water out of the water keg and discovered seawater had seeped into it and turned it salty. I mixed the water with condensed milk and passed it around in tin cups. My companions all agreed it tasted like parrot piss. I wondered who among them had ever tasted parrot piss. Already we were having a hard time of it but could still laugh at a vulgar joke. Also a school of porpoises sprang above the water's surface and began to amuse us. We were sailing fast, but they were swimming faster. They came at us ready to ram the canoe and tip it. Then at the last moment they dove under it to come up on the other side. Bobbing and bouncing, they seemed to be laughing at us.

"The porpoises are fun to watch, but we'd better try to reach land somewhere," said Jules backed up by Ludo. "We can't drink salty water, it'll kill us. We can get some good water and shove off again."

"The water isn't all that salty," I replied, "not 100 percent, maybe only 10 percent at most. It won't kill us."

"Let's try the jungle," inexperienced Jules offered. "I'd rather take my chances in the jungle. At least we can find water and shade there and not have to worry about sharks or drowning,"

"We've been gone how long?" I asked, my lips drawing tight across my teeth in disdain. "Three days? I won't call you cowards, but already you want to go ashore? Didn't we agree that under no circumstances, for no reason whatever, would we be turning back? If we land on that coast, we'll be arrested and put on a road gang until they decide to send us back to Cayenne. The water isn't entirely salty. It won't harm us."

"Well, even if the water isn't all that salty," Ludo argued, "we could die out here of just plain exposure. I'd rather be back in prison serving more time than drowning and being eaten by sharks."

"Don't speak nonsense," urged Cluseau. "You're the oldest among us and should be the wisest. Relax, take it easy, we'll be all right."

And so we quarreled off and on all day. Any friendly camaraderie that had developed among us earlier had turned sour and melted away. We endured long periods of silence, and then suddenly without notice a fiery outburst would come from Jules or Ludo. Our navigator Cluseau was on my side, and so we were split down the middle. The fourth night was cruel. Subsequent nights were equally hard to bear. After a week we were clearly losing strength. Our hands and faces were swollen and tender from too much sun. Our lips were parched and swollen and our throats very dry. We gave up speaking to each other. When eight more days slipped by, we were scarcely human and yet had managed to stay inside the cramped canoe. Magically, it remained upright as it rode the crest of an angry wave and plunged downward into a deep trough to be lifted and thrown against another wave, repeating the maneuver. Dazed and half delirious, we began to lose feeling in our legs and feet and lost all desire to eat. The torment would have to end soon.

Chapter Twenty-Three
La Isla de la Trinidad

The first day at sea I told my companions we were heading for Trinidad. I didn't tell them it was more than 700 miles beyond the horizon. That little nugget had to be kept under wraps. To reveal how far we had to go would have brought doubt and indecision. In school I loved geography, and as we sailed I remembered Columbus gave the island its religious name. At the time of our grand adventure Trinidad was under British supervision. My comrades were surprised to learn that La Isla de la Trinidad was located only seven miles off the coast of northeastern Venezuela. They had thought a vast ocean surrounded the island.

"That's good to know," Ludo ventured. "But wouldn't we be in for trouble if a Venezuelan patrol boat should happen to see us? Don't they send convicts, freed or not, hastily back to Guiana?"

"Well, not hastily," I replied. "Not long ago I heard they are now in the habit of requiring escapees to work on their roads for months before sending them back. It's slave labor, but it's a risk we have to take. If we keep well out to sea and move in from the east we can avoid them. The Venezuelans stay close to the coast, seldom go into Trinidad waters, and the British will grant us refuge. They will allow us to rest a few days and replenish our food and water before we move onward. I've looked into all this carefully, did my homework before we left."

I had their trust and compliance for a couple of weeks. Then complaining began. "Dammit, Maurice!" Jules at the bow grumped. "We've been doing what you tell us far too many days now, and we're getting weaker every day. I'm ready to go ashore. Point this thing westward! I've had enough! I want my feet on the ground! What's it called? Terra firma? I'll take my chances on land. Even the deepest, roughest jungle is better than dying out here."

He began crawling aft to grab the tiller. I reached into my shirt and withdrew a small revolver bought without their knowledge from a liberated convict. It was wrapped in oilcloth and taped to my chest. I pointed the weapon at Jules's head and then at Ludo.

"I'm sure all of you have noticed I'm smaller than any of you. I'm a little man, it's the unvarnished truth and undeniable. But this thing in my hand makes me bigger than any of you, and don't you forget it. Our course is northward to Trinidad and will remain unchanged. Believe me, we'll find rest and security there and freedom too."

For a moment all three, even Cluseau, glowered at me fiercely. Then mulling over what I said and respecting the gun more than me, they fell silent. When night came I thought I might have to stay awake to protect myself. But soon I realized no mutiny would take place. They were brave men but feared the unknown. Settled down and more in control of their senses, they believed I would lead them to freedom or die trying. That for a time resolved the issue. Their behavior was the product of desperation, not animosity toward me. The sun had roasted every face. Our water was in short supply, and throats were parched. Every one of us was hungry, thirsty, exhausted, and fearful of sharks that seemed to be trailing the canoe. I tried to reassure them.

"The coast is Venezuelan territory and hostile. You'll be arrested and sent back within a day or forced into slave labor for months. Venezuela has learned how to improve its roads by exploiting escapees, and so it could be months. Now listen to me. Trinidad may seem far off, but we can make it. The people there will give us safety, rest, good food, and even medical attention. I promise you this. If we don't sight the island in a few more days, we'll go ashore and shift as best we can. Suffer with me just a few more days. Is that too much to ask?"

Jules and Ludo scowled as they heard my words but said nothing. Cluseau glanced at me calmly and looked downward. We sailed on with Cluseau and me at the tiller until late afternoon. The wind was steady from the southeast and filled the patchwork sail nicely. At the helm I sat amazed at how well the dugout canoe, once the trunk of a big and healthy tree, performed. Cluseau said the way the sail was rigged had a lot to do with it, but I speculated four men in the canoe instead of two made the difference. It might have capsized in a rushing wave with only two but didn't with four. As the day wore on, the wind diminished and I was thinking we might have to start paddling. Then suddenly in the brilliant blue sky we saw seagulls flashing white. Seagulls whirling in flight! Didn't that mean we were close to land?

"Not necessarily," said Cluseau, our nautical expert, in that studious tone he often used. "Marine scientists tell us the birds often fly hundreds of miles from shore. Depends on wind currents and the species."

"Well, we do know they came somewhere from land," I said. "They are not sea creatures. They live on land. It's a sight for sore eyes!"

The wind had diminished and the ocean was like a millpond, so calm it was becoming glassy. We thought of paddling but lay back instead and looked at the gulls wheeling and dipping in flight. In half an hour or less they were gone, and with them went our excitement. Another hour brought cat's paws on the water. Then suddenly Jules at the bow stood up shouting. In his excitement he had forgotten the cardinal rule I had tried to brand on everyone's brain: *Do not stand! You could tip the canoe.* He was gesticulating wildly and pointing at something in the distance. The canoe was becoming unstable.

"Look! Look! It's land!" he cried. "Oh my God, it's land!"

"Only a cloud bank," Cluseau called, "but looks like land."

"No, no! I see it too," Ludo yelled. "It's land, by God, it's land!"

"It's Trinidad!" Jules bellowed. "Trinidad, Maurice! I can't believe it, but you did it, man! You brought us to Trinidad!"

Crouched over the tiller and behind the sail, I couldn't see that part of the horizon where they were pointing. I pushed the sail to one side and saw green mountains against a blue sky. It wasn't a joke as I had suspected, and no mirage. It was the Island of Trinidad! Our destination was in sight! After long suffering that almost decimated us, at last we were making landfall. That glorious sight quickly replaced all the backbiting with joyous shouting and laughter. We were friends again, comrades celebrating a victory over forces much stronger than any of us, children of fortune riding high on a cloud. Cluseau took over the helm and caught a rising breeze expertly. The little canoe surged across the blue-green water like a mare galloping homeward. Water dashed over the side and set us to bailing. Not a soul complained. The land on the horizon grew larger and larger. We could see clusters of white houses with red roofs against the green of mountainous terrain.

A couple of hours later with the sun about to sink below the western horizon we were riding the swells offshore and about to enter the surf. I steered the bow forward toward the shore. The canoe lifted in back, began surfing, and shot through the veil of water well up on the gently sloping beach. As the surf receded, my companions in a frenzy of excitement tried jumping from the craft to the beach. All three were too weak to make the leap and fell flat on the white sand in shallow water. While they lay there sprawled and panting, I climbed out laughing and stood with eyes shaded to survey our surroundings. It was a crescent beach wide and white with a pinkish cast and unusually free of the detritus delivered by the sea to most beaches. In a moment of supreme elation, I ripped away the revolver taped to my chest and threw it into the sea. It had become an unnecessary burden. We were children now and celebrating. Joyous children, I said to myself, do not bear arms.

Some islanders fishing on the beach came strolling toward us but gave us a wide berth as they passed. They stared at us in disbelief but said nothing. In their eyes we were strange creatures to be avoided. I called out to them in English and begged them to climb a tree and toss down some coconuts. A lad not more than fourteen scampered up a nearby tree and began dropping coconuts the size of my head to the ground. His companions rolled them like bowling balls in our direction and hurried off. Each of us had two or more but no way to get at the meat or milk. Then I remembered the Chinaman had included a marlinspike in our supplies. It was the perfect tool for splitting the coconuts. Searching the canoe, I found it and hacked open coconuts for my friends. We drank the cool sweet liquid and devoured the white meat pried off with the marlinspike. We sat or reclined in the sand all the time we were eating. Then like drunken zombies we toddled toward a grass hut away from the beach half hidden in the trees.

The round hut with its thatched roof appeared deserted. No one answered our call, and so we stumbled inside. We found a big kettle filled with something that looked like gray mush. Its smell was strange but not unpleasant. We dug our sunburned hands into it and discovered fermented rice and pieces of boiled fish. Ravenously we gulped it down, grunting and groaning with satisfaction. On the brink of starvation when we found the food, we stupidly stuffed ourselves with no restraint. Minutes later we were rolling on the dirt floor with ubiquitous bellyaches. Despite the digestive pain, all four of us fell into profound sleep born of exhaustion. Through the night with room to spare we slept on the sandy floor, so different and far more comfortable than the restrictive canoe. Ludo was the first to awaken and waddled outside to relieve himself before daylight. I suggested we go immediately to the nearest town. My companions resisted that idea, fearing we could be arrested.

"Why can't we stay here for a few days?" they asked. "We can eat coconuts and forage for other food and gather our strength? Then we won't look like walking cadavers when we meet the people."

"It's a good argument," I explained, "but not a good idea. It's much better to report in person than have the villagers talk. That way we lessen suspicion. You can stay here if you like, but after I eat a little more mush I'm following that path to see where it takes me."

At daybreak we were walking down a narrow road all dusty with red earth. Later in the morning we encountered a group of blacks traveling by wagon in the opposite direction. They pulled over to the side of the road to let us pass and eyed us with suspicion. An old woman in colorful clothing said something in English that sounded like a question. We couldn't understand her, and they went on their way. In a couple of hours we came to a village with a police station and went directly to it. The constable, a black man with bulging muscles under a thin white shirt, sat behind a broad and bare desk in a rather crude office. He had heavy golden rings on his fingers and was wearing khaki shorts. Stripes denoting rank were on the sleeves of his shirt.

"Where do you come from?" he asked.

"From French Guiana," I replied in my best English.

"And where are you headed?"

"We're hoping to get to the United States."

"That's a long way from Trinidad. Why did you land here?"

"Because we were in a canoe two weeks on the open sea."

He was recording my answers in some kind of ledger. When he had finished he stood up, looked us over, and gave instructions to a deputy.

"Go to the store, James, and buy these men some beer and cigarettes. Have the storekeeper put it on my tab."

He gave us bread and beef, bottles of beer, and a place to rest. Assuring us we had nothing to fear, he said he would take us in the afternoon to Port of Spain, the capital of the island, to be processed. We had entered the country abruptly and illegally, but the processing would supply a legitimate explanation as to why it was necessary.

As we made ready to travel a few miles to the capital, the constable, who called himself Donny Adams, decided to tell us about our rights and legal obligations on the island. Rummaging in a drawer, he found a thin pamphlet and read from it: *"No French convict escaping Devil's Island and reaching the shores of Trinidad will be arrested unless he breaks the law or disturbs the peace. If he arrives by a boat deemed seaworthy, he will be given supplies to continue his journey. If the boat is deemed unseaworthy, a police officer will transport him to Port of Spain to petition the Port Authority for a replacement. He may remain on the island eighteen days. At the end of that time the law requires him to leave. If sick as determined by a doctor, he may stay longer."*

"The main thing to remember," said the constable, putting the pamphlet away, "is you won't be arrested. We believe the French are very much in the wrong as they continue to support and supply Devil's Island. It dishonors a civilized nation. The citizens of France should rise up against it. We've heard of the horror existing there and oppose it."

"Horror does indeed exist there, sir. One glance at the brave men who escaped with me will certainly confirm it. All of us served our sentences of hard labor under harsh conditions and were supposedly free, but we were not free. We were not allowed to leave Guiana."

"We on this island have heard of cases like yours and you have our sympathy. Tell me about your boat, Mr. Bonheur. Is it seaworthy?"

"It is not seaworthy, sir. Absolutely not!"

"I would like to take your word for it, but regulations compel me to inspect it. Do you mind if we go over and take a look?"

His deputy came back with beer and cigarettes and we went down to the sea in his old car. The canoe lay on the sand exactly where we had left it. He looked it over, carefully poked it with a walking stick, kicked the hull for soundness, found it soft and pliable, and shook his head.

"Would you go to sea in that?" I asked. "Look! Near the bow it's beginning to split open. And the makeshift sail hangs limp in tatters."

"I myself will take you to Port of Spain," he said. "I'm reasonably certain you'll be given a boat far more seaworthy. You will not have to pay for it. When one is fleeing Devil's Island in a no-good boat, our policy is to replace it. No one in the capital will go against me when I say this boat is a wreck. It's a miracle you got here in this."

Chapter Twenty-Four

A Boat For the Briny Deep

During the afternoon we drove along narrow roads across the island. En route we passed a gang of field hands prodding their slow-moving donkeys forward. The workers stood beside the road and broke into good-natured banter as we passed. Their lilting language was English even though I couldn't understand much of it. They were cheerful people and seemed quite satisfied with their lot in life and where they lived. I asked Mr. Adams if they were as happy as they appeared to be. He flashed an engaging smile, exposing white even teeth in a dark face, and nodded.

"They are indeed," he said. "If you could hear their music you would know as I know that blacks on this island have a good life. I'm black, as you can see, and I have the authority to arrest any white man, any yellow man, any man or woman of any color needing arrest. We've come a long ways since the days of abject slavery. When the British took over some years ago, things got a lot better for the people here."

In Port of Spain he drove us to the federal prison. The guards there were friendly but searched our meager belongings carefully for illegal drugs we might be carrying. Finding none, they recorded our names, ages, place of birth, and last occupation. We told them we were freed convicts forced to survive as best we could in the jungles of French Guiana. They placed us in a spacious cell while insisting we were not under arrest. We were being held only until our case could be resolved. A courteous jailer gave us meat and potatoes with bottles of beer, and we soon fell asleep. The cots were not as good as a bed but clean.

At ten o'clock the next morning an Englishman in civilian clothes opened our cell. He was affable and talkative, asking many questions in fluent French, questions I tried to answer frankly and truthfully. At last he led us out of the prison and down the street to what he called a halfway house. A man named Acker Bilk introduced himself and his wife Tilda. The time was nearly noon and a table was set for four. Though we insisted she not do it, the gracious lady served us a delicious meal with wine. None of us had tasted such a meal in many years, especially one with wine, and humbly we thanked her.

"You have the right to stay on this island eighteen days," said the plain-clothes officer. "This place could be your home during that time at no expense to you, or you may go to any other place of your choosing. You are not prisoners here. I'll see you tomorrow."

Living in the halfway house, we were free to come and go as we pleased. People came by and gave us toilet articles and clothes and even small donations of money, saying they were in sympathy with our cause. We were amazed at what a simple toothbrush could do for the teeth and mouth, even more amazed that we had never had one during all our years in prison. My teeth were in bad shape. Brushing them made the gums bleed but left a good taste in the mouth. We ate heartily and began to put on weight. We showered every other day and wore clean clothing. We had forgotten what a luxury it was to be clean and to wear clean underwear. With so much leisure, we soon began to plan the next phase of our adventure. Cluseau had money to buy passage to Europe to see his ailing mother, who had moved to England, but had no passport. A barber told us to see a man who lived above a drug store. The man, a Venezuelan political exile, fashioned for my friend within three days a Venezuelan passport with visas. It was simply a matter of money, and having the money Cluseau gladly paid the price.

Ten days after arriving in Trinidad he boarded a ship for Southhampton. I saw him off at the pier, thinking in time I might be able to book passage on a vessel headed for the United States. Jules and Ludo had no money and no plans. Late at night as we talked before sleeping, they said they might petition the government for citizenship and remain in Trinidad. They could learn English and find work and live a good life. I spoke of my dream to gain citizenship in the United States and forget entirely my French heritage. Hearing that, my companions expressed a wish to come along with me. When I said I had money for only one passage, they replied we could get ourselves a better boat and continue our journey by sea. After all we had been through I felt I couldn't desert them. I gave some thought to it and reluctantly assented.

A week or so later I paid a visit to the Chief of Police, the inspector general of the entire island. A suave British army officer who spoke beautiful French, he chatted with me for an hour.

"Two things about the French I don't understand," he said with a wink and click of the tongue. "Their Foreign Legion and Devil's Island. Their love of women and good literature I do understand."

He got on the phone and spoke rapidly in English to someone he seemed to know very well. Though not intending to eavesdrop, I found myself understanding his English as well as I had understood Donny Adams. The blacks we met on the road had spoken a special brand of English I couldn't understand. The Chief turned to me, smiling.

"You will have your boat, M'sieur! All you need to do is go to the harbor and look for one that's up for sale. A fisherman's boat, I should think, would serve you admirably."

Before noon the next day we had a boat. It was a ship's lifeboat more than thirty feet in length with a wide beam and rigged with a tall mast, a long boom, and sturdy sails. A naval officer authorized the government to purchase the boat and ordered a carpenter to modify it according to our instructions. Then he gave me a chart showing the seas we would travel and said the government would pay for any supplies we needed for our voyage. Never had anyone treated us so well.

Back at the halfway house I spread out the nautical chart on the dining-room table. The three of us hovered over the table for a good look. Jules and Ludo found it hard to believe we would have a road map, as it were, in our hands as we sailed. Before leaving for England Cluseau had told me what he knew about nautical charts, and so I was able to read this one with few problems.

"We can make it to America," I said, "by sailing through the Caribbean to Miami." With a pencil I pointed to islands on the chart. "Tobago is fifty-two miles north of Trinidad. Grenada is a hundred miles or so. Then we come to Saint Vincent, Saint Lucia, and Saint Kitts. Those are friendly islands. We'll have to be careful to avoid Martinique and Guadeloupe. If by some misfortune we should land on a French island, we'd be sent back to Devil's Island in a hurry."

"What about that island right there?" Jules asked, placing his finger on the chart. "It's much bigger than the others. Will we run into trouble if we happen to land there?"

"Puerto Rico is American," I explained. "We shouldn't have a problem landing there. Haiti, I'm reasonably certain, will be safe too. As for Cuba, I think we'd better keep our distance from that island and go on toward Key West, southern-most tip of the United States. It's a little village from what I know, but the people are friendly."

"Looks like for most of the journey we'll be in sight of land!" Jules exclaimed happily. "We'll be hopping from one island to another and often sheltered by land. Ah, that sounds good! I like it!"

"Call it Freedom Street!" Ludo exclaimed. "It's our road to living as men instead of beasts. Oh my God! After fifteen years of misery and suffering, I can't wait to live my life as a respectable human being once again. I'm ready to go right now!"

"I'm ready to have some fun on this island before we go," said Jules. "It's a lively place and them mulatto girls are hot and pretty. Why don't we see the sights and have some good food and a beer or two in a good bar before we even think of going to sea again?"

Ten minutes later we had put away the chart and were in the street. We needed to be close to people, to jostle them on the sidewalk and become part of them. Isolation for years in prison demanded it. We went into a bar and ordered three beers. A smiling East Indian girl in a low-cut dress, her black hair tumbling to her shoulders, served them to us. We guzzled the beer in a minute and ordered three more. Doomed associates of the living dead were living again, really living as free men! The beer was tart, slightly bitter, but deliciously cold.

We left the bar and walked down the main street that runs from one end of the city to the other. Outside a café on a bed of ice were oysters, sea urchins, shrimp, clams, mussels, and several varieties of fish. It was an amazing display to tempt the passerby, and we couldn't resist. I got some francs exchanged for Antilles dollars, and we treated ourselves to an orgy of seafood, the best I ever tasted. We washed it all down with a fine white wine. Then back to our lodgings we went, a little drunk when the drinking got out of hand but full and happy.

Three days later the boat was ready for launching. The bow had been decked over to give us a cuddy cabin in which to sleep. The gunwales had been raised to keep the sea out. The standing rigging (stays and shrouds) had been replaced with new cable. The running rigging (the ropes) was new and strong, and to my delight we had a new jib and mainsail. Also we were given a wonderful assortment of supplies — pots and pans for the galley, a broad and readable compass for steering, two lamps for night travel, several nautical charts depicting the entire region, a stove for cooking our food, and enough food to take us to Key West. I wanted a document stating the boat officially belonged to me as skipper, should naval authorities ask questions, but was told it was not available. Venezuela and Colombia had complained, and so Trinidad stopped issuing documents of any kind to fugitives.

Early in the morning a powerboat towed us out of the harbor into the open sea. The day was balmy, clear, and quite warm. A moderate breeze swept across the water from the southeast and filled our sails as soon as hoisted. On his way to becoming perhaps a citizen of England, Cluseau was not on hand to navigate the boat or help with the steering. I was glad to have learned the basics from him and felt I would have no trouble navigating by the stars at night. He had spoken of celestial navigation, taking a noon sight to discover latitude, but that I had never learned. I had my charts and a rudimentary knowledge of dead reckoning. Sailing among the islands of the Caribbean that seemed enough. We would eyeball each island as we came to it and find it on the chart.

"Stay east of the Lesser Antilles and north of the Greater Antilles," a seasoned sailor told us. "If you keep to the north of Puerto Rico, Haiti, and Cuba, you'll be on your way to Key West. Stop and rest at islands owned by the British and Americans. Avoid the Dutch and French."

Checking the chart I could see Tobago situated northeast of Trinidad. We would sail northeasterly toward that island and later northward to Grenada. "Northeast," I said to Jules at the tiller.

"Aye, aye skipper!" he responded. "Woohoo! We're on our way! And this time in a boat that can handle everything!"

"Wind from the southwest and rising," Ludo cautioned. "Keep an eye on the sail, Jules, and don't let that boom knock you over."

"I can handle this baby, old man! So go below and take a rest!"

"Listen up!" I yelled above the wind. "There will be no quarreling on this leg of our voyage, no show of disrespect from anybody. If you accept me as your skipper and each other as mates, you'll survive. Go against me or each other and you won't."

"Aye, aye, skipper!" Jules replied after some hesitation.

"And you, Ludo?"

"I'm your man, skipper. Count on me."

Chapter Twenty-Five

Lost at Sea

J ules was in his early twenties and Ludo was in his late fifties. The age difference made them wary of each other and likely to generate conflict. Jules with the exuberance of youth had been in the habit of teasing the older man, and that had to stop. Ludo had suffered terribly fifteen long years in a place that prided itself on robbing men of their dignity. Now on his way to freedom, he was not about to suffer insolence from Jules or anyone young or old. I could understand but couldn't be sure young and cocky Jules understood. So when Ludo went below to rest before taking his turn at the helm, I had a little conversation with the younger man. I made it clear to him that we would die if we didn't work together. He said, nodding his head, he would remember Ludo's suffering and his struggle to assert his worth as a man and make an effort to get along with him. Then he changed the subject and began to talk about how well the kind people of Trinidad had treated us. I agreed they had been kind and generous to a high degree. I would remember for the rest of my life the time we spent with the extraordinary people there.

I looked over my shoulder at the benign island that had given refuge to four desperate men. It was slowly disappearing in the mist. Our sturdy lifeboat converted into a sailboat was in harmony with the wind and waves and moving fast. All provisions were safely stowed below, and we had no worries about food or drink or heavy weather. The sun was far less hot than on shore and the breeze was steady under balmy skies. We were passing Tobago and on our way to Grenada. There as planned, the Salvation Army would replenish our supplies. When the sun fell below the horizon in a gorgeous display of orange, red, blue, green, and purple, we made ready for the night. The nocturnal sailing we divided into three watches of three hours each. Our chronometer, by which we could measure the hours, was an ancient alarm clock a woman in Trinidad had given us. Ludo would take the first watch, I the second, and Jules at the helm would greet the morning. Not one of us had known anything about how to sail a boat before our escape. Now Necessity had made us seasoned and hopefully intrepid sailors.

"Keep an eye on the compass and steer northwesterly," I said to Ludo before finding my place to sleep. "You won't see much and neither will I on my watch, but after we've put behind us maybe seventy-five miles, Jules in the morning will see the Grenada Light."

I slept better on that sailboat than ever in my life. It must have been the motion that induced deep sleep. I would have slept till morning but was awakened after Ludo's stint. He had done a good job of keeping us on course even when the wind shifted almost directly behind us. Now it was off our starboard quarter, and the boat was plunging along with a jerky motion that wasn't very comfortable. I sat at the tiller almost dozing when a hand holding a mug of coffee in the semidarkness appeared before my face. Ludo had thought I would need it and made it before sleeping. I thanked him heartily. A man robbed of humanity was showing restored humanity. It was a very good sign. The stars had disappeared. The sea around us was black with streaks of green and violet phosphorescence. A small lantern supplied light for the compass. I was glad we had more than just a star to guide us.

Half way through my watch the wind became erratic, shifted in speed and direction, and ceased altogether. I tried as best I could to fill the sails with a breeze, but they fluttered and luffed lamely with no wind at all. The black seas with waves of one to two feet earlier were confused for a time but soon settled into calm. The boat sat in the water in heavy silence, our mainsail drooping, the jib silent. I heard nothing but a gentle lapping of water against the hull. Then Jules appeared in the companionway and asked what was going on.

"No wind," I replied. "Marooned with no wind. Aggravating but better than too much wind I guess. Go back to sleep, Jules. I'll wake you when it's time for your stint at the helm."

"I'm not sure I can sleep," he muttered, climbing into the cockpit. "I'm beginning to think we've bitten off more than we can chew. I ain't afraid, mind you, but do you really believe we can make Miami?"

"I do believe we can if we work together as a team and help each other. The boat is small but seaworthy. Professionals modified her for the open sea, for any kind of weather. So this vessel is a far cry from the dugout canoe that could have killed us."

"Well, I hope we don't lose our way and head for Africa without knowing it. I can't see a damn thing even though on the eastern horizoia is a flicker of gray. Guess that's a sign of a good day in the making."

"Yes, absolutely. A good day is coming. Now try to get some sleep. It's important for us to get as much rest as we can."

Two hours passed and he was up again for his watch. I gave him coffee as Ludo had given me a mug. He thanked me but complained of no sleep. I went below to crawl under a blanket but couldn't sleep either. The silence almost hurt and the boat became a seesaw in the swells. Then Jules cried out he was certain a gigantic shark was bumping the boat. He couldn't see the shark but knews it was trying to get to us. I tried to comfort him, saying sharks in warm waters don't prowl at night, but he was certain he felt a bump. I could see that fear of the unknown was rubbing against his reason and causing him distress. Not knowing where we were and what lay ahead weighed heavily on us, and there was little we could do about it. After tossing in the narrow bunk for an hour, even counting backwards, I got what seemed a few minutes of sleep before being jostled awake.

When the sun quickly peeped above the horizon, we could see no land whatever. In still air Jules had given up trying to keep a course, but with the sun came the wind and we began to move again. We now had a northeast breeze off the starboard beam as we resumed the northwesterly course. The boat picked up speed and began to heel with Ludo at the helm. I went below to prepare breakfast. I didn't do a very good job of it. We had no gimbal for the stove, and the frying pan every few seconds wanted to slide off. Against the odds I managed to cook up some bacon and eggs. We ate our fill with bread dipped in bacon grease and afterwards felt stronger. No sight of land caused us to worry. At the end of the day, and the sailing was good, we had not seen land. All day long we had searched for it but found nothing. That brought on more worry. My companions thought we might have come close to Grenada at night and somehow missed it. That I couldn't believe. Winds were favorable and we made good headway, but mile after mile the next day we stared at the horizon and saw no land. We had to admit we were lost.

"We should keep sailing northwesterly anyway," I said, "because according to the chart we can reach Haiti and Cuba that way. Or we may run into Puerto Rico toward the east. I want my crew to keep a close eye on the ocean at all times. Land could appear at any moment."

My companions objected loudly when I called them "my crew." It reminded them painfully of prison work crews. And so another delicate adjustment had to be made. They thought if we continued on the north-northwesterly course we could run into a French island and be arrested. They insisted we should forget the northern part of the course altogether and head westerly toward land. I had no grounds on which to argue with them, and so I swung the helm over and set the course they wanted. The wind was not as favorable in that direction, but in time our little boat found her traces and galloped along. The wind increased and we found ourselves battling gale-force winds for most of an entire day. At the end of the day when the storm passed on we were exhausted, but our boat had performed wonderfully well and was as perky as ever. That's when we realized the boat could take a lot more than we could. Early the next day we expected to spot land but saw nothing. Departing Trinidad, we thought we could hop from one island to another all the way to Miami. Sadly, we had sailed a week with no sign of land, such as the gulls we saw approaching Trinidad, and no sight of land.

Another day we spent on the wide ocean with nothing in sight but a round horizon where the blue sky met the blue water. Then in late afternoon as I lay resting below I heard Ludo hoarsely shout, "A ship! I see a ship!" I scrambled into the cockpit to see for myself, and sure enough on the distant horizon we saw what appeared to be a cargo ship moving in our direction. We could see smoke from her stacks and the stacks a few minutes later, and then the black hull of the ship itself. At last the massive bow with white waves on either side approached us. The big ship had spotted our sail and had come to investigate.

"What boat is that?" came an accented inquiry in English.

At the stem of our boat, Jules shouted in French, "Help us, please! We need assistance! *M'aidez!*"

"Can you come alongside? We'll drop a ladder."

"We can and we will, sir! Give us ten minutes!"

Because of her size the ship appeared to be much closer, and more than twenty minutes passed before we were able to drop our sail and nudge up against the steel hull. Skirting her stern, we saw that she was flying the German flag. A rope ladder with wooden steps had been lowered from the deck, and I climbed it.

Jules and Ludo stayed in our sailboat to keep her from banging against the ship. We had two rubber fenders for that purpose, but strong arms were needed also. On deck I spoke with a young officer who escorted me to the bridge of the ship. There I came face to face with the captain who had the bearing of a German military officer. Though his face was young looking, his long hair was gray and his beard flecked with gray. He spoke to me in German, a language I didn't understand. Then realizing his error and learning I was a Frenchman, he spoke French with a Germanic thrust.

"How big is your boat, M'sieur Bonheur? I'm astonished to find a vessel so small in these vast waters. And you hail from where?"

I hesitated before replying, but in a moment decided to tell all. The captain was our benefactor and deserved to hear the full story.

"We sailed from Trinidad," I explained, "after all the kind people there extended heart-warming hospitality. They also gave us a sturdy boat with ample supplies for a long voyage. I won't deceive you, sir. We sailed to Trinidad in a dugout canoe from French Guiana. We had served our sentences there but were not allowed to leave. We escaped in a canoe and made it all the way to Trinidad."

"Ah! I've heard of your kind. You are desperate fugitives from Devil's Island! Worst prison on earth I'm told. Sad story, that. My country and your country have never been the best of friends. I'm sure you know that. So I could say it's no business of mine what your country does, but that atrocious prison dishonors a nation and its people."

I nodded my head in agreement, remaining silent. I had heard the same sentiments from others. In his chart room the captain drew from a large drawer a chart that covered most of the table. At a glance I could see it displayed most of the islands of the Caribbean. He pointed to an island well to the west of Grenada and close to the coast of Venezuela.

"That's the Dutch island of Curaçao," he said, "and nearby, sixty-five miles or so, is Aruba also owned by the Dutch. We found you more than one hundred miles north of those islands."

I stared at the chart in amazement. Our northwesterly course had taken us more than 500 miles from Trinidad to open water well to the north of the Dutch island. Had we sailed more westerly, as my companions suggested, we might have entered a hostile harbor. Dutch Guiana was known to arrest convicts trying to escape French Guiana. A Dutch island probably had the same policy.

"I'm doubting you'll ever make it to Miami from here," the captain was saying. "With no engine the Gulf Stream would keep pushing you back. You would sail up to it and be pushed backward by the current. We can lift your boat on deck and take all three of you to Curaçao."

"I appreciate your kind and generous offer, sir, but must refuse it. My comrades and I believe we'd lose our freedom there and be sent back to Devil's Island. It's because Dutch Guiana arrests convicts from French Guiana, and it's probably a general policy among the Dutch."

"Perhaps it is," he said, "and of course you don't want to take unnecessary risks. I admire your grit and wish you luck. The steward will give you a keg of water and some food supplies."

I thanked the good captain sincerely and returned to our sailboat with a large bag of food, a big keg of water, some bottles of wine, and a generous supply of cigarettes. Two sailors loaded all the stuff on board, and turning to climb the ladder, wished us well. We pushed off with no difficulty and hoisted sail. A new leg of the voyage had begun. This leg, we hoped, would take us to Panama. We would sail due west for several days and then southward. To keep track of the miles, I marked our progress on the chart and hoped for the best. Because I had seen the captain's professional chart, I knew our exact position. Also he gave me a little booklet in English on "dead reckoning" and urged me to study it in my spare time. Necessity and the thin booklet taught me basic nautical navigation beyond what Cluseau had taught me. I knew nothing of celestial navigation. Had I known more about navigating a boat when we left Trinidad, we wouldn't have missed Grenada. We wouldn't have sailed for many days without knowing where we happened to be in a vast desert of water. I must take all the blame for that colossal failure. If Ludo and Jules wanted a scapegoat to blame, they surely had one in me.

Chapter Twenty-Six
Things Fall Apart

I t was getting dark when I left the German ship, and ahead of us was a new course to follow at night. We attached a lantern to the forestay and used the second lantern for reading the compass. Because the seas were mild under steady breezes, we decided to stand four-hour watches to give the two men off duty more sleep. Jules took the first watch running from eight to midnight, and I volunteered for the second. Ludo would take over in the early morning and be at the helm at first light. At that time he would scan the horizon for any sight of land. We were feeling better after talking with professional mariners, and our boat skipped across the water as if knowing where she was going. If we could reach Panama, we were fairly certain the Americans wouldn't hinder our moving overland through Central America and Mexico to reach Texas. If immigration officials allowed us to enter Texas, it would place us more than a thousand miles from Miami, our original destination. Getting to the east coast would be another obstacle to overcome.

We struggled against strong currents that came and went, but the wind held all night and into the next day. It was a favorable wind blowing at moderate speed from the south. As we sailed due west, the wind on our portside beam heeled the boat well over but also gave her steady speed. Each day I tried to plot our course to determine how far we had gone. At a fixed position we would have to tack and move southwesterly near the coast of Colombia to reach Panama. Three days went by after we left the German ship. On the fourth day we sighted land to the south of us. I was relatively certain it was the Colombian coast and urged caution. We could sail along the coast but far out so as not to attract attention. Then we could veer off a bit and head toward Panama. My exhausted companions insisted we move into a little cove, drop anchor, and try to find out exactly where we were. As before, they were victims of not knowing. Their state of mind interfered with sound thinking and left them indecisive and apprehensive.

"We really need to know our location," Ludo exclaimed. "It's important. When we know where we are, we can move with confidence."

I tried to tell him my dead reckoning penciled on the chart gave us a good idea of our position, but he found that hard to believe. I had studied the little booklet given me on dead reckoning, and was reasonably certain I was doing it right. To him and Jules it was an esoteric thing, a mind-numbing mystery not to be trusted.

"That squiggly line on paper don't tell me much," Ludo asserted. "I'm for putting in to shore now that we're close enough."

"I'm with Ludo on this," said Jules. "We don't often agree on anything, but this time we do. With the shore so close, we'd be fools not to take advantage of it. We really need to be on dry land again."

"I'm wary of moving to a shore that could be hostile," I trie to argue, "and yet after all these days at sea it's hard to resist."

In front of us was a barren stretch of sandy beach. We sailed toward it, slowly at first and then faster. Our intention was to drop anchor in calm water and possibly swim ashore, but the breakers caught the boat, lifted it, and sped it forward. All we could do at that moment was hang on. A rushing wave hit us broadside and capsized our sailboat, throwing the vessel on her side with the mast and boom digging into sand. All three of us tumbled into the surf and were carried head over heels to the beach. Minutes later we lay battered and water-soaked on hard sand. Our boat lay swamped a few yards from us. Knowing our lives depended on it, we plunged into the breaking waves to rescue as many provisions and equipment as we could. We placed the stuff away from the water and sprawled exhausted and half conscious. By the time we were up and moving again, the tropical sun had dried our clothes.

Away from the beach we found plenty of dry wood to build a fire. I lit it with a match kept dry in a bottle and prepared a dinner of rice and beans. We had water to drink from a full keg we had rescued. As we were beginning to eat we looked over our shoulders to see a band of wild-looking Indians staring at us. I called to them in Spanish but got no response. They moved away and we assumed they were leaving us alone, but they later returned and boldly approached us. Again I spoke to them in the Spanish I had learned in Panama. They understood not a word and jabbered in a language we didn't understand. For a few minutes none of us moved, neither they nor us. Then several went over and began inspecting our rescued supplies. When we moved as if to stop them, they threatened us with spears and helped themselves to all we had. They grabbed our blankets, lamp, personal effects, food and clothing, even the compass we had managed to save. Then giggling among themselves they danced off and disappeared over the dunes.

"What brave men we are!" Jules squawked, slapping his forehead in disgust. "Why in hell didn't you shoot them bastards with that revolver you threatened us with a while back?"

"Oh, that!" I responded. "I threw it into the sea as soon as we landed on the beach in Trinidad. It had become a burden, and I didn't think I'd have use for it any more. Also it wasn't a good idea to be armed when entering a new country. Now I'm thinking I should have kept it."

"Oh my God, Bonheur! What a dumbass thing to do! Dumb! Just plain dumb! You had a good weapon and you threw it into the ocean? Trinidad ain't French Guiana, you know. Very doubtful a policeman would have searched your clothing. Dumb, Bonheur, dumb! You're not the skipper any more, and so I can say what I feel like saying."

"Well, you've said enough, kid," Ludo cautioned. "Now put a cork in your piehole! It's them black bastards we need to worry about. I'll slit their slimy throats when they come back again!"

"With what?" I asked. "You don't remember they put a spear to your chest and ran off with your knife? You getting senile?"

Just as I began to apologize for my unseemly remark, Jules ran into the surf and swam out to our boat. It was battered and beaten and almost entirely under water. He dove down looking for something inside and came up with a machete. I didn't even know it was on the boat; he had hidden it in the bilge. He swam ashore waving the big blade triumphantly and shouting gleefully.

"Now let them savages mess with us! This is the equalizer!"

"Better than nothing I guess," Ludo groused, "but too bad our skipper threw his goddamn revolver away."

So the three of us had some protection, but what could it do when pitted against a bow and arrow or long spear? Even so, I was glad we had it, for we had almost nothing else. We moved away from the beach to a grove of trees, hoping to find a secure place to sleep. Hidden by the undergrowth, we slept fitfully on empty bellies. When morning came Jules killed a big lizard with his machete, and after struggling to build a fire and light it with the last match we had, we shared the lizard. The tiny bit of meat only made us ravenous, and then Ludo remembered the bottles of wine we had stowed on the boat. Jules, a good swimmer, went in search of them and swam on his back to shore holding two bottles. Then he returned for two more. The Indians had broken open the water keg, and so the wine imprisoned in sturdy bottles was all we had to slake our thirst. Desperation will often turn a dull man into a genius, and it happened with Ludo. He opened the corked bottles with the prong of his belt buckle. We drank our fill of good wine, left the beach and our boat, and began walking inland.

For an entire day we trudged along with no food and no water. We expected to find a river we might have trouble crossing but found none. At last we came upon a stream of fresh water, drank and drank, and filled our wine bottles with water. Then we bathed in the stream to cool off and get clean again but also to alleviate the pain of many insect bites. We were now some distance from the sand dunes and surrounded by jungle, yet close to the shore. For several days we saw no other human being but had a nagging suspicion from time to time that someone was observing us. We ate fish speared with a pointed bamboo stick, and we ate frogs we managed to spear. In a large seashell we carried coals to make a fire. Rubbing sticks together for half an hour was no longer necessary. All three of us had festering insect bites and bleeding feet. On the boat the soles of our feet had become tender, and we had no footwear. Happily, we had not begun to quarrel again.

Near sunset on the third day we came upon a grass hut in a circular clearing with jungle all around. Some fishing nets were drying in the sun, and a sea turtle lay upside down in a tub nearby. With one blow of his machete Jules hacked off the shell. He boiled the turtle in the tub, and we ate thick hunks of tasty meat to our hearts' content. Ludo found an old calico dress inside the hut and on leaving wrapped chunks of meat in it. Walking on the beach beside the jungle, we came to a small native village of maybe twenty huts. We crept into the village at night but quickly exited when dogs began to bark. All night long we walked along the beach in cool air, stopping only to relieve ourselves now and then but not to rest. When morning came with dazzling light filtering downward, we crawled under a jungle thicket and slept.

I thought I was dreaming when I heard a man speaking angry words in Spanish. "Don't you dare move, hombres, not a one of you!

Who in hell are you and what you doing here? Sleeping obviously but why here? Give me answers and give them fast!"

A very brown young man in a soldier's uniform was confronting us. Another soldier stood behind him. He ordered us to walk. They had tied their horses to a tree on the edge of the jungle, and soon we were on the beach. After an hour of trudging behind their horses we reached the Colombian coastal town of Santa Marta. They took us directly to the police station that served also as an army barracks. A crowd of noisy children, talkative men and women, and barking dogs followed us through the town. Three pale-skin strangers, obviously foreigners, bedraggled and sparely dressed made a festive occasion for them. At the barracks, behind a large mahogany desk, sat the soldiers' commanding officer. He was a little man, thin and wiry, but with a loud, authoritative voice. No ordinary soldier, he wore a military jacket with gaudy epaulets. On the jacket spread across its left side were numerous medals. His rank and name I soon learned was Colonel Mateo Lopez.

"Your passports, please," he said in polite Spanish. We had none. "Fugitivos de Cayenne!" he announced to his soldiers. "Fugitivos!"

Ludo had been ailing for several days and was now shivering. I explained that my comrade was sick of the fever. The colonel had an orderly call a doctor who gave us all quinine. Native women brought us food and drink. Colonel Lopez picked up the phone and asked to be put through to another city some miles away.

"Tengo tres fugitivos de Cayenne. Notificar el Cónsul Francés."

Jules, feverish Ludo, and I stared blankly at one another. He was asking someone to notify the French Consul. After two fearful stints with the unpredictable sea, and after sailing hundreds of miles in the open ocean in a small boat, we were losing our bid for freedom. The misery we had suffered for many years had killed our ability to cry, and yet in disgust and sadness we felt like crying. It was my seventh attempt to escape the horror that was killing me, and I thought it would surely succeed. Like all the others it had ended in failure. I would have neither the will nor the strength for another. I felt old and tired.

"I'm finding no pleasure in this matter," Colonel Lopez explained. "But it's the law, and as a public figure I must obey it. You will be sent to Cartagena. There, if you can present your case forcefully, you may not be deported. I feel no pleasure detaining you, and yet I must."

The next day we found ourselves behind bars in the colorful old city of Cartagena, a key port in colonial days where pirates found refuge. Our mood was one of sad resignation until the warden paid us a visit with good news. If we had arrived only two days earlier, he told us with a glint in his eye, we would have gone back to Cayenne under guard on the French mail boat. So even though most of the time fate, nature, and human society seemed against us, we now relished an interval of good luck. There wouldn't be another vessel going to French Guiana for another month. That gave us time to think of something that might help us squirm out of our predicament.

"You will have to wait, gentlemen, but don't try to escape," the warden warned us, pointing to armed guards. "My men are sharpshooters, the best in the business. You wouldn't have a chance."

That afternoon, looking through the tiny window of my cell at the lush green jungle, I told myself I would indeed try to escape. I might be courting death, as the warden had warned, but every day for a month I would make an effort to escape. I had tried it seven times and failed, but with each try, as I thought about it, I had come closer to succeeding. The latest attempt had taken me hundreds of miles from Devil's Island. The last leg of the journey would have brought me to Panama. My final attempt would take me to Panama and beyond. I would place my battered shoes on the soil of the United States of America, or die trying. The guards were crack shots, the warden had said, and would shoot me on sight if I made a false move. But I reasoned it would be better to be dead in Colombia than alive in French Guiana. I would try again, my eighth attempt to escape. I would find a way to live free of degradation, oppression, pain, and human misery or find peace in death.

Chapter Twenty-Seven

My Eighth Attempt

Day after day I gazed fixedly at the green jungle. It seemed to beckon and was becoming an obsession. Each morning in groggy imbalance I stumbled to the small window and stood staring at the scene outside. I ate the breakfast they gave me and went back to stare at the stretch of green. My companions in the somber cell refused to look through the bars at the outside world. They were worn out, despondent, defeated, cursing their fate and each other. They seldom spoke, but when they did it was to complain bitterly of what lay in store for us. They were certain we would soon be on a ship headed to French Guiana and death in solitary confinement. It was over for us, they just knew it. Our little lives were as good as ended. Countless men had died or gone mad in the solitary cells, and so would we. As the days passed, they became more gloomy and quarrelsome. They found fault with each other but mainly with me. Impulsive Jules in a fit of anger triggered by something I said struck me with his fist between my shoulder blades. I backed off in pain, declaring I was in no mood to fight him. He glared at me with fists clenched and moved closer. Ludo sided with me. He wrenched off a table leg, saying he would smash the young man's skull to mush if he punched me again. Jules calmed down and lapsed into sullen silence.

I was more hopeful than my companions because I knew something they didn't. For half a century or more the Colombians had hated the French penal system in Guiana. So from time to time depending on circumstances, instead of arresting runaways they helped them. A few days after our capture the editor of a leading newspaper in Cartagena asked the warden if he might interview me. He had read an article by Ellen Thornhurst acknowledging me by name as a major source. The editor spoke to me in private and said he would pay me generously if I wrote for him a series of stories exposing the abuses of the French penal colony. He said in addition to payment he might be able to use his influence to get me released from captivity. Of course I agreed to work with him, and a few days later he told me he had written to the French ambassador in Bogatá on my behalf. I wasn't surprised to learn the ambassador adamantly refused to grant even a semblance of freedom. Vehemently he insisted I be returned immediately to French Guiana.

However, events did not unfold that way. The captain of the guards placed me in a cell of my own with pen and paper and a table to write on. All day long and well into the night I scribbled paragraphs in French, thanking fate and the gods for making me literate. Altogether I produced in record time six articles. The editor had them translated, read perhaps four of them, and handed me a roll of bills the size of my fist. I stood amazed, dumfounded, but happy as a lark. Then I discovered something mystifying and troubling. Stuffed in with the bills was a note informing me it had been "arranged" for my cell door to be unlocked after midnight. Was it a ruse to get me in deeper trouble? I had heard of prisoners in Guiana egged on to escape only to be shot. The note was brief. I read it more than once. Then slowly I began to see it as entirely authentic. The newspaper editor was influential in the old city — his newspaper had become a powerful voice — and as a bonus to me he had persuaded prison officials to let me go.

I decided to bide my time and not become too excited. I ate the generous supper they gave me, and feeling warm and full I lay down to rest but fell asleep. Near midnight I heard a key turn in the lock, shuffling footsteps retreating, and silence. I went to the door, turned the latch, and pushed. When the door swung open, I looked into the corridor. Even though I saw not a single person in the hallway, I did see an iron gate in the prison wall slightly ajar. My heart raced with excitement. This was no scheme to kill me for trying to escape as I had thought. The Colombians were deliberately permitting me to leave unnoticed by anybody. I took a deep breath and ran for the gate. A few minutes later I was walking fast through the narrow streets of Cartagena. In the distance a dog was barking, but most of the people in the city were asleep. On the road leading to the seacoast I broke into a slow jog that quickly turned into a run. When I stopped to rest and sleep for an hour or two, I thought of Jules and Ludo and wondered whether they too would be allowed to escape. I never found out.

I had but one plan, to reach the Canal Zone in Panama where the Americans were in charge. I knew they staunchly opposed the prison system in French Guiana and wouldn't deport me. But how would I get there? And how would I defend myself against tribes of primitive Indians that lay between Cartagena and Panama? I had heard of human traffickers working out of Cartagena getting rich by taking people to Panama. It crossed my mind to use their services, but knowing they couldn't be trusted I decided to make the journey on foot. It would require walking along the coast hundreds of miles. I wasn't sure I had the physical strength or stamina to accomplish so gargantuan a task, but how would I know if I didn't try? At a little roadside store I bought a backpack and stuffed it with necessities. On the counter lay the owner's pistol, a small revolver. I asked if he would sell it to me. He quoted an outrageous figure, but after haggling half an hour I bought the weapon and a box of shells for a reasonable price. I loaded it with six bullets and stuffed it in my backpack. I reasoned it would serve me better, should I encounter hostile Indians, than a knife or machete.

As I was leaving, the shopkeeper called me back, speaking Spanish spiced with a thick Mandarin accent and displaying excessive politeness. "You gonna need machete walking through tough jungle, mister. You gonna need sharp machete to cut through jungle growth. I sell you very nice machete, good price, new as can be, never used."

What he was saying made sense. I needed that instrument to clear a path through swampy areas and fend off killer snakes. I bought it at three times its worth and left the owner satisfied. An hour later I was using it to make headway in a Colombian shore jungle. For several days I struggled through thick undergrowth and a number of swamps. Then one afternoon I blundered into a clearing filled with thatched huts. Indians clad in loincloths grabbed their spears and ran toward me. One of them understood Spanish and calmed the others when I spoke to him. They took me to their chief, a much older man in a faded yellow tee shirt with "USA" on it in big red letters. Around his neck he wore a necklace of boars' teeth. He questioned me through his interpreter and learned I was on my way to Colón in Panama. He said I would have to turn back. The land ahead was "closed country." No white man could enter it. "You die if you go near it," the interpreter translated.

A group of Indians had gathered around my backpack to examine its contents. A woman drew out the revolver and quickly handed it to the chief. Aware of its value, he giggled as it lay in his lap. He picked up the loaded gun and pointed it at me, smiling happily with a show of blackened teeth. To test the gun, he pointed it upward and pulled the trigger. The safety mechanism prevented the pistol from firing, and so nothing happened. The chief frowned and muttered *no bueno* in the little Spanish he knew. I released the safety latch and he fired the gun twice in the air. Then smiling broadly, he instructed the interpreter to tell me the gun was no longer mine. Fully aware I was in no position to oppose him, I said it would be my gift to him in exchange for his hospitality. His blinking old eyes lit up and he nodded with delight. In a tone of high authority he announced I could stay the night in his village and be on my way the following day. He put aside a hut for me, and a young woman brought me the lean pork of a wild pig, a hunk of sourdough bread, and a bowl of fermented guava juice. When night fell and the village slept, I made my way to the beach and stole a canoe.

I selected one with a sail and an outrigger. The sail would propel the boat and the projecting outrigger would make it stable. I put a couple of paddles in the craft and slid it off the beach into the water. I knew nothing about paddling a canoe alone and had to learn fast. In about an hour I got the hang of it, shifting the paddle from side to side to keep the canoe moving forward. For several hours I paddled furiously along the coast not having to worry about navigation. I tried to raise the sail in the choppy sea but couldn't do it. The canoe was too tender to move about in it or stand. It would capsize despite the outrigger and throw all my equipment overboard. So I paddled to shore and began working with the sail. It was gaff-rigged with a heavy yard that complicated the procedure, but at last I got it hoisted and set out again. A short tiller was attached to a makeshift rudder, and it was all I could do to keep the boat upright in building waves. Then I learned how to manage the outrigger, and that made the going easier.

I put behind me maybe thirty miles during the night and put in to shore when the sun came up. I was hesitant to move by day, knowing the Indians from whom I had stolen the boat would be looking for me. I hid the canoe in the bush and ate coconuts thrown down by the wind. With my machete I whacked open a few and drank the milk. I whacked them again to get at the meat, and it took the edge off my hunger. All day I remained in hiding and took to the water again as soon as darkness came. Shoal water made it easier to get back out to sea, but in the deep water curious sharks began to flash their fins. One mighty bump against the canoe was all they needed for a feast of human flesh. Although alone in darkness on a vast and silent sea, I didn't relish them as my companions. Then I remembered something I had read. Because of poor eyesight, sharks in tropical waters seldom scavenge for food at night. Perhaps these were merely curious. They circled the boat once or twice, lost interest, and left me. Before daylight came I beached the canoe and hid it in a tangle of vines and brush. I slept hidden in the brush and didn't become wide awake until noon.

In my knapsack I found two hard biscuits and pieces of dried pork and bolted them down for breakfast. Walking resolutely on the beach in the heat of a blazing sun, I saw in the distance three human figures. Rapidly they approached, and I could see they were Indians with no love for white men. Scowling, they danced around me and asked questions in a dialect I couldn't understand. In a matter of minutes they were pushing me along to their village at the mouth of a wide creek. Scores of Indians emerged from huts to look me over, a strange white man almost never seen in their territory. Naked children driven by curiosity prodded me with sticks and shrieked when I yelled at them. One or two touched me with their hands and ran frightened to their mothers. Had I not been hungry and exhausted, I would have found their antics amusing.

In the chief's hut was a man who knew Spanish. He helped me tell the chief I was a runaway from a terrible prison and meant no harm to him or his people. The old chief, clad only in a loincloth and wearing painted tribal symbols on his arms and chest, nodded but said not a word. With a flick of his hand a pretty young girl came forward to stand in front of him. Except for a skirt hanging from her hips, she was naked. At his command, she went away and came back with a basket of fruit and other food for me. An older woman with a child in her arms led me to a hut for the night. They were granting a man on the run extraordinary hospitality for which I felt guilty. To continue my journey, I knew I would have to steal from them a canoe they valued highly.

Chapter Twenty-Eight

Panama Lights

Inside the Indian hut was a mattress stuffed with the feathers of tropical birds. Even though when I nestled into it a strange odor filled my nostrils, I slept as one dead until midnight. Awake I found a wooden bowl of fruit and a pan of water near me. The woman who led me to the hut had apparently taken it upon herself to leave the refreshment. I put the fruit in my knapsack, crept away from the hut, and ran toward the beach just as a dog began to bark. I stopped in my tracks and held my breath. The dog could awaken the village and give me away. As I was about to hide in the brush, I heard a yelp from the animal, and the barking ceased. A rowboat near several canoes lay close to the water in the moonlight. It was a sturdy boat with a wide beam and strong oars but without a sail. It was heavy and demanded all my strength to lug it to the water. In waist-deep breakers I jumped into the boat and began to row. I followed the coastline, clear and silent in the moonlight, and rowed all night. Pieces of cloth torn from my ragged trousers saved my hands from severe blisters. Above my head was a brilliant display of stars so close I thought I could reach up and touch them.

In the early light of day I landed on a spit of land extending eastward for miles. I couldn't row around it and thought I might get to the other side by portage. But the boat was too heavy to drag across dry land. I had to leave it, hoping the owners would eventually find it. I walked mile after mile along the beach and through the jungle. While the beach was easy except for the sun, the jungle trek was difficult. I had to cut myself free of vines wanting to entrap me and was glad I had bought the machete. Thorns dug into my feet and legs, and leeches attached themselves below the knee. My trousers had become shorts. When night came, it brought with it a palpable darkness very different from the moonlit beach. I wrapped myself in sailcloth from the outrigger canoe to fend off the mosquitoes. Tired and hungry, I lay down between the roots of a gigantic tree to sleep.

The next day I saw big cats that looked like jaguars and also wild boars. I wanted desperately to kill a boar and roast the meat but didn't dare get in its way with nothing more than a blunt machete. I remembered the old chief had confiscated my pistol, but what I really needed was a good rifle. A day later, weak from hunger and thirst, I killed a large land turtle and ate its raw meat soaked in coconut milk. I had never thought I would be reduced to eating raw meat, and yet it wasn't bad. My hunger and the coconut flavor made it sweet and digestible. The turtle meat quickly restored my strength to move onward. After three days of cutting through the jungle, I heard the roar of pounding surf.

Trudging toward the sound, I found myself on a sunny beach approaching several men. Offshore in the blue-green water were several islands. Later I learned they belonged to Panama, were called the San Blas Islands, and were peopled by Kuna Indians. In the past, because white men had stolen their goods, raped their women, and enslaved their men, they had learned to hate any person who spoke Spanish. Brandishing spears, the men came fiercely forward as if to harm me. I stood waiting to defend myself to the end, thinking I could die. When they learned I was not a greedy prospector seeking to wrest gold from them, nor a slave hunter with shackles, they treated me kindly. With elaborate sign language I managed to tell them I was a poor runaway from a vile prison, and their behavior showed they believed me.

Not one of them knew a word of Spanish. It was the language of brutal men who had tormented them in the past, and they had decreed it would not be heard in their village. Before my fourth attempt to escape failed, my native wife Leywa had taught me much of her language. In solitary confinement I constructed imaginative scenes with her and me on the beach chatting, and I told myself I would never forget her language or its terms of endearment. Now much later I was listening to the speech of other Indians and thought I might understand it. But the dialect spoken by them differed from any other tribal language in the region. That barrier caused sign language to be common among them, and it seemed to work all right. I went with them to their island and remained there several days. They fed me their native food to make me stronger. I rested there with good people, watched a ceremonial dance, and got half drunk on fermented guava juice. When time came for me to leave, a little girl gave me a bunch of flowers. In the middle of the flowers was a gorgeous orchid. Their hospitality was rare indeed.

For several days — I lost track of the number — I worked my way northward with only one thought in mind: Colón on the Caribbean. I had visited the town during my year of freedom and knew it was Panama's second largest city. At last I reached that part of the Panama coast opposite the island of El Porvenir, *the future* in English. The Indians had told me a garrison of soldiers was quartered on that island, and I tried not to be seen by them. Since I could show no passport, I feared their commander would send me back to Colombia. I faded into the forest and walked all day under a thick canopy that shut out most of the sun. Near suppertime I came upon a crew of men cutting mahogany. A woodcutter who had killed a boar gave me a portion of roast pig and a mug of beer. He said Colón was seventy-five miles up the coast, and he warned me not to try getting there by canoe. A lone man in a little canoe would be in great danger trying to negotiate strong currents and tides. Don't do it, he advised, but I had to try.

I went along a trail he said would take me to an Indian village. It was a well-used trail with no obstacles and no need to hack anything with my machete. I came to the village faster than expected and lingered on the outskirts. When night came with overcast and a moon behind it, I hustled to the beach hoping to find a boat. As expected, I found several canoes neatly lined in a row and selected one with a sail. I pushed it into the surf and after some struggle managed to get inside and get the sail up. I was glad to have heavy darkness and no moon, for in moonlight any person on the beach could have seen the white sail. Past the breakers I made good speed with the wind behind me but quickly took on water. I had to bail constantly with a big gourd an Indian had left in the canoe. Several hours passed and then to my surprise and mild alarm a bright light flashed across the water. Instantly I thought a patrol boat had spotted me, but then I saw the lighthouse on shore. It was a moment of high excitement, particularly when I turned to my left to see a glowing sky. The glow came from the lights of Panama!

As I moved in closer, the lights grew brighter and Colón began to rise up in full view. Steamers passed me several times, almost capsizing my clumsy boat in their wake. I had no light to warn them, and they wouldn't have seen me even with a light. In a breeze almost gone I moved in closer and closer to shore, aiming for a beach south of the town. It was important to avoid human contact. I couldn't be stopped or questioned. It was a needless worry. All the people on shore, except for a few authorities, were asleep; the night was late and dark. The canoe moved slowly until it hit the surf. Then it picked up speed and began to dash toward the sloping beach. I held on tight and held my breath. A few yards from the beach the craft overturned and dunked me in the water, soaking my clothing and all I owned. I struggled to the sandy beach and quickly removed my knapsack. Because it was made of canvas, some of the stuff inside was still dry. Concealed in bushes I made a pillow of the knapsack and slept as one dead within minutes.

How long I lay there, huddled under the brush and cuddling my knapsack, is anyone's guess. I woke in broad daylight groggy from too much sleep and tottered to the beach. I was looking out at the ocean, intensely blue and shimmering in the sun, when a man in uniform approached and asked me if I was okay. I think he was surely an American policeman because of the way he spoke English. He smiled when I replied in my schoolbook English that I was a stranger in town and didn't quite know my way around. I was speaking a white lie, of course, because I had lived briefly in Colón during my year of freedom. I think I must have told the policeman I was French because he mentioned the French quarter of Colón. I remembered how to get there.

It was an old historic part of the town near the waterfront, colorful and peopled with some of the most amazing outcasts one can possibly imagine. I had been there earlier but now found an assortment of people I had never seen before. However, as soon as I spoke a few words in French they accepted me as one of their own and declared we were friends for life. A woman named Agatha with remnants of feminine beauty that must have turned heads when she was young offered me a change of clothes. Because the red shirt with white stripes and broad white pants reminded me too much of the south of France, I politely declined her offer. Another fed me a delicious stew with French bread and good wine. I wanted to reward her for her kindness, but she refused to accept from me anything more than heartfelt thanks. A man who sold leather goods offered me his bathroom to shave and shower. I was glad to rake off a growth of beard that was itching and glad to be clean again. Among those good people I felt at home but needed to move on. The train for Panama City would be leaving soon.

Chapter Twenty-Nine

Golden Skulls and Butterflies

When I reached Panama City, I found myself in a familiar town. On the Pacific side of the isthmus, it was as modern and progressive as ever. Again I felt like a free human being at home. In Trinidad I had enjoyed feelings of freedom but nothing like the ones I felt in Panama. Recalling what I had done, I myself couldn't believe it. I had walked more than 400 miles to get to Colón. I would have walked to my old haunts in the capital had I not remembered the Canal Zone was restricted government property. I went immediately to the house of a man recommend to me by an expatriate of the French quarter. He had written two books and worked as a well-known journalist. I was certain he would befriend me and allow me to rest until I could move northward again. I found that he was away for a month on assignment and had left his house in the care of a good servant. Serena was a woman in her late forties with smooth, clear, olive skin but copper hair that had once been jet black. She spoke fluent Spanish, labored French, and some English. I spoke fluent French, labored Spanish, and some English. We got along famously from the beginning. She was a gregarious woman easy to know and glad to have my company. She fed me well and I learned how to laugh again. She gave me a room with a very comfortable bed.

Serena was knowledgeable about current events, probably because her employer was a freelance journalist. Although she had little formal education, her mind was sharp and she was curious. She told me political turmoil in the region would make it dangerous to continue my journey northward. Costa Rica appeared to be on the brink of revolution. The authorities, fearing an uprising at any hour, were particularly vigilant in regard to strangers who might cause trouble. She advised me to wait until solutions could be found for current problems and until the tense political situation cooled down. I should go when the country was no longer in uproar and the government more stable. I asked how long that would be, and she replied maybe six months or so.

"My boss," she said, observing my show of disappointment, "owns a banana plantation not far from here. A boat will leave for the plantation tomorrow. Why don't you go there for a while? It'll do you good, and you can rest up until it's safe to move northward again. I'll give you a letter of introduction, and the people there will treat you well."

So after only a few days happily immersed in civilization, and with the good wishes of Serena, I was back in the jungle. The boat went into the Pacific, up the coast a few miles, and then up a river. It was more like a flat barge than a boat and carried many supplies to the settlement. It moved slowly up the river with a man at the bow signaling natives on shore with a loud horn. I asked why he was doing that and was told the barge would be collecting green bananas from Indian villages on its way back. The horn was to let them know the banana boat would be with them soon to do business. In the afternoon when the barge had gone as far as it could go, its supplies were put on boats with outboard motors to go even farther up the twisting river. Near sunset we reached a long dock built along the riverbank and walked into the jungle to find a clearing with three large buildings perched on stilts. In back of them I could see acre after acre of Cavendish banana plants.

At another time I might have liked the place very much. It was as far away from the prying eyes of authority figures as humanly possible and peaceful. However, it was a place of refuge when I needed no refuge, when I felt compelled to complete my journey. And as it turned out, the camp wasn't as pleasant as I thought on first arriving. At the end of the day dozens of fruit cutters, released for a few hours from hard labor, crammed into the houses and began drinking raw alcohol distilled from sugar cane. They gambled, quarreled, shared bawdy stories, broke into brawling, yelled at one another, and set going a stream of vulgar noise that lasted for hours. I sat in a corner to listen and observe and couldn't help but think I had come a long way from Devil's Island only to find myself once more consorting with riffraff, the dregs of humankind. The only difference between them and the convicts I had known for so many years was their believing they were free. It was a very small difference because their work didn't allow them genuine freedom. They were obligated to labor at low pay until physical strength expired.

The Indians were freer. They came to the clearing painted and naked save for loincloths, but courteous and smiling. They spoke softly and listened when I spoke of catching butterflies for money. I showed them a giant morpho I had caught just recently, and they said where they lived one could find even bigger butterflies with blue iridescent wings even brighter. They found it hard to believe one could catch the butterflies and sell them for their wings. Yet when they began to ask many questions I knew they wanted to give it a try. They were primitive people and their Spanish wasn't as good as mine, but of a sudden I decided I would rather spend time with them than with the boisterous banana cutters. As the Indians began walking to the river dock I walked with them to explain how to catch the butterflies, how to prepare them for sale, and where to find buyers. When they got in their boats to leave, I asked if I might come with them. Surprised by my request, they huddled to talk it over and finally agreed to take me to their village.

So began a seven-month adventure that changed me as a man. For the first time in many years I began to feel every day an emotion related to peace and contentment. It was a feeling so foreign to me that initially I didn't recognize it or label it. Feelings of peace and self worth came first and through them came feelings of contenment and happiness. For the first time in my adult life I calmly accepted the reality around me, one very different from Paris or Cayenne, and found it better than either. When the Indians learned they could acquire money and creature comforts selling butterflies, they showed me sincere respect and allowed me to move freely among their villages. I passed from one village to another deep inside Indian country, and not a person raised a hand against me. They had learned I was not a white man looking to rob them of gold and not a scout on the lookout for slave labor. I was merely an escaped convict who loved butterflies.

After some hesitation they escorted me to their most populous village where their chief lived. In that village every man and many of the women wore ornaments of solid gold shaped like human skulls. A larger number than expected spoke Spanish with me but when talking to each other used a language I didn't understand. In his youth the old chief had been a splendid warrior, but in his golden years he seemed half infirm and not quite with it. He had lost all vision in his left eye, and his right eye appeared to be in trouble too. His potbelly effectively hid his loincloth, and his brown skin had the tone of fine leather. He glared at me with a firm hard eye when I offered to shake hands. It was the white man's custom, and he hated white men. The members of his tribe who brought me to him spoke on my behalf to soften his attitude toward me. In time he asked me to show him my collection of butterflies.

He gazed at them with a look of surprise and asked why I killed them. Why in the world would I want to kill a thing so beautiful as a butterfly? Shrugging his shoulders, he looked at me sternly.

"I can understand killing a mosquito" he said. "It causes harm. The butterfly doesn't cause harm, doesn't bite or sting. It is merely a pretty thing, a flower that flies. We catch pretty things too but put them in cages to be admired. Why don't you do that? Why must you kill a gorgeous butterfly just to display its wings?"

I explained that morpho butterflies had no commercial value alive. Their beautiful wings had to be dried to become coveted ornaments almost like pieces of jewelry. He shrugged to show his displeasure but finally said I could settle down in his city as long as I followed certain rules. I couldn't penetrate the jungle on my own but would require a companion when hunting butterflies. I couldn't have anything whatever to do with gold, couldn't dig for it in their region, couldn't steal it or trade for it. Gold I couldn't touch in any form. I couldn't bathe in the river with the villagers but had to do it alone. I couldn't look with a lustful eye at the native women, and if I stayed longer than two moons I would have to take a wife.

"A man without a wife is liable to get in trouble with another man's wife," the chief intoned through his interpreter. "Without a wife how you find time away from house chores to hunt butterflies? I say to you, Monkey Man, you need a wife even now."

A girl in her teens wearing only a strip of cloth around her hips looked me full in the face, smiling coyly. Her black hair fell almost to the small of her back, and she moved with a fluid motion pleasing to watch. Without speaking she left and returned with a gourd filled with sliced bananas and berries in coconut milk. She offered the gourd to me, causing all the children to laugh. They understood what I did not.

The chief made them silent with a flick of the hand and said, "This woman would be a good wife for you. She works hard. Her offer of food is her way of offering herself to you as your wife. What do you say?"

I was in no position to quibble. Certainly I would need a partner to keep house for me and teach me their customs and way of life. Moreover, I didn't want to make a mistake that might insult the old chief and bring about hard feelings or worse. So nodding my head I spoke in Spanish loud enough for all to hear: *Tendré esta mujer. Ella es buena.* "I will have this woman. She is good."

Lowaki! grunted the chief in his own language. And from the natives who knew some Spanish came *Bueno! Bueno!*

"Now eat some of the food the woman has given you," the chief commanded through his interpreter. "It signifies in our culture that you take her for your wife as she takes you for her husband."

I dipped a wooden spoon into the berries and bananas and began to eat. The food was delicious. Anyone who has never eaten a banana picked exactly when ripe doesn't know bananas. As I made the gourd empty, the chief spoke softly to the girl in their language. She listened politely, then turned and began to walk gracefully through the crowd.

"Follow her," enjoined the chief. "She will take you to the house I am giving you for a home. Be kind to her. You are right, Monkey Man. The woman is good. She works hard and will make your life easier."

I thanked the wise old man in the way I had seen others thank him. To show humility and respect, I stood at attention in front of him and bowed my head. He smiled in appreciation of my gesture and beckoned me catch up with the girl. I did and we walked to a dwelling raised eight feet off the ground. I tried speaking to her in Spanish. She understood not a word, nor could I understand any word that she spoke, but somehow all that didn't really matter. We understood each other in spirit, and we got along well. I lived with that gentle, healthy, good-looking girl for several months, and I do believe those months were as happy as any I've ever known, including those I spent as an errand boy in Montmartre. Those fleeting days of my youth were exciting, carefree, and happy. Then regrettably my penchant for thievery caught up with me, and misery fell upon me. In a tranquil native village with that pretty girl supporting me, I climbed out of that pit of misery to live again.

Chapter Thirty

Nikata Fulewo Sawiki

Hand in hand we walked rapidly to the dwelling the chief had so generously given us. A log with notches for steps led up from the ground to the flooring of the house. With no banisters on either side it required a great sense of balance for anyone daring to mount it. The girl pointed to the open door eight feet above me and indicated I should enter first. I found the steps too small for my feet and with nothing to hang onto I slipped and fell to the ground. My bride uttered a merry little laugh and helped me to my feet. On the second try with my shoes removed I managed to ascend without falling. The house was spacious and clean. In the middle of the large room was a stone hearth for cooking. Flat rocks covered with embers formed a square of ample size. She fanned the embers to make a fire and began to cook our supper. We had plenty of food on hand, but she seemed to think the way to cook a meal was to toss all the food into a pot, pour water on it, and boil it. When I saw what she was doing, I decided to cook the supper myself.

"You get more wood," I said with gestures she could understand. "I'll do the cooking and soon we can eat!"

A look of deep puzzlement crossed her young and pretty face. Why would I want to do her work? Had not she become my woman to keep my house, look after me, and cook for me? Reluctantly she went into the forest for more wood, stopping to chat with native women and apparently telling them her new husband was cooking supper. Two or three came to the house, shyly mounted the steps, looked at me preparing the food and giggled. How strange! A man doing the cooking! It was unheard of by anyone in the tribe. It was perhaps scandalous!

Word spread through the village like wild fire. The crazy white man was doing woman's work! Several women and girls had to see it to believe it. They crept up the log steps, giggled, slipped easily to the ground, and ran off. The children picked up the excitement and wanted to see also. They came running in groups of five or six and had to be chased away by their elders. The hullabaloo reached the old chief who believed his sworn duty was to set me straight. He seemed unduly disturbed, deeply puzzled, as his interpreter translated.

"What is this I hear about you, Nikata? What are you doing in your new home to upset the women folk? Will not your woman work?"

"She's a good worker, my chieftain," I said humbly, "and a good wife, but she doesn't know how to cook."

A few days later I learned that she was celebrated as the best cook in the village. At all the great feasts when natives came from outlying villages, she and her mother always did the cooking. Several times each year she authored the ceremonial banquet and was revered for doing it with perfection. I made it known to her that I was very sorry for having usurped her honorable position. She did the cooking from then on, and slowly I learned to like her fare. She was also good at many other things and performed her duties as a wife skillfully and dutifully. Her behavior in bed was excellent except for the kissing. Instead of pressing her lips against mine to show affection, she bit them hard as Leywa had done. And always she murmured, "Nikata fulewo Sawiki," *Nikata deeply loves Sawiki.* It was the name the chief had given me at the moment I accepted her as my bride. He had called me "Monkey Man" (*Nikata*) because of my size and because I was pale and different. I didn't learn her name until I began to learn her language. It was Sawiki, *Sleeping Flower* in English. She was indeed a flower but seldom sleeping. Tender and gentle but strong of body and mind, she was dedicated to work and loved it.

In the world as I have come to know it, millions of people dream of living in opulence and hate their wretched existence. Primitive people have known for centuries the key to a happy life is simplicity. In the village where I lived simplicity in all its forms was practiced as a cardinal rule. It wasn't what one owned that defined a man or woman but what he or she did with what they owned. That was the rule I soon learned to live by in Chief Catu's village. If a woman found she needed sweet potatoes for her evening meal, she went to her neighbor and came home with more than enough. The potatoes she didn't borrow. They were given to her simply and generously because she needed them. The person doing the giving expected nothing in return, and yet was often richly rewarded. As I denied my French heritage and became a member of a native tribe in Central America, I understood for the first time in my life what it means to have peace of mind. Having divested myself of what civilization calls essential, I found exceptional peace. Never had my days begun so pleasantly and ended so well.

In the shade the tropical heat could be endured, but like all the other men of the village I wore few clothes. I passed my days much as they did, and no one suffered want. The river was full of fish. The forest had an abundance of game. Small clearings in the jungle produced fruits and vegetables of every variety. Fields on the edge of the jungle yielded cotton for clothing. Tobacco hung drying in the sun. Medicinal plants healed one of aches and pains but were used with caution. Even though some of the men got high gnawing on a jungle plant that blackened their teeth, not a person in the village had ever heard of drug addiction, or drinking alcohol to get drunk. For the first time in my life I was truly free and living with good and caring people. I feared nothing and needed nothing.

With a lovely young woman at my side and supporting me every way imaginable, I had it all. At last after many years of hardship, I was tasting the simple pleasure of living. My work was rewarding, and I was learning to speak my wife's language. I would point to an object and listen to her repeat its name. In little more than a month, each week dissolving into the next, we could sit in the shade and talk a little.

I fished and hunted and spent many hours seeking butterflies. My collection of jewel-like wings grew larger each day. I soon began to value them at several hundred dollars. Since there was no market within easy range to take them, their value increased with each morpho caught. I attended tribal conferences and ceremonials and sat next to Chief Catu. Like him, I painted my face and chest but wore cut-off trousers instead of a loincloth. Natives who had never seen a white man asked many questions. A white man in their midst was an anomaly they found hard to accept. They had been taught to hate white men, for didn't those men rape and burn their villages, steal their gold, and cast their young people into slavery? I carefully made it known to them that the Spaniards were guilty of those abuses. I was a Frenchman and different. Moreover, I had escaped privation and almost certain death in a horrible prison to come to them. I was not a plunderer. I chased butterflies and lived peacefully with a native woman. As the months passed all the Indians I met became my friends. I wore a necklace of wild boars' teeth, and silver ornaments. I couldn't touch their gold, but silver wasn't off limits.

As the months passed, in spite of what seemed in every way an idyllic existence, I began to feel it was necessary for me to complete my journey. I had struggled too long and come too far to replace my sustaining dream with a repeat of the life I had so thoroughly enjoyed with Leywa, my first native wife. And yet the more I thought about it the more indecisive I became. Was it not better to reject a world that had been very cruel to me for a simple world of peace and harmony? Could I find greater peace anywhere else? Certainly

I couldn't find more freedom to live day after day without fear of French injustice. It was a conundrum demanding resolution. I worked on it for hours and was inclined to stay with Sawiki and the tribe that had become my tribe. Then on my thirty-ninth birthday I decided the primitive life, however appealing, was not what I wanted. I had survived fifteen years in a vile institution that had tried to destroy me. I felt at thirty-nine I could live happily for another thirty-nine by turning the larger world to my advantage. Maybe the United States would help me achieve my dream. Didn't the Americans call their vast country the land of opportunity?

Between my jungle home and America lay thousands of miles of very difficult terrain and the borders of many countries. If I could get back to Panama City and take a plane to New York, I could be there in a day. But I would need money for air travel, which I didn't have. Also I had no passport. To travel thousands of miles in a good car would be expensive and take several days. To do the journey by foot, even if it were possible, would consume months. Maybe I was tilting at windmills. Yet somehow I felt I had to reach the end of my pilgrimage. So one evening as we sat outside to catch the cool breezes, I turned to Sawiki and told her I would soon be leaving.

"Do you go to catch more butterflies?" she asked. "Many butterflies are in the mountains, and they are big and beautiful. I will go with you and help you catch them. I will go wherever you go, sleep wherever you sleep, eat whatever you eat because I am your woman."

"I won't be catching butterflies on leaving," I replied after a long silence. "You've been very good to me, Sawiki, and good for me, but I belong in another country. I love you and your people, and yet we both know I'm not one of you. Also I must complete the odyssey I began many months ago. Something within me is driving me to do it. I may return and raise a family with you, and live out my days with you and our children in peaceful understanding. But that I can't promise."

Nothing more was said. She didn't ask more questions and didn't seem unduly upset. Even so, she put her head between her knees and sighed deeply. That was the extent of it. Tribal custom had taught her not to show emotion. When morning came I spoke to the chief and asked if he would have some men take me down river to the trading station. His one eye squinting, he looked me full in the face and grunted but said it could be arranged. He spoke no word of regret, nor did anyone else. Not a person thought my leaving Sawiki was a betrayal. She told me she would wait eight moons for my return. If I had not returned by the ninth moon, she would take a new husband. She spoke softly and with feeling, but with no tears. It was the way her tribe embraced life and the hardships it brought. Stoicism was in their blood.

The entire Indian village gathered to see me off. Chattering children danced around me as if in celebration. The women called out to me in friendly voices and waved, "Goodbye, Monkey Man! Goodbye beloved Nikata!" The men made a friendly fist and raised it to the sky in salute. Gesticulating with broad movement, as they had taught me, I communicated my thanks to them all. In the canoe we moved away from the village fast. All day we paddled, often fighting swift currents and bouncing through rapids. As night came we camped under tremendous trees. The next day we reached the trading post and found the monthly banana boat at the dock, a stroke of good luck. A day later it was plying its way downstream loaded with green bananas for the Canal Zone. The captain, a stocky fellow with very short legs, was glad to have a paying passenger and fed me well. Two days later an American who owned a little curio shop in Panama City bought my butterflies at a good price.

With my wallet stuffed with money, I left the city as a hitchhiker in a truck. The affable driver was big and fat and jovial, but sweaty and smelly. His right arm was almost as big around as my leg above the knee. He said his name was Carlos, and he spoke his brand of Spanish rapidly. Though I couldn't understand much of what he said, I listened politely. He was in the habit of speaking strings of words that seemed quite serious, but at the end of each sentence he'd roar with laughter. Every sentence he spoke, instead of having a period at the end, had a peal of laughter. Perhaps it was his way of saying he was enjoying life or found it funny. I think he liked his job and what life offered him, but I couldn't see pleasure in driving a truck over dangerous roads eleven hours a day. He said he carried a load of new furniture for a store close to the Costa Rican border. I hoped as we bumped along that I might be able to cross the border unobserved. Then I would move without delay toward Nicaragua. It didn't happen. The reality of life, as my gloomy old grandma was fond of saying, has a way of crushing the dream of life.

Chapter Thirty-One

Walking My Shoes Away

C arlos let me ride with him in his truck all the way to his destination. It was night when we arrived, and I had no place to go. He said if I didn't mind, I could sleep with the furniture. I lay on the hard boards within inches of a comfortable sofa, but the sofa was upside down. When morning came, stiff and groggy, I paid Carlos for my ride, said goodbye, and began walking. In a town with a railway station I took a train to a border town called Palo Seco, getting off unobtrusively with other passengers. Dry Stick lived up to its name as a dry and dusty little place, and I must have stood out like a sore thumb among the brown residents. They eyed me as they passed, probably thinking I was an American gringo, but said nothing. I was now in Costa Rica, a new country I had never seen before, and was glad I could speak and understand Spanish. Outside a restaurant I met a boy of fourteen or so who looked hungry. We had a lunch of rice and black beans, and Pablo gladly agreed to guide me through the town and put me on the main road northward.

Soon after we started walking, however, two policemen stopped and searched us, insisting we might be smuggling drugs. They saw the pack on my back and politely asked if they might inspect it. A policeman rifled through everything in the pack, leaving my small belongings in a pile exposed to the dusty wind. He seemed disappointed when he found no drugs. Then the other asked to see

211

my papers, my identification and passport. That I couldn't provide. So they hauled me off to jail, admonishing the boy to choose his company better in future. They gave me water to drink in their jail but no food. In the morning they lost no time escorting me back across the border and turning me over to the Panamanian police. I was jailed in a place called Concepción for two nights before being taken to the Governor of the province. That really scared me. If the Governor sent me back to Panama City and the authorities turned me over to the French Consul, I would be on my way back to prison in French Guiana. My eighth attempt to escape, so promising until that moment, would quickly become a failure.

The Governor belonged to the highest social class in the country and had the manners of a gentleman. Thin and angular, he was immaculately dressed in a white suit that matched his white beard, white hair, and white shoes. He sat behind a huge desk twiddling a silver fountain pen and looking at me over his reading spectacles. In excellent Spanish he asked me to tell him all about me, and I decided to be frank and honest. I told him without going into a lot of detail that I was French and a fugitive from Devil's Island. I had served my time but was not allowed to leave the penal colony. He had heard of that unjust law and felt sympathy for any man daring enough to break it. I spoke of my desire to reach the United States, and to my surprise without saying a word he signed a form releasing me of criminal intent. His assistant advised me to go to a seaport on the Pacific coast where I would find Costa Rican smugglers ready to take me on one of their nightly trips up the coast. He cautioned me to pay them only a few dollars.

"They will state an enormous sum but will do it for less," he said.

A few hours later I found myself in a dingy café bargaining with swarthy bandits intent on smuggling into Costa Rica an extensive collection of Japanese shirts. They had stolen the expensive shirts from a shipping container left on the dock beside an Asian ship. After much haggling they agreed to include me in their cargo for ten dollars. They made it clear that I would go as cargo and would not have the amenities of a passenger. I could have water to drink and a beer if I bought it, but no food. Soon afterwards we were at sea moving fast up the Costa Rican coast as far as a port called Jaco. A few miles south of the port their shallow-draft boat put into a sandy beach, and we jumped into the surf. Every man knew exactly what to do, and before daylight the merchandise was unloaded on the beach. Two associates waited in a parked truck. They came as soon as the boat was back at sea and picked up the wooden crates along with me. As we rode toward a town, I asked the men how I might cross the Nicaraguan border.

"Pay some money to rent a horse and guide," they said. "You got money to pay us smugglers, so pay a guide for help. Then you ride four days northward and cross the border at San Juan del Sur. Hire a guide. You'll get lost and run into a ton of trouble if you try to do it on your own. Bandits up that way don't like the looks of white men."

When daylight came I was alone in a dusty little town that sizzled in the sun. I went to a little restaurant called *La Cocina de la Abuela* (*Grandma's Kitchen*) and talked to the owner. In less than an hour he arranged for his cousin to guide me for a few dollars. In all my life I had never been on a horse and was expected to ride one in wild terrain for four days. Fortunately I had a sluggish horse and a good saddle. Even so, at the end of each day my buttocks and thighs were so painful I could barely walk or sit. But remembering an old family motto — *when you have to do it, son, you do it* — I persevered. Certainly in years past I had suffered worse abuse and was able to take the latest in stride. Then one day in a narrow canyon my guide asked for his seven dollars and told me I would have to travel on foot to the other side of the mountain blocking our view. If I could somehow make it over or around the mountain, he said as he rode away, I would find Nicaragua sleeping in the sun.

I wanted to ask him a few questions about what lay ahead, but he was gone before I could collect my thoughts. So I began walking along a hot and rocky trail. Soon to my relief I lost the saddle pain and began to feel normal again. All day I walked alone in a hot and dusty and barren country with cacti as the main vegetation. Along the way I saw the bones of goats and donkeys at a watering hole that had long been dry. Near sunset I began to look for a place to bed down for the night. Hoping to get a few hours' sleep and too tired to think clearly, I stumbled unwittingly into a nest of bandits. They were sitting around a sputtering campfire and numbered maybe a dozen. Every man, or so it seemed, held a big rifle pointed directly at my head. More confused than fearful, I raised both hands and stood as still as a statue.

Their leader had a big wad of tobacco in his mouth and spit a dollop of brown juice at my feet. He came up close to question me, thrusting his ugly face close to mine. I could smell his foul breath above the tobacco odor. On his left cheek was a festering sore and his fat lips sagged at one corner. He was in dire need of a bath, and his clothes were very dirty. But in spite of his appearance, in that setting he was a figure of authority to be obeyed. I answered each one of his questions truthfully, and he softened his attitude visibly when I told him I was a runaway convict trying to get as far away from Devil's Island as I possibly could. He turned away and seemed ready to let me go on my way, but then another bandit, one of his lieutenants, decided to frisk me.

He found a handkerchief, a pocketknife, and a pack of cigarettes. He missed my prison knife strapped to my leg. I had dropped my backpack to the ground in the gathering darkness and was hoping he would overlook it. He didn't. The leader's henchman searched through my belongings and found all my money, the cash I was using to finance my escape. When they were satisfied they had seized all I had of worth, they beckoned me to leave. I gathered from the dirt the contents of my backpack and slowly moved away. It alarmed me to lose my money, and I kept thinking how I might get it back. I was one man and unarmed, and they were many. They were killers and could have murdered me on the spot with no one ever knowing. One aggressive move on my part meant certain death. I thought of an old saying, *you don't enter a gunfight with a knife,* and instantly saw the wisdom behind it. Though angry and astounded by what had happened, I was glad to go with my life.

I stumbled along the trail in darkness for maybe half an hour and decided it would be foolish to go farther. So I curled up between the roots of a massive jungle tree and went to sleep. In the middle of the night I awoke with a start, thinking the bandits had caught up with me to pummel my body with heavy clubs. Yet I felt no pain. All was very quiet. I was suffering a nightmare. I hid in a thicket so no one could find me in the morning and went back to sleep. With first light I walked and walked, eating almost nothing. For two days I walked and finally came to Managua, the capital city of Nicaragua. It was a pleasant place, a sleepy town one might call it, especially at midday. I had no money even for a cheap hotel room but just enough hidden in a shoe to send a telegram to the American shop owner in Panama City. I explained that bandits had robbed me of all my money. Could he send me a hundred dollars for butterflies I would collect for him valued at two hundred or more? I couldn't believe it, but within a few hours I had money in my pocket and was no longer a vagrant. I promised myself I wouldn't betray the trust he had shown me. Years later, learning he was still in business, I sent him $300. It pleased me to imagine his surprise.

Hanging outside a fish market was a net. I bought it and hoped I could use it right away. Since I would be in the tropics for months, there would be ample time to catch and prepare the collection of brilliant wings I hoped to send him. But of first importance was finding a way to move onward and northward. Between the capital of the country and the border were many little towns. I would have to get through them without causing suspicion. They were sleepy towns filled with peasants who would see me as a stranger right away, and that could mean trouble. I solved the problem by hopping on a crowded train heading for Honduras and losing myself among the many people on it. I found a seat, slouched in it, and pulled the brim of my hat over my face. In the midst of noisy women and children and old men hustling live hens in burlap bags, no one noticed me. So without a great deal of effort I reached Honduras, another country on my endless itinerary. There I found no train going northward but also no Custom House.

For more than two weeks I trudged northward. I walked until my shoes began to fall apart, and I traded my prison knife for used boots. I went down paved roads and up steep mule roads of gravel and dirt. I climbed tall mountains, descended into ravines, and skirted banana plantations of many acres. At night when I had to find a place to sleep, poor people offered me space in an outlying building, a barn or shed. When morning came they shared a spare breakfast with me. One evening a family of eighteen invited me to have dinner with them. We sat outdoors at a rustic table loaded with food. Though some of the dishes seemed strange to me, I ate my fill and went away with food. Some days when I felt hungry I found bananas growing beside the road. I was able to move into El Salvador with no problems, but on more than one occasion well-meaning persons warned me not to try crossing into Guatemala. Civil unrest existed there. A new regime in the country had tightened the borders. Policemen were on the lookout for strangers even in the cities. Special permits were needed to enter and leave the country.

The mayor of a town where I spent half a day drinking cheap cold beer advised me to go to La Libertad on the Pacific coast. He and his son were going there to visit relatives, and he offered me a ride all the way. It was a long ride through the mountains, but in late afternoon we arrived at the port city. I thanked him heartily and offered to pay for the ride, but he said they had to make the trip anyway. Although he refused to accept money directly, he allowed me to buy gasoline for his truck. El Puerto de la Libertad, one of the first ports in El Salvador, was a pretty town with beautiful tropical beaches, a long pier, and a harbor for nautical traffic. I hoped that by hanging around the waterfront I might be able to get on a ship heading north. Somehow I had to get past Guatemala, and the obvious way was by sea. It wouldn't be a long voyage because Guatemala's coastline was very short compared to Mexico's. I had heard the Mexican authorities wouldn't be asking for identification. There was a bandit problem, however, and that I had to consider.

Chapter Thirty-Two

Stowaway and USA

On the waterfront I looked for smugglers but found none. A man in a bar told me they were lying low after a big operation. An hour later I found a freighter bound for Canada loading cargo. I didn't have enough money to buy passage on the big ship, but thought I might sneak aboard and stow away. So I went to a store nearby and bought two loaves of bread, a few cans of sardines, and some candy bars. I put the stuff in my knapsack and went to a restaurant to fill my belly with native food. I figured it could be days before I'd be eating another meal. The waitress, a shapely young woman with sensual red lips and yellow hair, noticed how much I was eating and came over to chat.

"I will top off your meal with a big slice of lemon pie," she said in good Spanish, "and it won't cost you extra. It's on the house."

"It's awfully kind of you to offer me that," I replied. "I'm sure the pie is very tasty, but I've already eaten more than I can hold."

"I will give you a rain check. Come back tomorrow, and your pie will be waiting for you. I'll be here too."

She was pleasant, simpatico, flirtacious, and alive. At another time I would have accepted her invitation, but on that day I had important decisions to make. I thanked her cordially and went back to the docks.

As soon as it got dark I joined the men who were loading the ship and went on board. Then I slipped away from them, holding an empty box I had found on deck, and walked to the stern of the ship. If anyone accosted me, glibly I would say I had been ordered to take the box aft. No one stood in my way, and I went down a companionway to a lower deck and through a small trapdoor into the hold. It had a flickering light at the time I entered, but an hour or so later a sailor quenched it. I was in darkness so thick I couldn't see my hand in front of my face. That's when I began to doubt the wisdom of stowing away. It had not occurred to me that I might have to spend many days in damp and darkness. Also I remembered rats occupy the holds of most ships. I shuddered at the thought of one gnawing on my face as I slept, but the thing couldn't be undone. I would have to make the most of it.

The ship's engines throbbed with a rhythmic thrum, and I knew we had moved away from the dock to enter the open sea. In the darkness I got undressed except for my underwear. The hold wasn't a clean place for a stowaway, and I knew if I didn't remove and protect my clothes they'd become filthy. I would have to get off the ship later, and to be seen in very dirty clothing would be a dead giveaway. Hour after hour I lay against the steel hull sleeping as much as possible to pass the time. In the black hold I had no way of knowing how much time was passing, but when my bread and sardines ran out and I had only two candy bars left, I knew I would have to find something to eat soon and particularly water to quench my thirst. Though salty, the sardines had supplied enough liquid to stave off rampant thirst. The candy bars could offer a bit of nutrition but no water. I decided if it were night I would sneak on deck and make a search. Slowly I climbed the ladder, opened the trapdoor, found it was night, and looked for food and water. Only a few feet away sat a bowl of table scraps beside a pan of water. The food had been left for a dog sleeping against the deckhouse.

I drank the water in one gulp, dumped the scraps in my underwear, and scurried back to the hold. It would have been easier to snatch the bowl and take it with me, but that I had to leave. Anyone feeding the dog later would wonder what happened to it, might even decide to feed the mutt in another place. Eight or ten times or more — I lost count — I was hungry and thirsty enough to sneak on deck and steal the dog's food and water. Its owner must have thought the animal was eating wonderfully well though sleeping too much. Fortune was my friend on that trip; I didn't get caught and I didn't starve or die of thirst. Also because the climate was in my favor I remained fairly comfortable nearly nude.

Twice, however, I came close to being discovered by two sailors when they came into the hold to check the security of the cargo. In rough seas they had to make certain the heavy cargo didn't break away and shift position. I hid behind some wooden crates and could hear them talking. They didn't like the ornery job they were ordered to do but were fully aware of its importance. Loose cargo in the hold could sink even a large ship in heavy weather. I held my breath when they checked the crates where I was hiding. Flashing their lanterns here and there, they passed without seeing me and exited. In the dark, my heart racing, I felt enormously relieved. For more than a week I lay against the hull in darkness but managed to evade them both times. Then one day or night, as I lay dozing with my backpack as a pillow, I heard a blast of the ship's horn. It meant we were moving into a harbor, but where? I began to put on my clothes. Slowly the ship came to a halt and cut her engines. I heard water slapping against the hull and the sound of hawsers made fast to a dock. We were no longer moving.

I took my time to dress carefully and climbed the ladder. I opened the trapdoor and faced a morning so bright it blinded me. The dazzling sunlight compelled me to sink downward on the ladder with the door slightly open to let my eyesight adjust. I feared someone might see what was going on, but again luck was on my side. When I could see again I peeked along the deck to view sailors busy at work. Not a one was nearby. I had double vision when I climbed to the deck, but it soon disappeared to give me confidence.

With the wondrous eyes of a child I stood at the rail and looked at the landscape, brown and green in the sun. I thought we had come to a Mexican port and was thinking I would have to walk again. Later on shore I learned with amazement that in ten days we had come much farther than I ever expected. The ship had docked in San Pedro, California.

I had never heard of the place and asked about it. I was told it was once a separate city but had since become a community within the city of Los Angeles and served as its seaport. So again I received news that left me dumfounded but excited. I had come as a stowaway all the way from El Salvador to Los Angeles, California in record time. I had eaten dog food to stay alive and had endured total darkness for more than ten days. Then dressed in presentable clothing I had emerged into dazzling sunshine. It was an indisputable highlight of my life. I was delighted but had trouble believing it. At last I was a free man in America!

Looking down from the deck, I saw a man in uniform at the foot of the gangplank. He appeared to be checking the pockets of sailors as they left the ship. I fell in behind an officer and followed him down the gangplank. The man in uniform greeted the officer cordially and let him pass with no frisking. I stepped forward and opened my knapsack to indicate I was ready to be searched. The inspector ran his hands over my pockets, glanced at my scraggly beard, and motioned me to move on. At the end of the wharf I saw a gate. On the other side was another uniformed man performing the same work. He made a quick search, running his hands rapidly over my clothing, and nodded. I strolled nonchalantly into the streets, came to railway tracks, and walked along them.

A work crew was nearby, and I asked one of the men a question, "Can you tell me where these tracks go?"

I spoke with an accent and he must have thought I was an immigrant, lost and demented. He looked at me for a full minute before answering, "To Los Angeles, old man, Los Angeles."

I was in America, in California, in the City of Angels, and free! I could forget the past, the long years of captivity, and plan a future.

Hesitantly, blinking in the bright sunlight, I asked the same man another question, "Can you tell me what day this happens to be?"

Stopping his work and looking me squarely in the face, he was clearly annoyed but gruffly replied. "It's a Wednesday, you moron! Now get lost! Can't you see I got work to do here? Where did you come from anyway? A booby hatch? Get back there and take a bath and shave."

He picked up his tools and walked away to join the rest of his crew. As he did so I noticed something on the ground that looked like a leather wallet. I picked it up and rifled through it. Neatly tucked inside were eighty American dollars, two weeks' wages. I needed that money to add to the little I had left. I needed it to make my way in my new country. I could pocket the money and move on. Who would know? The answer was obvious. I would know, and I wouldn't live in America as a thief. The man had called me a moron and crazy, but I returned his wallet. With a show of surprise, he thanked me sincerely.

To this day he probably tells an amusing story of meeting a lunatic on railroad tracks in San Pedro, asking crazy questions but returning his wallet with its money untouched. And I think I was truly a lunatic to have attempted what I accomplished. For more than two years, fronting unbelievable obstacles as a fugitive, I had overcome them all to reach a nation of tolerance and opportunity. I remembered Lafayette helping the young country become a sovereign nation in its time of most need. I would help it too, though beyond forty and toothless, should I be lucky enough to become a citizen. I wanted to renounce my identity as a Frenchman and become a brave American. Of necessity I had learned to speak Spanish fluently. Now in this nation of English speakers I would work on my English.

Printed in the United States
By Bookmasters